REVIEWS OF *GHOSTLINES*

Winner, Victorian Premier's Literary Award for an Unpublished Manuscript

Winner, Ned Kelly Award for a debut crime novel

"*Ghostlines* is rough-cut, grainy and good ... Earthy and exciting, with a bluesy, wistful air."

– *The Australian*

"Gadd's novel is all crime and intrigue ... He understands the the magical effect that a dud story coming good can have on a once-great but now disengaged reporter – the thrill of the hunt, the accidental discoveries and the growing understanding as happenings slowly add up to an intriguing, dangerous whole."

– Seamus Bradley, *The Sunday Age,* 'Read of the Week'

"A ripping yarn of art theft, corruption and murder. This is an atmospheric, intriguing and spooky debut."

– *The Sun-Herald* (Sydney)

"A thriller with a neat psychological twist. Gadd's Trudeau is a convincing central character whose own story is just as compelling as the mystery at the heart of the story."

– *The Herald-Sun* (Melbourne)

"Crime fans will enjoy the compelling narrative, the succinct writing and the pleasing lack of blood, gore and psychopathic behaviour that mars most contemporary crime stories. FOUR STARS"

– *Bookseller & Publisher*

"Unforeseen twists and a spine-tingling supernatural element leave the reader anticipating more from a promising new author."

– *Adelaide Advertiser*

REVIEWS OF *DEATH OF A TYPOGRAPHER*

"This clever, stylish, and very funny novel will appeal to anyone who loves the printed word."

– Kerryn Goldsworthy, *The Age*

"A romp of a book, both sprightly and erudite. With in-jokes scattered joyfully about, it's easy to be drawn into its 'typomania', and Gadd delivers a novel that combines detective mystery and letterform aesthetics."

– *The Sunday Age*

"*Death of a Typographer* is a joyous book – from a word nerd's point of view I've never seen such fun being had with the sheer joy of fonts, and it's a cracking yarn with great characters."

– David Astle, presenter, Evenings, ABC 774 Melbourne

"Set primarily in Melbourne with excursions to overseas destinations including a Tibetan monastery, the Peruvian plains, and Naples backstreets, Gadd's novel is both a celebration and a gentle satire of typography. The typographical gags are a delight to discover."

– *The Sunday Sun-Herald* (Sydney)

"This is a smart and funny book that revolves around typefaces. Lest you think that no one could possibly make a story out of such an arcane speciality, fear not – Gadd's book is a whole lot of fun. It's a mystery full of wonderful in-jokes that bibliophiles will love."

– *The Big Issue*

"It's very smart. Very funny. Deserves a big international release. An excellent summer read."

– Michael Cathcart, presenter, ABC Radio National

"You might start thinking that Jasper Fforde has hit a new high, but Nick Gadd's brilliant blend of humour, mystery, and, yes, typography is all his own. A compelling read, whether or not you know your Comic Sans from your Zapf Dingbats."

– Nick Earls, author of *Zigzag Street* and *Wisdom Tree*

"A smart, witty, riveting read that made me laugh out loud and changed the way I see fonts."

– Angela Savage, author of *Mother of Pearl*

GHOSTLINES

NICK GADD

ARDEN

Published 2020 by Arden
the international general books' imprint of
Australian Scholarly Publishing Ltd
7 Lt Lothian St Nth, North Melbourne, Vic 3051
Tel: 03 9329 6963 / Fax: 03 9329 5452
enquiry@scholarly.info / www.scholarly.info

First published by Scribe 2008

ISBN 978-1-925984-72-9

Cover design: Stephen Banham

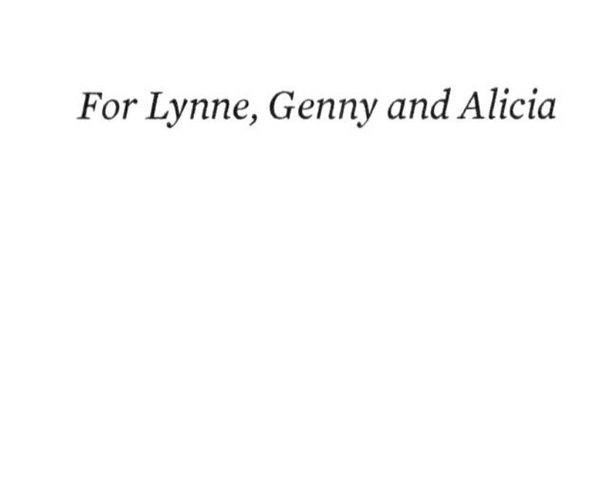

For Lynne, Genny and Alicia

1

The kid never saw the train that hit him. The citybound 11.05 had passed through the level crossing and was standing in Yarraville station when the kid came riding towards the tracks, head down, legs pumping. Witnesses said the bells had been ringing and the lights flashing in the darkness. The boom gate had descended on cue, but without slowing down the kid had swerved around the boom, past the back of the stationary train, and headed for the other side. He was hit by the second, southbound train, a non-stopping express. Nobody had time to shout a warning, and anyway he would not have heard.

Philip Trudeau stood leaning on the boom gate while the police and ambulance crew went through their procedures. Sirens, orange tape, fluorescent jackets – the paraphernalia that always follows violent death. Philip had seen it hundreds of times, and it bored him. It was a foul night, wet and cold, a night to be in his flat with a glass of Jameson's, listening to jazz, not hanging round a suburban station. He lit a cigarette and walked over to a squad car in which a policewoman was sitting. Bending down he tapped on the glass.

'Got anything for me, Sue?'

She opened the window half a centimetre. 'Not till we've finished.'

'Taking your time, aren't you?'

'It's not easy. There are bits of him everywhere.'

'At least give me a name.'

'Can't help you, Phil. We're not releasing any details yet.'

'Come on, Sue. You know I'll find out anyway.' He grinned. 'Give me a hint?'

'Yeah, don't play on the train tracks.' The window closed.

'Ha bloody ha.'

He pulled his jacket tight and glanced around. You could count on seeing people hanging out near the station most nights, but over the last half hour the usual characters had melted away, offended by the presence of the cops. Philip strolled towards a group of less familiar figures that had gathered. Their coats, thrown on over pyjamas and slippers, proclaimed them as local residents drawn away from their televisions by the more exciting drama outside their front doors.

'Do you know who it was?' he asked them.

An elderly woman, her hand to her mouth, said: 'Young Michael.'

'Michael who?'

'Michael Maher.'

'Do you know where he lived?'

'Bentley Street.'

'What number?'

'Somewhere down the end.' She darted a look at him. 'Are you with the police?'

'I'm a reporter from *The Messenger.*'

'Well you should put something in the paper about this. That crossing's a deathtrap. I've told the council again and again.'

'Have Michael's parents been called?'

'His mum's there.' Her finger jabbed towards the ambulance parked beside the tracks. 'His dad flew the coop.'

Philip nodded. The story was coming together: *Boy tragically slain in crossing horror.* The local council angle was good. Ron, his editor, would like that — he had a long-running feud with the mayor. All Philip needed now was a picture of the dead kid. No problem, he'd do the deathknock tomorrow. 'Mrs Maher, *The Messenger* wants to ensure this tragedy never happens again. We will give Michael's story prominence as a warning to other parents and children. If you could possibly find a recent photograph ...' Piece of cake.

He flipped his notebook closed. Not bad: it wasn't yet midnight and he was out of there. The ambulance was making its way up the street, not bothering to turn on the siren. The cops were leaving, the bystanders were drifting away. *The Messenger*'s photographer, who had been there when Philip arrived, was packing up his gear.

Philip glanced at the scene a final time, and noticed someone new. A woman was standing by herself on the other side of the tracks. He paused and took a long look. Unlike the emergency crews or the other observers, she was openly weeping. Who, besides the mother, cared enough about the kid to stand here on a freezing winter night, her face crumpled? Perhaps it was worth finding out.

He walked across the tracks and stood beside her. She wore an old blue coat over her nightclothes, and her feet were bare despite the rain. 'What a tragedy,' he said. 'Poor Michael.'

She paid no attention, consumed by her own grief. Her hand was over her mouth, her body shaking.

He held out a tissue. 'Here. How did you know him?'

Still she ignored him, wiping her eyes. Her shoulder-length hair was reddish in the neon light. Philip's next question died on his lips. Something about her was familiar, like a musical phrase from long ago, something melancholy from a solo by Coltrane.

'Haven't we met before?' It wasn't the question he'd planned.

She looked at him without seeming to see, then began to walk away, down the middle of the road. Philip followed.

'I just wanted –'

'Go away!'

'I'm Philip Trudeau from *The Messenger*. What's your –'

'Leave me alone!'

She turned to glare at him, her face wet with tears and rain. Philip raised his hands in a calming gesture. A car of hoons screeched up behind them, horn blaring: *Heymoveyerfuckinarse*. Philip stepped out of their way, and the woman ran into the darkness. He followed her to a side street, but looking down it he couldn't make out which house she had gone into. He noted the name: Davis Avenue.

There was nothing more to be done. He walked back to his Kingswood and tossed his notebook onto the passenger seat. He coaxed the car into life, then braked as the bells on the level crossing began to ring. The last train from the city was about to come through. As he drummed his fingers on the steering wheel, he noticed a darkish stain on the sleeve of his jacket, where he had been leaning on the boom gate. He touched the wet patch gingerly, then held his fingertips in front of his face. They were red in the feeble light.

Do you feel numbed by his death? The question – which he'd learned on his first day as a cadet, twenty years ago – had served Philip well on many occasions. It did the job again when he paid a call on Sally Maher the following morning. An hour of sympathy was rewarded with a portrait of her son's grinning, freckled face. A trip to the school yielded more information. A quiet kid, Philip was told, with average grades that might have been higher if he hadn't been absent so often. *Bit of a dreamer*, one teacher said.

Philip's article portrayed the kid as a young prodigy with

strong community spirit. His editor loved the council angle: *Mayor ignored pleas on crossing of death*. A pity, Ron had commented, that the kid hadn't been killed in time for the council elections, but you couldn't have everything. Philip was happy, too: his story covered the whole front page and ran on to page two. It even got a small run in the metropolitan paper of which *The Messenger* was a suburban relative.

A few times Philip remembered the woman he'd seen crying beside the tracks. A couple of nights after the accident he awoke in darkness, her face in front of him. Red hair, pale skin, distraught expression. Why had she seemed familiar? He ran through a mental identity parade, but nothing checked. He gave up and went back to sleep.

A few days later, mid-afternoon, Philip's phone rang. He was sitting at his computer, about to complete solitaire.

'It's Sally Maher here.'

'And you are?' Red six on black seven.

'I'm Michael's mum. You came to my house.'

'Of course. What can I do for you?' When you were contacted by someone after a story, it was never good.

'I was expecting you to call me.'

'Why?' Black four on red five.

'You said you wanted to help ... Did you find out where he was going?'

Philip dragged his attention away from the screen. 'What?'

'The night he was hit.'

Philip covered the mouthpiece and groaned.

'Are you there?' Her voice had a touch of hysteria.

'Home?' Philip said.

'The police said he was riding the other way.'

'Maybe he was visiting his mates?'

'He never went out at night. He was a good boy. He went to bed early, said he was tired.' He could hear her choking back sobs. 'The first I knew he wasn't there was when the police called.'

Philip closed his eyes, put his head back and sighed. 'Look, he was your son, not mine. I've no idea where he was going.'

'But you talked to people. His friends, his teachers. Didn't you find any clues?'

Philip had gained little from his interviews with Michael's schoolmates. The kid had been a loner. He hadn't put that into his article, of course. Instead he had built up Michael's life into something special. His mother should be thanking him, not bugging him with crazy questions. Her voice sounded unsteady – maybe she'd been on the grog.

'Have you asked the police?'

'They weren't interested. Wanted to know if he was in any trouble.' She sounded angry now. 'But he was a good boy. A good boy.'

'I'll look through my notes, OK? If I come across anything, I'll call you.'

'All right.' Her voice was empty, defeated. There was a pause and he was about to end the call when she spoke again. 'I want to know why it happened, Mr Trudeau. Isn't that what you do? Find out why things happen?'

'That's what a coroner does, Mrs Maher. I'm just a reporter.' He hung up, and turned back to the solitaire. No, he'd lost it now: it wasn't going to come out.

'Hey Phil, take a look at these.' It was Ted, *The Messenger*'s photographer, with a sheaf of prints in his hand. 'Took 'em the other night, at the station. Whaddya reckon? Good eh?'

Philip glanced at the pictures. Ted was an aficionado of death. The photographer had a legendary sense for accidents – he kept his ear glued to the cops' radio, and often arrived on the scene before they did. It was said in the office, only half jokingly, that he sometimes turned up before an accident had even happened. When a truck overturned, cars smashed, or a builder fell off scaffolding, Ted would be there snapping away. Decapitations, mutilations and stabbings all made good material. Most of his work was too gruesome for publication but that didn't bother Ted, who kept the images for his own vast collection. Philip flipped quickly through pictures of the boy's body and handed them back. 'Very nice, Ted. You've excelled yourself. Reminds me of that Dylan album.'

'Which one?'

'Blood on the Tracks.'

Ted guffawed. 'Drink later?'

'Sure.' Philip's mind turned to the Irish pub. Another half hour and he'd be able to slip away. But his plans were shattered by a voice yelling down the hallway.

'Phil!'

He got slowly to his feet and dragged himself towards Ron's office, where his editor was pacing up and down. Ron's face was a banner headline proclaiming heart disease. 'Christ, Phil, what's going on?'

'What do you mean?'

'I've just copped a spray from Town Hall. Your story's full of holes. Didn't you talk to them?'

'I thought you wanted us to have a go at him.'

'Jesus!' Ron held a copy of *The Messenger*'s competitor, the *Post,* in Philip's face and smacked it with his knuckles. 'Seen this? A history of all the accidents at that crossing, plus the times it's been before council. And *she's* only just out of uni.' Ron flung the newspaper down on the desk and sank into his chair.

'They told me I was taking a risk when I hired you. I was prepared to make allowances because of your record, but I can't cut you any more slack. We may not be *The Biz & Fin*, but we have our standards.' Gloomily he flipped through the pages of the rival paper. 'The *Post* is leaving us for dead on this one. *Kids out of control!*'

'That's a beat up, Ron.'

'You don't say. That'd be why their circulation's double ours. You've gotta do a follow up.'

'What follow up? Is he gonna rise from the dead?'

'Lift your game, Phil. I don't like getting my arse kicked by the opposition. Any ideas?'

Philip reached for his smokes. 'Put those away,' Ron said. 'If I can't, you can't. What was he doing round the station at eleven at night? All the junkies go there, don't they?'

'He wasn't a junkie, Ron.'

'Well, what about the park? You know what that's like at night. Maybe he was ...?'

'Will you snap out of it? He wasn't doing that either. Three words: No Fucking Story. He was just a normal kid.'

'A normal kid who goes joy-riding round the station in the middle of the night?' Ron glared at Philip. 'Look into it, Phil. And for Christ's sake, get it right this time. You're running out of chances, mate.'

2

Philip's Friday evenings followed two patterns. Occasionally he spent the evening at the pub, alone or with Ted. More often he stayed home, listening to CDs and drinking whatever was in the house. It wasn't uncommon for him to go from Friday evening to Monday morning seeing and speaking to no one. The Friday night after his argument with Ron was shaping as the start of just such a weekend. He had half a bottle of Jameson's that he'd planned to drink as an accompaniment to Miles Davis' *Live in Stockholm*. But he couldn't focus on the music: he kept hearing the voice of Sally Maher. *I want to know why it happened*. Once there had been more to his life than filing twenty routine pieces – stories that wrote themselves – every week. *Didn't you find any clues?* Once he'd been fired up with the need to know.

By half past nine the Jameson's was finished. It wasn't too late: the bottle shop would still be open. He went into his bedroom to retrieve his shoes. Looking under the bed he noticed a dull gleam. He reached for it and his fingers closed around his sax. Twenty years ago now, having outgrown the instrument he played through high school, he'd answered an ad in the *Trading Post*. On Grand Final day, while everyone else was glued to the box, he'd driven to an address in a far northern suburb. The guy selling the sax was over sixty, a retired postman with crippling arthritis, but he played ten times better than Philip ever would. He couldn't believe Philip had never heard Coltrane and refused to let him leave until they had listened repeatedly to *A Love Supreme*.

'You're not walking out of here with my Selmer till you know what saxophone playing is,' he'd said. He took up the sax and played along with the record, making the hairs on Philip's neck stand up and his temples prickle.

By the time Philip staggered away, clutching the instrument, all he wanted to do was play like that. He wore out his own copy of *A Love Supreme* attempting to master it. One phrase he practised for weeks, repeating it over and over like a drunk with a grudge. It seemed to contain all the emptiness, all the longing – for what, he didn't know – in his life. In the end he let the obsession go: he could play the notes, but the magic was beyond him. He went back to normal life, picking up the sax a couple of times a week. He'd never be Coltrane, or even that postman, but he'd learned what music could do.

Now he lifted the sax from its resting place. How long since he'd touched it? Six months? A year? Longer still since he'd wrung any notes from it. Despite that, he'd never been tempted to sell it. His computer, sound system, furniture – all the stuff he and Sarah had bought together – was long gone. But not the sax. Cautiously he lifted it to his lips and tried a scale, like a kid at his first lesson. The keys were sticky, the reed was brittle, his lips had lost the muscle of regular playing. He attempted a riff – one of the first he'd ever learned. It was no good, he was thinking about it too much. He tried again, more relaxed this time, realising his fingers and lips had not forgotten everything. And as he played the slow, melancholy phrase, the woman by the railway lines came to mind. Her distraught face, red hair and bare feet. Who was she? He played on. He wished he'd got her name.

Banging exploded from the upstairs flat. His neighbours' enjoyment of a reality TV show was being disturbed. A man yelled: *Shaddupyacunt!* Philip blew a long loud fart in B flat, and tossed the sax aside.

Giving up the bottle-shop plan, he reached for a newspaper on the floor. Michael Maher's face grinned up at him. *Rail Tragedy* by Philip Trudeau. *Michael, 13, was always ready with a smile and a friendly word ... promising footballer ... community demands answers ...* He flipped through the rest of the paper. It provided the typical fare of the suburban press: golden wedding anniversaries, petty crime, zoning disputes, press releases published verbatim, all wrapped in a hundred pages of real estate. The same stories were recycled over and over — only the names changed. Philip sometimes wondered whether anyone would notice if they repeated entire articles word for word every few months.

He returned to the front page and looked again at Michael's face. *Isn't that what you do? Find out why things happen?* Wrong, love. I just sell real estate. But he knew she was right. A real journalist would have asked more questions, instead of leaving it all to the cops and the coroner. Philip flung the newspaper at the rubbish bin and emptied his glass.

He found a pen and paper and began sketching a crude map of Yarraville, starting with the railway line, which was traversed by Anderson Street. The kid had been riding up Anderson Street from west to east. His home was a few blocks behind him in Bentley Street. Back there were houses, the new supermarket, yuppie apartments, a few shops. On the other side, the side the kid hadn't made it to, were the pizza place, trendy cafés, the Irish theme pub, more streets and houses and the park. Why would he be heading that way? Sure, a few drugs were dealt around the station at night, but that didn't square with what he knew about Michael. What about the streets beyond the shopping strip? Philip tried to remember the names. The first was Hunter. The second he couldn't recall. The third ... Day? No, Davis. The barefooted woman had run to Davis Street. What if Michael had been heading there, too? Philip had made no attempt to find and interview the woman. Maybe she was a relative, or a teacher. But why would Michael sneak out to see her at eleven at night?

He yawned, scrunched up his map and it followed the newspaper into the bin. The next day was Saturday. He'd get up late. Then he'd drive to the bottle shop for a healthy breakfast. From there it was only a few hundred yards to Davis Street. Maybe he'd check it out. He'd sleep on it and see.

Davis Street typified the changes underway in Yarraville. Once working class, the area was gentrifying as young couples moved in, attracted by its faintly bohemian atmosphere and relatively cheap period housing. Philip parked his car and walked slowly along the street, glancing to left and right at small weatherboard and brick homes with tiny front yards. The Greek families grew olive trees and vegies; the newcomers grew ornamental roses. A few kids about Michael's age were kicking a football.

In front of one house a garage sale was in progress. Piles of old clothes and broken toys were spread around. Philip opened the gate and strolled in. He picked up a CD and approached the woman running the sale. She had a toddler pulling at her hand and a baby in her arms. Philip smiled at the kids, patting the toddler on the head. To the mother, he said: 'I'm looking for the place where my friend lives. It's somewhere on this street, but I just can't remember the number. She's about thirty, reddish hair ...'

The woman looked at him, distracted. Handing over a fiver,

Philip went on, 'She sometimes wears a blue coat with a kind of '60s look ...'

'Oh, you mean Nina? Hush darling.'

'A handful at that age, aren't they?' Philip said sympathetically.

'Yeah, Nina, that's right.'

'From the flats?' the woman pointed towards a nondescript two-storey apartment block across the street.

'The flats, of course. Thanks.'

Parked outside the building were an old yellow Mazda with a 'no nuclear' sticker on its bumper, and a smart Toyota four-wheel drive. Glancing up Philip noticed a balcony with clinking wind chimes and a few potted geraniums. The main entrance was locked. At the door there were four buzzers, not labelled with names. He pressed the first and a woman answered.

'Nina?'

'She's number two.'

There was no answer from number two. Philip walked back down the drive, past a row of letterboxes. Surreptitiously he opened the second box. He found an envelope addressed to Nina Fletcher, which opened easily. It contained a cheque in her name, with an attached note: *For photographic services.* Did that have anything to do with Michael? A few possibilities flickered. He resealed and returned the envelope, and studied the front of the building more carefully. The door to the wind-chime balcony was open, and inside he detected movement.

He returned to the buzzers and left his finger on number two for a full thirty seconds. *Come on, answer.*

Nothing happened. Christ, why was he bothering with this? At that moment a man came down the stairs, carrying a stroller and a small child, and opened the front door. Philip obligingly held it for him, then slipped inside. He jogged up the stairs. Putting his ear to the door of number two, he heard low voices. He knocked briskly and the voices stopped.

'Nina?' he called.

There was no answer for a few seconds. He knocked again, and was about to repeat her name when she spoke.

'Who is it?'

'Philip Trudeau from *The Messenger.* I want to ask you about Michael.' Silence. 'His mother's very distressed, Nina. She asked me to help.' He decided to take a punt. 'Why was Michael coming to see you, Nina?'

Silence. Finally, her voice: 'Go away, please. I can't talk to you.'

'His mum's devastated. She just wants to know what was going on.' He waited. There was no response, but he had her now: he could take his time. He bent down and slipped his card under the door. 'I'll be back, Nina. Call me when you're ready to talk.'

He waited for a few seconds at the bottom of the stairs, then continued down the drive. Reaching the street, he turned and looked up and, as he had expected, a figure in the window was watching him. The figure immediately retreated, but not before Philip got a good look. It wasn't Nina, but a smallish guy, middle-aged, fair-haired, leather-jacketed. A guy that Philip recognised. And on placing him, Philip realised why Nina, too, had seemed so familiar.

3

Six months earlier, Philip had received an unwelcome surprise when, about to depart for work, he had flipped open his letterbox. Inside he found a letter from Queensland, marked with the logo of Elsworthy & Elsworthy, waiting for him like a bomb. No, worse. A bomb would kill you straight off, but lawyers inflict a lingering death.

He had pocketed the envelope and headed to the office. He didn't open it until he had steeled himself with strong black coffee and was sitting at his desk. Then his eye hurried over the ponderous phrases: *financial obligations, initiate proceedings, access rights*. He sat silently for ten minutes, his head resting in his hands.

He opened his wallet and took out the creased photo of Amy, aged five, riding on his shoulders at Luna Park. She was laughing, her pudgy hands gripping the top of his head, her face painted as a tiger, her mouth frosted with fairy floss. These days Amy was a spindly thirteen-year-old and he knew next to nothing about her life. Each time he visited he was more of a stranger. But to have his occasional visits reduced to zero — that he couldn't stand.

Finally he roused himself. The light on his phone was blinking. He hit replay to listen to his messages. Another burglary: one hundred dollars taken. Delete. Rotary holding a charity barbecue. Delete. The matey tones of the local MP's press officer. Instant delete. One more message. 'My name is John Price.' An old bloke, by the sound of it, his voice high and tremulous. 'I have a business proposition for you, Mr Trudeau.' Philip's finger hovered over delete. 'When you ring me back, we'll discuss terms.' Philip hesitated, then scribbled down the number.

The day passed slowly. Conscious of Ron's requirement that every journo file twenty stories a week – conscious, too, that he was well down on that figure – Philip went through his usual drill: phone calls to his network of cop shops, council departments and community centres; checking his inbox for emailed press releases to which his sole change, before flicking them on to the subeditors, was the addition of the words *by Philip Trudeau*. His eye kept falling on the Queensland letter. By three o'clock he was ready to crack. He dialled John Price.

'I'm hoping you can help me, Mr Trudeau. I'm seventy-six years old and I've lived a very full life. I've got an enormous amount of material here and since my wife died I've been busy sorting it out. Quite a job.' He gave a breathless laugh.

'I'm sure it is,' Philip said. 'You mentioned a business proposition.'

'I'm not much of an author, Mr Trudeau. I require the assistance of a professional to write my memoirs.'

'You want a ghostwriter?' Philip said, and laughed. 'I don't do that kind of work.'

'You've been recommended to me, Mr Trudeau. And I remember your work for the *Business and Financial Review*.'

'You must have a long memory.'

'I think you'd find the job interesting. I've known some eminent artists in my time.' Price reeled off names.

'I've never heard of those people. My background's business, not art.'

‘I’ll pay you well for the job, Mr Trudeau. Won’t you at least come and discuss it? I’m only down the road from you – Clarke Street, Williamstown.’

Philip wavered. But pride wouldn’t settle his debts and get Elsworthy & Elsworthy off his back. Maybe this offer would give him breathing space, if he could stand it.

So the next Saturday he had driven to Price’s house. It was a couple of suburbs away, only ten minutes’ drive from Yarraville. There’s plenty of money round here, Philip thought, parking behind a four-wheel drive: company directors with sparkling wives and cello-playing children. Approaching the front door he heard the swell and crash of an orchestra and choir. He leaned on the doorbell. There’d been a time when he was a welcome guest in houses like these. *Nice to see you, Phil. Got any good tips for us? Where’s the market heading?* But this place, although old and solid, appeared neglected. Weeds and creepers ran riot in the garden, the gutters overflowed, the paint was peeling and there were cracks in the brickwork. Around the front step were piled numerous cardboard boxes, spilling papers and books. And the door wasn’t opened by a pink-faced host, drawing him into a room bubbling with laughter and champagne. Instead a small, crumpled old man stood there, stains on his lapels, tears streaming down his face. ‘Mozart’s *Requiem*,’ he said. ‘It always has this effect on me.’ He put out his hand. ‘John Price.’

He led Philip down a dim hallway. They had to weave between more stacks of boxes. But this was nothing compared to the room into which they emerged. There was hardly space to move. Besides several thousand books, there were mountains of newspapers, magazines and yet more boxes. The walls were jammed with pictures and every surface was taken up with papers and bric-a-brac. The room reeked of damp and something else: Philip noticed plates with ancient food crusted to them and cups of undrunk tea that had grown cultures of mould. 'Impressive,' Philip said, thinking: *Christ, the old bugger's off his head.*

Price chuckled. 'This is only a fraction of it. There's lots more in the back rooms.'

'What is all this stuff?'

'Papers, documents, items of historical interest.'

'Interest to whom?' Philip opened a leather-bound volume. It contained a collection of local newspapers from 1953. *Fight to stop noxious trades*, ran the headline.

'Public interest. Some day I'm going to donate all this to the museum. I just have to get it in order first.'

'I'm sure they'll be delighted.' Philip sat down on a chair that Price had cleared for him and coughed as a cloud of dust rose. 'Now, what about your memoirs?'

'I've led a very full life, and it's time to put some of it down, with the help of an expert.'

'You've always lived round here?'

'Yes, all my life. But this area used to be very different. The docks, you know. Factories, rail yards, abattoirs, quarries. Mostly gone now, of course.'

'You said something about artists.'

'That's right. I was a member of the Maribyrnong Group,' Price said, gesturing towards the walls. 'Look around you – this is the largest collection of their paintings anywhere.'

On the walls hung a couple of dozen pictures, brown and covered with dust. They struck Philip as drab. 'What was the Maribyrnong Group?'

Price stared. 'The group headed by Jimmy West – you've heard of him, of course? Sir James, as he became later?'

'Vaguely.'

‘I’m amazed that a man of your ...You know, friend of Picasso ... No? Well, never mind, never mind. I’ve got all that here for you anyway. Later on Jimmy went to England and we didn’t see much more of him. What about Bill Shearwood? Vic Smith? Tom Zylinski?’

‘Sorry. What about you — are you an artist, too?’

‘No great talent, I’m afraid. My role is as a collector. And I’ve done a good deal of singing. I’ve got some programs somewhere. Gilbert and Sullivan, you know. Would you like to see ...’

‘Please don’t trouble yourself.’

‘Oh, it’s no trouble.’ Price leapt to his feet and began rummaging among the boxes, humming ‘I am the captain of the Pinafore ...’ In mid-rummage, something distracted him. ‘Ah yes, I was forgetting my photography. I’ve got a huge amount.’ He held up a box full of glass slides. ‘My collection of pamphlets. My correspondence. And then there are my books, yes, my books. Take a look at this edition of Matthew Flinders’ *Voyages*. It cost me ten shillings in 1964.’

‘Amazing,’ Philip said. Ghostwriter for this old bore? Never in a million years. God, he needed a drink. He cleared his throat and began to rise from his seat, but there was no stopping Price.

‘My health isn’t too good, so I’ve been sorting my collection, getting rid of a few non-essentials, putting the rest in order. I’ve decided to go through the lot, writing down my memories. That’s why I need your help, Mr Trudeau.’

‘I’d love to help, but this isn’t my thing,’ Philip said decisively, and began to back out of the room. ‘Good luck with the memoirs, but ...’

‘I’ll pay you well, Mr Trudeau ...’

‘Look, I’m not a ghostwriter ...’

Speaking simultaneously they shuffled towards the door, Philip in reverse, his hands held up to ward off the old man. Close to the door, Philip’s heel kicked over a small painting leaning against the wall. He bent and picked it up, and stared.

It was a portrait of a young woman. She was sitting in a plain room, looking straight ahead. She had reddish hair, a small face and dark eyes. The woman was attractive – or had once been – but something about her was wrong. She was too pale, and when Philip looked closely he saw swellings under her skin. Portraitists, he thought, did their best to hide blemishes – to make the ugly look beautiful, the dull seem fascinating. This artist seemed to have gone to the other extreme, putting in every unpleasant detail. And she had sat there and taken it. But there was still a radiance about her, and defiance glittered in her eyes, however weak her body was. She was not someone to cross.

'What's this?' Philip asked.

Price looked at it, his flow of words interrupted. An expression crossed his face that mingled surprise with apprehension. 'It's one of Jimmy's portraits. *Valerie.*' He took the picture from Philip's hands and placed it on a table, face down. 'I was thinking five thousand dollars.'

Philip turned his gaze from the painting to the old man. 'For the picture?'

'No, no, no. For the job.'

Five thousand dollars. Enough to make a dent in his debts. To avert, at least for now, legal action. To maintain access rights to Amy.

'That's generous,' he said. 'But I'll have to think –'

There was the sound of the front door opening, footsteps in the hall. A voice called out 'John!' Philip and Price both turned. A man was picking his way carefully through the towers of boxes. 'Afternoon,' the newcomer said. 'We did say 2.30, didn't we?'

'Hello, Stefan, good to see you.' The old man shuffled forward. 'Oh, let me introduce Philip Trudeau, he's going to help me with my memoirs.'

The man put out his hand. 'Hello, Philip, I'm Stefan West.

Aren't you with *The Biz & Fin*?'

'Used to be.'

'So you're writing the memoirs? John's a lucky man.'

'Actually we're still discussing that.'

'Stefan has a gallery in the city,' Price put in.

'My skills are more on the business side,' Stefan said. 'Helping people acquire an artwork they love, watching an artist's career develop ... It's not like being an artist yourself, but it gives me satisfaction. Unfortunately my dad didn't pass his talent on to me.'

'Your dad?'

'James West.'

Philip looked again at Stefan West, more carefully this time. He was a small guy, around Philip's age, neatly dressed in a black t-shirt and jeans, dark jacket and white tennis shoes. 'I'm sure you'll enjoy the job,' Stefan said. 'John's lived an amazing life, and he's got an incredible collection.'

'Oh, really, Stefan,' the old man said, dancing around like a geriatric elf.

'Well, it's true.' Stefan turned to Philip. 'John was my father's closest friend. He's kept *everything* from the era. He's one of the city's leading collectors.' Price was laughing and making self-deprecating gestures, but he had gone pink from vanity and excitement.

'John, why don't you trot off and get us a drink?' Stefan said. 'He's got a rather good collection of single malts in the next room.' Philip cheered up at this news. As Price went to get the whisky, Stefan went on: 'I appreciate you helping the old bloke out – it means a lot to him.'

'It's not really settled. I'm not sure I'm the right person.'

'I understand. His memoirs are pretty dull.'

'I'm a journalist, not a ghostwriter. I don't know these famous artists he talks about.'

Stefan grinned, as if he and Philip were in on a private joke. 'Oh, really? Actually, only one of them was famous – or any good. My old man. The rest were nobodies.'

'So his collection's not really valuable?'

Stefan shook his head. 'He's just an eccentric old bloke, with a few ordinary paintings. I mean, look at this place! I keep saying he should get someone in to clean up, but he won't hear of it. He's got a couple of minor pieces, but as for the rest of them ...'

'What about this one?' Philip lifted the picture of the woman that Price had placed on the table. The sickness in her face and the relentlessness of her stare made him shiver. What name had Price given her? Valerie. Who was she?

Stefan took the picture from him and smiled. 'Nothing special, mate.' The word 'mate' sounded strange from him, Philip thought, almost a word from a foreign language.

'But John said it was by your father.'

'Did he?' Stefan rolled his eyes. 'He doesn't have much idea. But he *was* a friend of dad's, so I try to give him advice where I can.'

'Advice?'

'I'm planning to bequeath the best pieces to the State Gallery,' Price said, pottering back into the room with three glasses and a bottle of Scotch. 'Stefan's helping with the arrangements.'

Price dispensed the glasses and poured a generous measure into each, an action which seemed to confirm Philip's appointment.

Stefan raised his glass in Philip's direction with a grin. 'Cheers, Philip. Here's to the memoirs.'

Here's to the memoirs. Well, they had never happened. Philip's career as a ghostwriter had been mercifully brief. Although Philip vaguely remembered one more visit to Price's house, where he had endured hours of tedious reminiscences, the project had stalled. Philip's initial reaction had been correct – he wasn't cut out to be a ghostwriter. He'd made his excuses to Price, sent some money to Queensland, and let the matter drop. But that hadn't stopped the old bloke from continuing to call him and leave messages, which Philip had deleted unheard. Eventually, though, the calls had stopped, and the subject of John Price and the Maribyrnong Group had slipped out of Philip's mind. Until now.

Sitting outside Nina's place, he recalled John Price and his bizarre offer. The five grand would have come in handy. He was only just managing to keep a step ahead of the lawyers. And thanks to his fuck-up with the story about Michael, his standing at the paper was in jeopardy. He needed a good story now. He needed it badly. He needed Nina Fletcher to talk to him. But she was hiding in her flat – in the company of Stefan West.

Stefan and Nina. How could they possibly know each other? Stefan was a gallery owner. His natural habitat was the moneyed suburbs of the east. He couldn't have much business in this part of town. It was one thing to find him in John Price's house, ramshackle but solidly middle-class; Nina's place was a cheap flat. Casting his mind back, Philip remembered Stefan with the painting in his hands. *Nothing special about this, mate*. Something about Nina reminded him of that portrait. It wasn't just her reddish hair – it was some other quality, like a melancholy solo in a minor key. He wondered, now, if that was what had struck him about Nina the first time he had seen her.

Half an hour later, two figures emerged from the flats. They were leaving together. They crossed the road and got into the four-wheel drive.

Philip allowed them to reach the end of the street, then started the engine and cautiously followed. He stayed a few vehicles behind Stefan's car, which was easy to pick out. Philip assumed Stefan would cross the bridge and head back to the city. But instead of turning onto the freeway the four-wheel drive continued straight on towards Williamstown, the beachside suburb where John Price lived. After a few minutes it pulled up in a shopping strip. Philip stopped fifty metres further on. In his rear-view mirror he watched Stefan get out of the car and enter a door fronting the street. Nina was waiting in the passenger seat, staring through the windscreen. When Philip was about to light his second cigarette, Stefan reappeared, got back into his car and made a U-turn. Philip turned, too, and drove back past the place Stefan had entered. A bronze sign at the front read: *Gordon Parker, Solicitor.* The name meant nothing to Philip. He continued to follow. This time Stefan took the slip road onto the freeway and headed over the bridge towards the city.

Swerving from lane to lane, Philip tried to keep Stefan and Nina in sight. They left the freeway and were soon inching their way up a street in the CBD. The four-wheel drive took a couple of lefts and crawled down a narrow lane. Stefan pulled over to the side and parked illegally. Philip had little choice but to continue past. They were oblivious to him. They were about to enter a building with a plate on the wall: *The Stefan West Gallery.*

Philip decided to drive around the block. But further down the lane he got stuck behind a man trying to reverse a large truck into a small gate. A good fifteen minutes had passed before he was back outside the gallery. Philip parked and stood on the pavement for a while, checking the place out. It was open but he decided against walking in. He would prefer Stefan not to know that someone was on his trail.

'That your car, mate?' Philip looked up. A bloke in overalls was hailing him from the window of a removal van. 'Mind moving it? I gotta park the van.'

'I'm just going.' Philip scribbled the gallery's address on a Rizla paper, climbed back into his car and headed for home.

4

The kid's funeral attracted few mourners. There were no more than thirty people in the church on that cold morning one week after the accident. Philip took a position at the back from which he could see everybody. Besides the kid's mother and one or two people who could have been relatives – though no one looked likely to be his father – the congregation was made up of teachers, neighbours and kids from Michael's class. Just as the service was about to start, Nina Fletcher walked in and sat by herself at the back.

The service passed quickly. There were a couple of short eulogies, one by a teacher who referred to the kid as 'Mitchell' before correcting himself. He said that the kid would be a much-missed member of the class. The coach of the under-14s footy team said, 'He always tried his heart out ... he wouldn't give up', while admitting that the kid hadn't been around much lately. A pop song was played, said to be Michael's favourite. Philip watched Nina. Couldn't she add anything to this bland picture of a life? But she sat silently, pulling her jacket tightly around herself.

They left the church for the cemetery. The area devoted to recent burials had shining marble monuments inscribed in Polish, Vietnamese, Spanish and Italian, many of them heaped with flowers. Walking between them, Philip kept his eyes on Nina. She spoke to no one as she approached the group standing around the grave. The hole looked absurdly small. The sky began to spit with rain, and not far away a train whistled. The schoolkids stood silently, shocked by the realisation that a child could die. The priest, who had noted the dark clouds, spoke rapidly, like a race caller. 'Together let us earnestly pray that our God, who is rich in mercy, will forgive our brother all his offences ...' Does he really believe this stuff? Philip wondered. More than likely it was just a job. These formulas meant no more to the priest than Philip's stories did to him. They were two of a kind: believers once, but these days peddlers of meaningless words.

When the priest got to the words: 'O God, in whose presence the spirits of the dead have life ...', Michael's mother wailed, 'Oh God, oh God, Mikey ...' The priest stopped momentarily, all eyes turned towards the disturbance, and Philip was the only person who noticed Nina Fletcher step forward and drop something that fluttered onto the coffin. The priest nodded to a man in overalls who began shovelling earth into the hole, quickly filling it. Behind him lay a simple white wooden cross to be knocked in when the job was done.

The mourners drifted away. The priest glanced at the sky and put his umbrella up. Several people gathered around Michael's sobbing mother. Philip paused. He'd planned to get more quotes out of the relatives – *If the council had listened, he'd be alive today* – but he didn't want to lose Nina, who was now walking quickly towards the road. He began to jog after her, catching up just as she was about to reach the gate.

'Nina!'

She turned, saw him, kept walking.

He hurried after her. 'Look, I don't mean to hassle you.' Her expression told him what she thought of this comment. 'I promise this won't take long. I just need to know why Michael was going to your place that night.'

'I don't know.'

He was exultant: it was an admission. 'You must have some idea. What had you been doing together?'

'We were friends.'

'He was only thirteen.'

'So what?' She stopped, her eyes searching Philip's face. 'Did you think that ...? Look, he was just a kid. He was interested in photography.'

'So you took pictures of him?'

'Yes. I mean no. There was nothing ...' She put her hand to her face, kept on walking. 'Please, it's a funeral, I can't talk to you now.'

He caught up with her again as she reached her car. Fumbling in her pocket, she dropped her keys. Philip quickly bent and picked them up.

'Nina, I'm very sorry, I can see you're upset. But I promise, I promise, I will leave you alone, if you'll just tell me what Michael was doing at your place. Eleven o'clock is a weird time for a thirteen-year-old to go visiting. His mother said he went to bed early. Was he into something he shouldn't have been?' Philip was pretty sure drugs had nothing to do with it, but sometimes floating an outrageous idea would lead the unguarded to give something away.

'Don't be stupid.'

'How much were you paid for the photographs?' This was pure kite-flying, but he was feeling lucky.

'I wasn't p—' She stopped herself. 'Give me my keys.'

'What did you drop into the grave just now?'

'Give me my keys.'

'Why did you —'

'Give me my keys!' She managed to grab his hand and ripped

the keys out of it, cutting the skin on his palm. Angrily wringing his hand, he blocked her way as she was about to open the door. 'How do you know Stefan West?'

'What?'

'He was at your place the other day.'

She stared at him. 'It's nothing to do with Stefan. Mike was just curious. Too curious. And now he's ...' With a quick movement she forced the door open, climbed into the driver's seat, slammed the door. The car took off with a jerk, nearly hitting him.

Philip watched her go, sucking his hand. His old instinct for a story hadn't let him down. It was something a hack like Ron would never understand.

Looking back across the cemetery, he saw that everyone had dispersed. Never mind: he knew where Sally Maher lived. He'd talk to her tomorrow. He walked back to his own car. What had the kid been *too curious* about? Philip felt something awakening inside him that had been dormant for a long time.

Twenty-two Bentley Street was a small terraced house with a neat garden. It was tucked away in a residential street close to the station. Sally Maher was in her mid-thirties but looked older. Her hair was more grey than brown and as she talked to Philip she constantly plucked at it. He could see the beginning of a bald patch on the side of her head. Her eyes were dark-ringed. There was an empty bottle of aspirin on the floor beside the sofa. Three photos of Michael stood on top of the TV – the one that Philip had borrowed for publication was in the middle. Now it was time to find out what else she might know.

'I wanted to ask you about his friends.'

'I don't know ... he went round by himself.'

'What did he do?'

She shook her head. 'I had the bakery and the cleaning. I was out all day, sometimes nights, too.'

'Did he ever mention a woman called Nina?'

'A *woman*?'

'In her thirties, reddish hair,' Philip prompted. 'She was at the funeral.'

'Is she a teacher?'

'No. She says she was a friend – a photographer.'

She looked at him blankly.

'Try to remember, Sally. It could be important. Did he ever mention photography? Did you notice him having extra money to spend?' Philip tried to keep his impatience under control.

After a moment, she said: 'He mentioned something about making prints. I thought it was for school.'

Making prints? 'I think he was going to see her, the night he was hit.'

'Why?'

'I don't know.'

'Tell me where she lives,' Sally said. 'I want to see her. What was she doing with my boy?' Philip didn't answer. 'You mean – pictures? Oh God.' She lowered her face into her hands and began to sob, in an uncontrollable convulsion of grief.

Philip sat beside her and touched her shoulder. 'Don't jump to conclusions. We don't really know yet. But you can count on me. This stor– this tragedy is very important to me. I'll tell you the moment I find anything out.'

She recovered a little and took the tissue he offered her. 'What about the police?'

'No, no, no – not yet. Just leave it to me.'

She nodded. 'All right. Thank you.'

'Is there anyone else who ...'

She shook her head. 'I'm on my own. His dad left two weeks after he was born. Then I got retrenched. Did some cleaning here and there, then I got the bakery job. We were starting to get ahead. I was planning to buy us a place of our own. No point now. Maybe if I hadn't been working all the time.'

'Come on, Sally. You did the best you could.' She was sobbing again, head in hands. Oh, Christ. This could take forever. 'I'll make you a cup of tea,' he said.

He stood up, walked into the kitchen, found the kettle and turned it on. He took two mugs from a row of hooks – Bart Simpson on one, the Bulldogs on the other. As he waited for the water to boil he wandered into the hall, where he noticed a half-open door. This was Michael's room. Sally had allowed Philip to see it briefly on his first visit. Now he quietly pushed the door open and went in. It was a normal kid's room. A chest of drawers stuffed with clothes, all clean and folded. A tank with two goggle-eyed fish that swam ravenously to the surface, mouths gawping. A box of more-or-less broken toys. An ancient teddy. Old runners under the bed. A football. A couple of shelves of books – more, Philip suspected, than the average boy. Quite a few detective stories. Michael may not have got high grades, but he'd been a reader. On the second shelf, books on history and photography were mixed in among some about bikes and cars. Philip had believed that kids didn't read books anymore; Amy had shown little interest in the ones he'd given her. On the wall was a rally car, an American pop star, dinosaurs. Philip walked to the bed and sat down. A memory came to him of sitting on Amy's bed when she was three, reading fairy tales. She never wanted them to stop. And everyone lived happily ever after. He'd never seen Amy's current room: they only met on neutral ground. Philip wondered if Michael's dad, wherever he was, still thought about his son. He wondered if he knew Michael was dead.

Then he noticed something. Blutacked to the side of the chest of drawers was a black-and-white photograph. It showed two young men and a woman, sitting together on a sunny afternoon. Their appearance placed them in the 1950s or '60s, Philip guessed. What was Michael doing with this? He pulled the photograph from its place and focused his eyes on the woman in the middle of the group. Hers was a familiar face. Dark eyes. A cool, interrogative expression. It was the woman from the painting at John Price's house. Valerie. But here she looked in better shape; her face was fuller and made up, her eyes bright. Again he felt the prickling at his temples. Who was this woman, and why did Michael have her photograph?

In the kitchen the kettle clicked off. Philip stood up. He could hear sobbing from the next room. The photograph couldn't have any meaning to Sally – surely she wouldn't notice if it vanished. He folded it and slid it into his inside jacket pocket, then went and made the tea.

An hour later he was back at Nina's place with the photograph in his hand. He didn't need to press the buzzer this time: the outside door was open. When he ran up the stairs, so was the door to her flat. The place was bare. A young man in a suit was inside, pacing around with a clipboard. He looked at Philip with hostility.

'Yeah?'

'Where's Nina?'

'Moved out,' the young guy said, going back to his pacing. 'Without notice. She'll lose her bond,' he added with satisfaction.

'Where's she gone?'

'Do I look psychic?'

'I need to see her. It's urgent.'

'She's gone, that's all I can tell you. Some guy dropped the key off an hour ago. Know anyone looking for a flat?'

Philip trudged back down the stairs. Nina was gone and with her his best chance of finding out about Michael. He stood in the driveway and looked up at the window. For a moment he thought he saw a woman watching him from behind the glass. Then the sun came out and the shadow disappeared. Stuffing the photo into his jacket, Philip turned and walked back to his car.

5

Philip's eyes opened and instantly he was fully awake. He awoke at 7.15 every morning, regardless of what time he had gone to bed, even when he had a hangover, like today. Right now inside Castlemaine fists would be hammering on doors, boots tramping along gangways, keys rattling. Men would be cursing and rolling from their bunks, returning from dreams of freedom. For Philip it often happened in reverse: he dreamed of Castlemaine, and awoke to find himself free. If this was freedom.

Philip hadn't dreamed of Castlemaine last night though. Instead he had dreamed of a woman whose face remained in his mind. He sat up in bed and took the photograph he had found in Michael's room from his bedside table. The woman looked back at him, her face half hidden in shadow. Now she was gone, but he had the impression that she had been close to him a moment before. He had felt her breath on his lips as she had whispered something important. But the words were lost, washed away by the feeble sunlight. What did she want from him? Did she, too, want a ghostwriter to tell her story?

He swung his legs out of bed and made for the kitchen. In a few minutes he was gulping down strong tea and dragging on the first cigarette of the day. He placed the photo in front of him on the table, smoothed it out and stared. Why did Michael have this photograph? Was it one of the prints he had mentioned to his mother? Nina must know. She might have resisted, but he would soon have broken her down. She knew that, too, so she skipped her flat. OK, he would find out for himself. Starting with what the photograph itself could tell him.

It looked like a group of friends setting out on an excursion. They were sitting in a car. The men wore jackets and corduroys, and one was bearded. A bohemian look. The woman's arm was around the fairer of the two men. He looked faintly familiar. But what was that stuff piled into the back of the car? And was there anything significant about the building in the background? He could see a brick wall, iron railings, a tree and a house.

Philip sat back, and blew smoke at the ceiling. Memory flickered like a dodgy light globe. John Price. At their second, and last, meeting, Philip had unwillingly listened to the old bloke rambling on about his artistic friends and their excursions. The Maribyrnong Group. Valerie was in the painting at Price's house and in this photograph. So was this a photograph of the Maribyrnong Group?

Six months ago, after toasting Price's memoirs with Scotch, Philip had agreed to come back the next Saturday and interview the old man. He had returned to the crumbling old house armed with a portable Sony and recorded Price's chatter. Did he still have the tape?

Philip went into his spare room, which he used as a dumping ground for all the stuff he didn't need from day to day. He had never bothered to unpack or buy shelves; this was supposed to be temporary digs, although he'd been here for twelve months. If the tape was anywhere, it would be here. He rummaged through newspapers, bills, disks, empty bottles, paperbacks, shoes, uncovering half-a-dozen tapes in the process. He slotted them in turn into the machine.

Coltrane in New York: good to find that one again. Some councillor droning on about street lighting. An irate restaurant owner whose premises had been closed down by health inspectors. Philip's voice: 'Would you say this is a council vendetta?' Last one. On this tape, there seemed to be nothing at all, except a background hiss. Philip was about to give up when he heard John Price's quavering tones: '... most important years of my life!' This was it.

How much would he have to replay? He remembered Price babbling on for a couple of hours. There was nothing for it, he'd have to listen to the lot. He hit rewind and fetched his rollies from the kitchen. He pressed play and settled in for a long spell. Hearing that voice, faint but audible, he was in Price's library again. Musty smells of old books and mould mingled with the fragrance of jasmine that wafted through the open French windows. Birds yacked in the bottlebrush tree. Philip had sat in a rickety chair and the old man had been opposite him on a sofa. The tape recorder had balanced uneasily on a box between them.

'Let's make a start then,' Philip said, with an enthusiasm he was far from feeling. 'I'm sure you've got a lot to tell me.'

'Yes, yes, yes. I've lived a very full life, very full.' Price perched opposite Philip, frail, snow-haired, rubbing his hands together with a sound like rustling paper. 'I hardly know where to begin.'

'At the beginning, I guess. What's your first memory?'

'Let me show you this,' the old man interrupted, leaping to his feet and disappearing among the shelves. Philip heard a creaking noise and saw Price scrambling up a stepladder. 'It's up here somewhere ... yes, here we are ... one of the first books I ever bought. Got it from South Melbourne Market in 1951, or was it '52?'

Philip flicked through the tatty brown volume that Price

reverently handed him, while Price launched into the tale of where, how and why he had bought the book. Feigning interest, Philip wondered how much of this he could stand. But he concentrated on the money; he was depending on Price's dough. He jumped in, as Price showed no sign of shutting up.

'That's fascinating, but I need the basic facts. Birth, marriage, that sort of stuff.'

'The basic facts, yes. Name, rank, service number. Corporal Price, SX17180. Never forget that.'

'OK, the army, why not. Where did you –'

'I've got plenty of books about the war.' Price leapt to his feet again.

'Oh Christ,' Philip muttered. Price's high-pitched voice continued from deep among the shelves, scrambling the names of cities and battles and generals in a rapid monologue. Giving up, Philip let his eyes wander around the room. They alighted on the corner where he had seen the painting of the young woman on his previous visit. The picture was gone now.

For the next hour the old man was like a fly buzzing between his sofa and the shelves, never settling for more than a few seconds. Piles of books mounted around them. Price had an endless fund of stories, even if Philip couldn't see how they fitted together. For twenty minutes he listened to Price speak of the Kokoda Trail – my God, he thought, the old man's been through hell. Perhaps he could even get a feature out of it: *A Veteran Remembers*. Then it dawned on him that Price was recounting the story of some digger whose memoirs he'd read. Price himself had never left Australia; in fact, it was hard to specify anything he had done. He never mentioned family or career. Philip gradually realised that Price's books were his life. He spoke of the authors as if they were his friends, and their experiences as if they were his own. Price didn't need a ghostwriter

– his life had been ghostwritten already by the authors in his library.

'Look, John,' Philip almost shouted. The old man had disappeared into the next room in search of something. 'This isn't working. I need you to sit down here and tell me where you were born, school, jobs, all that.'

There was silence. Then Price reappeared. The energy had drained out of him. He walked slowly to the mantelpiece, on which there were an assortment of medicine bottles, swallowed a few pills and sat down.

'Are you all right?' Philip asked.

Price nodded feebly. 'My health's not the best ... sometimes overtire myself.'

'Perhaps we'd better carry on another day.'

'No, I'll be all right. I know I talk too much, Mr Trudeau. It's just that we don't have much time and there's so much to say. I've had a very ...'

'Full life. Yes, indeed. Packed with incident.'

Price picked up a bottle of Scotch and sloshed generous measures into two glasses. 'There's a lot I'd like to tell you.'

'That's what I'm here for.'

'Very lonely since Alice died. Not many visitors.'

'What about Stefan?'

'Oh yes, Stefan,' the old man said, brightening. 'He's very good to me, very good. Nothing's too much trouble.'

Philip stood up. 'Let's carry on another day.'

'Don't go yet, Mr Trudeau.' There was a note of panic in his voice.

'It's getting dark.' Philip looked out of the French windows. The sky was streaked with pink and dusk was falling on the wide lawn. Ice clinked in Price's glass: the old man was trembling as he stared into the garden. Philip looked at him. 'What is it, John?'

The old man's mouth opened and closed. Finally he managed to say: 'The curtains ... please ...'

Philip stood up and looked out into the gathering gloom. The garden was filigreed with shadows and shapes. For a moment he wondered whether a figure was standing in the middle of the lawn, staring into the room; then a car swept past, its headlights raking the garden, and there was nothing there. Philip closed the French windows, locked them and drew the curtains firmly.

Price took out a handkerchief and wiped his face. 'Just my eyes, playing tricks. You can stay a bit longer, can't you?'

Philip sighed and sat down. 'Tell me about your artistic friends.'

Price cheered visibly. 'The Maribyrnong Group. They were a great bunch. Jimmy West, Bill Shearwood, Vic Smith, Tom Zylinski and I.'

Philip scribbled down the names, despite his rising scepticism. No doubt this was another scenario from one of Price's books. Any minute now he would claim to be a mate of Vincent van Gogh and to have his ear in a jar. 'So what did the Group do?'

'We used to go on painting expeditions. We'd all pile into Tom's Ford and head out into the bush,' Price said, with the excitement of a ten-year-old recounting a trip to Disneyland. 'And we held an exhibition in Salvation Hall — I've got a review somewhere. I think it might be in one of those.' He gazed thoughtfully at a stack of boxes.

'Let's not worry about that right now.'

But Price was already on his feet and scrabbling in the top box, emerging with a bulging document, which he handed to Philip. 'Here, take a look at this.' It was a scrapbook, stuffed with yellow cuttings and photos. Philip skimmed the contents. *Exhibition shows promise. Parisian tour de force for young Aussie. West honoured in Venice.*

'I followed Jimmy's career all the way through,' Price said, pink from Scotch and pride. 'Those are from the early days, just local papers, but these are from *The Argus*, when he made his name in Paris. We were so proud of him.' He pointed to a photograph of a tall young man in overcoat and hat, a young woman on his arm, a painting in the background. Philip glanced at the date: July 1951.

'Who's the blonde?' Philip asked.

'That's Pamela Flett — later his wife. You probably know her as Lady Pamela West.'

'The philanthropist?'

'That's right.'

'Not bad, was she?' Philip said. Lady West had died only a few years earlier, and her saintly smile had beamed from the front page of all the papers. In her later years she had been a fixture of Melbourne's upper social strata. Her benevolent presence had graced the opening of every new hospital wing and the first night of every opera. It was unsettling to be confronted by her as a glamorous creature in her twenties.

'This was when Jimmy went to England,' Price went on, rapidly flicking pages. 'I used to get the English newspapers, so I could follow what was going on.' Philip registered a dozen or so photographs in rapid succession, showing James West, often with Pamela, in the company of well-known people. Price, who recalled them all, and who had clearly rehearsed this spiel many times, rattled off a list of names, dates and places.

'You must have been good friends, to keep all this stuff.'

'Oh yes, Jimmy and I were very close. But of course he was busy ... and he couldn't come back often.'

'Well, this is interesting, but it doesn't tell me much about *you*,' Philip said, handing the scrapbook back. 'I mean it's your memoirs you want me to write — not his.'

'Yes, yes, that's right,' Price said. But Philip's words had set his mind off on another tack. 'There's already a biography of Jimmy, by Peter McKendrick. I offered him my services, but he didn't take me up on it. Pity, because there's a lot he didn't know. For example, several of his photographs are incorrectly captioned. Would you believe there's a photo of Jimmy in Rapallo in 1956 with Sid Nolan, but it's been captioned as *Rome* in *1963* ...'

As Price jabbered on, his voice as high-pitched and repetitive as the birds outside, Philip glanced at his watch. He had been at Price's place for over two hours, learning little about his subject except that he was an obsessive old bore. Was Price's life so insignificant, his achievements so negligible, that all he remembered was his friendship, decades ago, with a man who had quickly forgotten him? And yet, Philip thought, did he have much more to his own life than this? He spent his days recording the deeds of other people, his nights chewing over long-gone events. Perhaps he and John Price had more in common than he'd supposed. He tuned in again.

Price was saying: 'They were the most important years of my life! The Maribyrnong Group, that's what we were called. We used to drive all over the place, painting in the open air – it was wonderful! Take a look at these.' He dragged a photograph album from his box. 'That was the day we drove along the coast. Another time we all went out into the country. We'd find a good spot, set up our easels and paint. A bit later we'd open a few bottles of beer. Oh, goodness me, look at Jimmy in this one! I remember one time –'

'Who's that?' Philip said suddenly. As Price flicked rapidly through the album, a face had momentarily appeared – a woman's face in a group shot – that brought to mind the painting he had seen on his previous visit.

'Oh, I can't remember. Jimmy always had a lot of girlfriends. I was about to tell you, once he put paint into Bill's beer glass when he wasn't looking, and when Bill drank it, goodness me ...' Price went off into convulsions of laughter at the story.

‘That’s hilarious,’ Philip said, handing the album back.

‘He didn’t realise it was paint, you see.’

‘No. And what about –’

‘He thought it was beer, and then he tried to drink it.’

‘What became of the others?’

‘Tom became a commercial artist. Vic went to sea. Bill drew cartoons for *The Argus*. Look, that one’s by Bill.’ He pointed to a pale watercolour above the fireplace.

‘Why did James West leave?’ Philip asked. West had been the only one who was ‘any good’, according to Stefan.

‘Ah, Jimmy was brilliant. Such originality! The ideas just poured out. He’d read everything, knew all the theories. I can see him now, sitting there, holding forth.’ Price’s eyes were bright. ‘But this town was too small for him. He wanted to be in Paris or London, so when he won the travelling scholarship he took off like a shot. We didn’t see him after that. Of course, things had also become a little difficult.’

‘What do you mean, difficult?’

‘Oh, nothing, really ... Jimmy and one of the other fellows didn’t see eye to eye. There was a girl, you see.’

‘Pamela?’

‘Oh, no, no, no. She was later. But you know what it’s like when two fellows are sweet on the same girl. There was a fight. Anyway, off he went, and everything sort of fell apart after that.’ Price was rummaging in the box again and emerged with a bundle of letters. ‘You see, Jimmy *did* keep in touch,’ he said triumphantly. ‘Here are his letters.’

‘Great, but I won’t read them now.’

‘Yes, all right, you can take them with you. Homework.’

‘OK.’ Philip stuffed the bundle into his bag, alongside an ancient jazz magazine and a stack of overdue bills. ‘I’ll have to be going soon, so what more can you tell me? What did you do after Jimmy left and the Group broke up?'

Price was silent for a few moments. His eyes strayed over his bookshelves and paintings, before returning, reluctantly, to meet Philip's. 'I got a job at the library. Stayed there till I retired.' Seeing Philip's expression, he added: 'I was never terribly interested in a career. But you see, I always had the house, and a small private income, so I could devote myself to my hobbies ... music ... collecting ...' His voice trailed away and he slumped back in his chair, exhausted.

Philip nodded. So that was Price's full life. Thirty years as a librarian, a room full of books and memories of painting trips. The whole story could be told in a hundred words – less than a sports report. But if his life had really been that uneventful, why did he seem so jumpy?

Philip pushed the question aside. 'I'll have to be going now. Got another appointment. This has been a good start.'

'You'll come back next Saturday?'

'Next Saturday it is.' Philip hesitated. 'By the way, John, my usual rates include an advance of ten per cent.'

'Oh yes, of course.' The old man went to his desk, fumbled around in the drawers, and after much fiddling with a pen and ink bottle, produced a cheque, which he handed to Philip with trembling fingers.

'Thank *you*, Mr Trudeau. I can't tell you how much it means to me to talk to you. I've got so much more to tell you ... Till next Saturday, eh?'

'Looking forward to it.'

Philip had left him there, shrinking into his chair like a snail retreating into its shell. It had got late. Leaving the house, Philip glanced around and shivered. The dark shapes were trees and shrubs, the figure he had seen was only a statue by the fish pond. What had Price closed the curtains against? Well, Philip was no psychologist. It was Saturday evening and he needed a drink. Tucking the cheque into his pocket, he walked quickly to his car.

The tape clicked to a stop. Philip picked up the photograph from Michael's bedroom and stared at it. Was this the Maribyrnong Group? Neither of the young men looked like Price, but the woman had to be the same as the subject of that striking portrait by James West. Valerie, Price had called her. But he had spoken the name only once, in his surprise at seeing the painting. If Philip was to find out who she was, he would have to get back in touch with Price and ask him directly.

Later that morning, he called Price's number from the office several times without success. It was typical of the man: constantly ringing when he wasn't wanted, unavailable when Philip needed him. Philip's deadline was approaching but he had nothing for the follow up. Ron was getting impatient. Lunchtime came and went. Philip tried again, still getting no reply. He worked on other stories, ringing round his usual contacts, trying to close in on the magic number of twenty. It was almost five o'clock, and the target was remote, when his phone rang. He recognised the voice of Alan Reynolds, a local police sergeant.

'Hey, Alan. Got anything juicy for me?' Philip said. His expectations were not high, but he was desperate, so the most routine mugging would do.

'Not exactly.' The policeman's tone sounded unusually formal, although he and Philip had shared a beer several times. 'Just a question you might be able to help us clear up. Do you know a John Price?'

Philip groaned. 'Yeah, I know him all right.'

'When did you last see him?'

'I don't know, a few months ago. I'm his ghostwriter, we're working on a book. He never shuts up. Why?'

'I'm calling from his house,' Reynolds said. 'He's shut up now. Permanently.'

'He's dead?'

'Just a little.'

'What happened?'

'He seems to have had a fall,' Reynolds said.

'Where?'

'In his library. I assume you've seen this place.' Philip could hear Reynolds' movements as he spoke, and visualised him picking his way around Price's labyrinth of junk. 'It's not exactly safe. A pile of boxes fell on him. He must've dislodged them. He had a whisky glass in his hand.'

'Dying for a drink.'

Reynolds began to laugh, then changed it to a cough. 'He was crushed to death. I've never seen anything like it. The place is filthy, smells terrible. Anyway, it has rats and he'd been here for over a week.'

Philip was grateful that for once Ted's nose for unpleasant death had let him down. For all his impatience with Price, Philip had no appetite for photographs of the old man's body gnawed by rats.

'So what's the question?' Philip asked.

'We found a Post-It on his desk with your name and number on it.'

'I suppose he wanted another appointment.'

'What's this book you were writing?'

'His memoirs.'

‘I didn’t realise you were a ghostwriter.’

‘My career’s over in that line.’

‘Well, it is now. Unless you work with actual ghosts.’

‘Let me get a few more details,’ said Philip, grabbing his notepad. If there had been little of note in Price’s life, the manner of his death would attract momentary public interest. ‘And Alan, would you mind not mentioning this to the *Post*?’

‘You’re way behind, mate,’ Reynolds said, with what Philip thought was unnecessary amusement. ‘She’s been and gone. We already gave her a statement.’

After Philip hung up he sat staring at the phone. Reynolds had said that it was uncertain when the old man had died. It was possible that he had lain there alive for days, unable to move or call for help, as the house darkened around him. What would it be like to die like that, alone, hearing cars pass outside, footsteps, the laughter of children? Where the hell had his family been? Was something like that lying in wait for Philip one day – an empty house, an empty glass, his body on the floor?

Then another thought occurred to him. Price had Philip’s telephone number, so perhaps he had been planning to call Philip just before his accident. What had Price wanted to tell him? If Philip had responded to that call, then he might have arrived in time to save him. But that was pure speculation; anyway, it wasn’t Philip’s responsibility to take care of every crazy old fool that crossed his path. Price’s home was a disaster waiting to happen. The old bloke had been a victim of his own obsession. At least Philip wouldn’t have to endure any more interminable afternoons in his library. For a moment Philip thought of the woman in the painting, and felt a pang of regret that he would never know any more about her.

‘Got anything on the kid yet?’ Ron had performed his usual trick of sneaking up without warning and was breathing Chinese takeaway over Philip's desk.

'Don't worry about the kid,' Philip said. 'I've got something better – you'll love it.' Turning to his computer he began to type: *Reclusive Williamstown collector and historian John Price has been found dead, buried alive in a tomb of his own making* ... It seemed he was to be Price's memorialist after all, though not as the old man had intended. He dashed off three hundred words, then called Ted and told him to go and take a photo of the house. That should keep Ron happy. Knocking off, he headed for the pub, happy with his day's work.

Once installed at the bar, Philip's satisfaction wore off. With Price dead, it would be tough to name the people in Michael's photo, making it harder to establish its significance. How had Michael got hold of it? And why had he put it on his wall? Say the photo did show the Maribyrnong Group. It could have come to Michael from Nina, who could have had it from Stefan. But even if that were so, it didn't help Philip with the woman's identity. Who might know? It wasn't Philip's scene. He never went to galleries. Never read the arts pages. He knew hardly anybody in that world – not a single soul.

Except for one.

Philip reached for his wallet. He pulled out a sheaf of crumpled cards and spread them on the bar like a suburban tarot pack: the Dentist, the Pizza Maker, the Irish Theme Pub, the Desperate Woman's phone number ... Among them he found a Rizla paper with an address scribbled on it.

Tomorrow he would renew his acquaintance with Stefan West.

6

Philip seldom visited the city. Once he'd practically lived in the CBD: how well he'd known the heavy stone buildings packed down like rugby forwards, and the glass towers giving one finger to the sky. But now he felt like an alien. First there had been Castlemaine, and now *The Messenger* limited his stamping ground to the western suburbs. He remembered the places where his associates used to drink, but had no desire to revisit them. These days he kept to the pubs and bars in the west, where the fact that he was largely unknown was just the way he wanted it.

Much had changed. Unfamiliar logos gleamed at the top of skyscrapers. At street level, greasy cafés had been transformed into sushi outlets and juice bars. The coffee bar he used to visit every morning had been taken over by an American chain. Even the trams were different: silver-grey bullets instead of green boxes. Through the windows of a former bank Philip could see people perched on large rubber balls, twisting, bending and stretching in unison.

A short, sandy-haired figure came rapidly round a corner and almost collided with him. Their eyes met, with a shock of recognition.

'Alex!' Philip said. 'How are you going?' Alex had once been a regular drinking mate. Back then he'd been a rapidly rising stockbroker with an astute sense of the market and an irreverent view of the world. From the look of him, he was now doing better than ever – his handmade Italian suit and gold silk tie told half the story, his well-fed physique the rest. But there was no answering smile on Alex's face. He backed away from Philip, opened his mouth as if to speak, thought better of it, and plunged into the stream of people heading in the opposite direction, leaving Philip with his hand stuck out and a half-finished sentence on his lips.

A removal van was parked outside the gallery. Philip passed through glass doors and entered a large space with white walls and polished wooden floors. Under Stefan's direction, men were lifting paintings from the walls and carrying them out. Philip walked over to him.

'Hello Stefan, I'm Philip Trudeau. We met at John Price's house.'

'Yeah, I remember.' After a second's pause, Stefan shook Philip's hand. Philip hadn't been sure what kind of reception to expect, but Stefan seemed friendly enough. 'Very good to see you again, Philip. What brings you here?'

'Just passing, thought I'd drop in. Hope it's not a bad time.'

'We're in a bit of chaos,' Stefan said with a grin. 'I've got two new shows starting soon – we're hanging over the next couple of days. But come on, I'll show you what we've got.'

He led Philip through several rooms, providing a commentary. Although Philip's knowledge of art was elementary, he recognised most of the names Stefan mentioned. He had seen loot like this before on the walls of mansions and boardrooms, placed there to prove the owners had taste as well as money. If Stefan was selling this stuff, he must be doing pretty well. He saw nothing that resembled the portrait of Valerie.

'It was sad to hear about John,' Philip said.

'Yeah, poor old bloke. It was a really tragic end. I hate to say it, but the way he lived, something like that was bound to happen.'

'He was fond of you.'

'Well, he was a friend of my father's.'

'Yeah, he mentioned that.'

Stefan grinned. 'I bet he did. Frankly, he was a lovely old chap, but I found his obsession quite wearing. I suppose he told you about the painting trips?'

'He did.'

'The famous paint in the beer glass story?' Stefan rolled his eyes. 'I didn't have the heart to tell him the Maribyrnong Group just weren't important. About a year ago he got in touch out of the blue. He wanted me to value his paintings. I went because he was a mate of dad's, but I doubted I'd find anything interesting.' The gap in quality between Price's collection and what Stefan had on show was pretty obvious, even to Philip's inexpert eye. 'He had a few minor things by the old man. The rest, well ... He wanted to donate them to the State Gallery.' Stefan's expression indicated how far-fetched this scheme was. 'I knew they wouldn't be interested, but I wanted to let him down gently.'

Stefan steered Philip towards a large bright painting, lowering his voice slightly. 'Look at this, it's a Bradley Black. One of his views of Sydney Harbour. That guy's handling of colour was just incredible. From a distance, it looks pure blue, but when you get in closer, you can see the under-painting in pink.'

Philip leaned forward to examine the picture, and realised that Stefan was right. The guy knew what he was talking about. He also had the flattering knack of making you feel that you were being singled out to see something special.

'Beautiful, isn't it?' Stefan led the way to the next painting. 'This one'll interest you — it's by my father. One of his *Slaughterhouse* series – I just sold it last week.’

‘Who to?’

Stefan smiled, and paused again before answering. ‘That’s confidential, mate. Let’s call him one of the country’s most successful businessmen. One of the most generous, too.’

‘Generous?’

‘He wants to donate it. Can’t say any more, but all will be revealed soon.’

‘Pretty grim choice of subject.’

‘Dad never forgot his working-class roots.’

‘When did he paint it?’

‘Late ’50s, in London. The pictures in that series were his masterpieces – Peter McKendrick agrees.’

‘What happened to the portrait of Valerie?’

‘Who?’

‘The woman with red hair. I saw it at John’s place.’

Stefan began adjusting a painting on the wall. Eventually he responded offhandedly: ‘No way was it a West.’

‘John thought it was.’

‘I didn’t want to upset him.’

Philip nodded. He wasn’t surprised. John Price had struck him as a man with many delusions. Still, the painting had seemed impressive – he was slightly disappointed to hear Stefan’s verdict.

Satisfied with the positioning of the painting, Stefan turned back towards him. ‘Well, I’d better be getting on.’

‘Just before I go’ – Philip reached for his pocket – ‘I’ve got this photo. I was hoping you could help me identify it.’ He handed Stefan the photograph from Michael’s wall.

‘John gave this to you, did he? Well, that’s my father all right.’ He pointed to the bearded man.

‘What about the woman?’

Stefan shook his head. 'Dad wasn't short of girlfriends, I'll tell you that much.' He handed the picture back.

'Could they be the Maribyrnong Group?'

Stefan laughed. 'Don't tell me you're getting obsessed with them, too.'

'So it is them?'

'I don't know.'

'John said something about a fight between your father and one of the others. Over a woman, apparently. Heard about that?'

Stefan paused. 'I thought I'd heard all John's stories, but I must have missed that one. Maybe there was a fight – my old man came from a pretty tough neighbourhood. How come you're so interested?'

'The Group's a part of local history. Even though John's dead, I may still write something.'

'Must be quiet at *The Messenger* these days.' Guiding Philip towards the door, he added: 'Did John give you anything else?'

Philip decided to see what the reaction would be. 'Yeah, actually he did. The letters James West wrote him from Paris.'

Stefan stopped. 'My father's letters?'

'For research. Haven't you seen them?'

'Of course I have. But Philip ...' Stefan's voice had dropped in volume. His tone was eminently reasonable, but Philip thought he detected a wavering in his assurance, like a tiny murmur in a regular heartbeat. 'I'd like them back ... if you don't mind.'

'No problem,' Philip said, making a mental note to read the letters, which until that point had lain untouched in his briefcase. 'I'll send them to you. I'm sure you're right, there's nothing much to John's stories.' About to leave, he stopped and turned, as if remembering something. 'There was one other thing: I wonder how you know Nina Fletcher?'

'Why do you ask?' Stefan was expressionless.

'We were chatting, your name came up.'

'Chatting? She told me you were stalking her. Nice way to make a living.'

'So how do you know her?'

Before Stefan could answer, an elderly couple arrived at the door. Philip recognised them as a former state premier and his wife. Stefan ushered them in, transforming his expression to a welcoming smile. 'Sir Roger, Lady Sterling, what a pleasure!'

The interruption annoyed Philip. He had just been getting somewhere. Not ready to leave, he took the opportunity, as Stefan and his visitors exchanged kisses and handshakes, to make another tour of the gallery, unaccompanied this time. Leading off the main room there was a smaller space, which Stefan had not shown him. A number of black-and-white photographs were casually spread out on a table – photographs of the western suburbs. Trucks leaving the refineries. Women at work in a textile factory. A group of protesters. Old men playing cards in a café. Teenagers hanging around the station. A boy riding a bike, up on the back wheel, showing off, grinning over his shoulder. It was Michael Maher.

Stefan led his visitors into the small room. 'I'd like to show you some interesting work by an outstanding new photographer. I'm planning to show her work.' The group came to a stop when they saw Philip.

'So this is how you know Nina,' Philip said.

Stefan didn't respond. 'Shall we do lunch?' he said to the old man.

'Excellent idea. What about my club?'

'No, let me take you to Bonetti's. Mr Trudeau's just leaving.' Hearing the name, the old man shot Philip a look as if he had noticed a dead dog in the corner.

Outside it was raining. Philip saw a hotel a short distance away.

He put his hand into his jacket pocket. The lining was ripped, but plunging his fingers through the hole he recovered a few dollars, enough for either a drink or a sandwich. He hesitated for a moment. Turning up his collar, he walked quickly towards the hotel.

Twenty minutes later he was seated at a stool, his second VB in front of him. The space was divided into a bar, where Philip and a few others were, and a restaurant, which was almost full. Philip remembered the place. He realised that he had eaten here regularly, years before. Glancing around he recognised a few people. They were mainly men in dark suits, with shiny pink faces and private school haircuts, scoffing porterhouse and guzzling shiraz. He doubted they would be happy to see him again, any more than Alex had been. The room hummed with conversation, tactfully masked by a jazz funk soundtrack. Philip knew how it went: as the food and wine worked its magic there would be explosions of laughter and raised voices, but at this stage it was no more than hints, smiles and murmurs. Later these men would go back to their computers and click millions of dollars around the world based on a few discreet words over the oysters. Philip hunched lower over his beer.

'Phil! Hey Phil! Is that you?' He turned, his train of thought derailed. A woman was addressing him. 'My God, it *is* you.'

'And it is *you*. Hello, Maureen,' Philip said, his pleasure at seeing her made all the sweeter by the fact that it was he, not the porterhouse-and-shiraz mob, being hailed by the woman on the next stool. Maureen was sexy, always had been. Her big smile, made brighter by lipstick, was unchanged, likewise her short dark hair with its red streak, and her clear voice.

'I was thinking about you the other day,' she said. 'I saw that bastard Stevenson on telly and I thought, *I know all about you, mate.* How long has it been, Phil? Three years?'

'More.' It had been a warm spring day in 1998, he remembered, when Graeme had walked into the newsroom of *The Biz & Fin* with a young woman in tow. 'This is Maureen Eastley – she's starting with us today. Just down from Queensland, where she's made quite a name for herself. I want you to take her under your wing, Phil.' The first thing he'd noticed were her clothes, so much more colourful than journalists usually wore – especially in this city, where funereal black was the norm. The second was the firmness of her handshake. 'It's great to meet you,' she'd said, with a smile. 'I always read your column. I'm looking forward to working together.' She was only twenty-two or twenty-three then, but she'd projected unshakeable self-confidence. Now she looked older, the bright Queensland clothes were long gone, and there was more watchfulness in her manner.

'Whatcha doing these days?' Philip asked.

'Freelancing. Just did some PR for Greenpeace. There's not much out there.'

'You're not in journalism anymore?'

'I'd had enough of those pricks. What about you?'

'I'm with a local rag, out west.'

'Are you kidding me?'

'It's temporary. Drink?'

'Whatever you're having.'

He beckoned to the barman, ordered two beers and rummaged in his pockets, praying he'd find some cash.

'Have you got enough?' Maureen asked.

'Shit, I meant to go to the ATM,' Philip said.

'We take plastic,' the barman said.

'Thanks, but I'm not sure my card ...' He retrieved a crumpled note from his back pocket. The barman looked at the note, made a point of straightening it and poured the beers.

'It's great to see you again, Phil.'

'You, too.' They looked at each other. She was wearing a denim jacket, short black skirt and black tights. A scarf was knotted casually around her neck. Philip cursed his old corduroy jacket, he wished that his hair wasn't in retreat from his forehead like a lake in times of drought, and that his eyes weren't red from sleeplessness and booze. He managed to fashion a smile. 'You're looking great.'

'Thanks. It's the pilates.'

'Is that the one where you sit on a big ball?'

'That's Swiss Ball. Jeez, Phil, where have you been?' He grinned into his beer. She touched his arm. 'Oh shit, I'm sorry. I wasn't thinking.'

'You can take the kid gloves off, I'm over it,' Philip said. 'You do look great, though.'

'You should try it.' She stretched her arms above her head and twisted to each side, like an athlete before a race. Her small body was firm and compact – she'd been a dancer, a netballer.

'Can you see me doing anything physical?'

They were both silent for a few seconds. She took out a packet of tobacco and papers and began to roll a smoke with the cigarette paper stuck to her lip like a Post-It.

'Hey,' she said, 'ever play your sax these days?'

'Haven't touched it in ages.'

'Pity. You were good. So what are you doing in these parts?'

'Just chasing up a story.'

'Anything interesting?'

'A kid was killed by a train. We don't know why he was out that night. My editor wants me to follow it up.'

'Getting anywhere?'

'Nah. My contact's disappeared.'

'Who's that?'

'A woman who saw the accident. Nina Fletcher. Now she's vanished.'

'How are you gonna find her?'

'She knows a guy called Stefan West. Heard of him?'

'The art dealer? He's so Map 58.'

'Map 58?'

'That's Toorak in the Melways. Get anything out of him?'

'Not cooperating.' Philip raised his glass, decided he was drinking too quickly, swilled the beer around and put it down again.

'Where are you living?' she asked.

'Yarraville.'

'Very aspirational,' she said with a grin.

'Not me. I'm desperational.'

'What's your place like?'

'Shit, but it's only me. What about you?'

'I'm on my own, too.' Her eyes rested on his for half a second. 'Hey, Phil, I've gotta go. But it was great to run into you. Do you want to catch up some time?'

He hesitated. 'If you like.'

'What's your email address?'

'Can't remember it.'

'Mobile?'

'Dead.'

'Jesus, Phil, you haven't changed have you? Give me the number anyway.' He scribbled it down on a beer mat. 'I'll call you,' she said. 'I bet I can still out-drink you.'

'In your dreams.'

Quickly she kissed his cheek, slid off her stool and walked away. Her legs were as good as ever. 'See ya,' Philip called after her and she looked back over her shoulder with that big grin he remembered.

Philip noticed the barman watching him quizzically. Philip returned the look. *Didn't you think a girl like that would talk to me, mate?* Maureen hadn't touched her beer. Ah well, shame to waste it.

He raised the glass to the barman, then to his lips. 'Cheers.'

Later that afternoon, back in the office, Ron yelled for Philip. The editor's hands were trembling even more than usual as he took a swig from his flask. 'Guess who I've just had on the phone.'

'Who?'

'Fucking *Callum*.'

Callum didn't require a surname. He was known to all as the heir to the newspaper empire built by his famous father. Part of the empire, a very small part, was a family of suburban newspapers that included *The Messenger*. A phone call from Callum would trouble the most respected of editors; on Ron the effect was as if the sergeant of a remote Roman garrison had received a communication from the emperor.

'What did he want?'

'To know why one of my reporters has been hassling Stefan West.'

'What's it got to do with him?'

'They went to Grammar together. What in Christ's name have you been up to?'

'It's about that kid who was killed. You told me to follow it up.'

'So?'

'I saw a woman at the scene. I think she's West's girlfriend.'

'What does that prove?'

'I'm not sure. I'm trying to find out.'

'Does West know the kid who died?'

'Dunno.'

'So he's not involved at all.'

'Then why are his mates calling my editor?'

'Because you're a pain in the arse,' roared Ron, standing up and pointing his finger. Clutching his chest he slumped down again. 'Sorry, mate. I can't stand those bastards any more than you can. But I can't afford to get offside with 'em. Where would I get another job at my age?' Ron began opening drawers and searching through them until he found a small plastic bottle. Putting it to his mouth he sprayed the medicine under his tongue, taking the taste away with whatever he had in the flask.

'But Ron, you told me to –'

'I don't care what I told you. Now I'm telling you to leave Stefan West alone, understand? Look, Phil, this business is like snakes and ladders. Find the right ladders, you'll keep going up. You trod on a snake, so now you're down at the bottom. You were a bloody good journalist once, and you can be again. But keep away from Callum – he's a boa constrictor.'

'I'm thirty-nine years old. No big paper's going to touch me. This is it for the rest of my career.'

'Give it up if you don't like it. Sell *The Big Issue*. I don't give a shit.'

Philip walked to the window and looked out. His heart rate had accelerated, but it wasn't an unpleasant feeling. It was a sensation he recognised: the excitement that came from being on to something.

'Ron, think about it. The woman knows the kid. West knows the woman. The kid dies. I ask a few questions, suddenly Callum's all over us like a rash. Why would that happen if there was nothing to hide?'

'Listen, mate,' Ron said. 'If you carry on with this, you're on your own. I can't protect you. Right now it's only a warning, but if Callum wants you out of here, you're out of here.'

'So if he whistles, you jump.'

'He's the owner's son, Phil. And we're *The Shitkickers Gazette*. This is no place for heroics.'

'I see. Thanks for sticking up for me,' Philip said and left.

But once out of the office Philip had to admit to himself that Ron was right. What chance did he have against Callum? If there really was a story, what was it? A dead kid. An eccentric old man. A photograph. And a woman in a painting. What could bring these elements together? If he'd been younger, or smarter, or less disillusioned, maybe ... As it was, it was all too hard. Over the road a man was chalking the words 'Happy Hour' on a blackboard. Quickening his step, Philip crossed the road and entered the pub.

Later that evening, as Philip slumped in his armchair, wondering whether to play *Kind of Blue* one more time or go to bed, there was a hammering at his door. He stumbled down the hall and opened it.

'Hope we didn't disturb you, Philip.'

'Stefan?' Philip blinked at his visitor, who stood at the top of the concrete steps. With him was a heavy-set guy with a bikie's beard and a face that belonged in a court artist's sketch.

'I've come to pick up those letters,' Stefan said.

'I said I'd send them to you.'

'I don't much like waiting for things. Particularly when they belong to me.'

'OK.' There was nothing else he could say. 'I'll get them.' He went back inside and found the letters.

Without being invited the men followed him in, looking around at the bare walls, the tatty furniture, the dirty clothes and crockery. The bearded guy stood with his arms folded, staring at Philip like a dog waiting for a word from its master. Philip handed over the bundle. Stefan leafed through it. 'Is this all of them?'

'Yeah.'

Stefan nodded and tucked them into his jacket.

'How'd you find my address?' Philip said.

'Come on, Philip. I thought you were a journalist. Finding an address is the easiest thing in the world.' He noticed a photo in a frame and picked it up. 'This your daughter?'

'Yeah.'

'Very cute. How old?'

'Six in that picture. Thirteen now.'

'And doesn't live here, obviously. From the look of it, I'd say this is a bachelor pad.' The bearded guy grinned, and Stefan handed him the picture. Disliking seeing his daughter in the hands of this gorilla, Philip tried to move them towards the door.

'See much of her?' Stefan asked.

'Every few months.'

'Must be tough for you. Still, I hear Queensland's great for kids.'

Philip returned his stare. 'So I'm told.'

When they had gone, Philip looked at the picture again. It had been taken on Amy's sixth birthday; she was dressed up in a fairy costume. Philip remembered the occasion not for the party itself, but for the row that had ensued when he failed to turn up, despite many promises, having been detained at work. *There'll be other parties,* he'd said, confronted by his daughter's tears: *I'm sorry sweetie, I'll definitely be there next year.* But as it turned out there were no more parties, at least not for him. He rubbed some grime off the picture frame and put it back in its place.

Why was Stefan so keen to retrieve a bunch of old letters? And why was he issuing clumsy threats now, on top of the phone call from Callum?

Philip's curiosity was aroused. He reached inside his briefcase and pulled out some sheets. He had, in fact, been intending to return the letters, but not before he'd photocopied them. With a stubby at his elbow, he began to read.

7

8 Feb '51

Dear Johnno,

Well, here I am — writing from my room on the fourth floor of Hotel Cujas, a little place in the Latin Quarter. It's after midnight, but I can't sleep for the bloody racket from the restaurant next door. Other characteristics of the place: they turn the water off at midnight in case it freezes in the pipes; the only place to relieve yourself is a Turkish john; and last night I found three bugs in the bed. But its greatest virtue is that it's cheap — the cheapest I could find — and I'm overjoyed to be here! If I stand on my chair and stick my head out the window at an angle of sixty degrees I can see a corner of the Notre Dame — assuming it's not raining, as it has been most of the time. Feel like I'm really on my way now — it's true what they say, for a painter this is the only place. I've been wandering the streets with my sketchbook. If I had a camera like yours I'd be taking hundreds of shots, but as it is I depend on my eye and my pencil.

It was damn nice of you, Johnno, to come and see me off. I must say, though, as I stood at the rail watching Australia disappear, all I could think was: thank Christ I'm out! When I told the old man I'd won the scholarship, his first reaction was: 'But will Murphys take you back afterwards?' — as if I ever wanted to see the place again. Thirty years of loyalty earned him nothing but ruined lungs. I won't ever be back if I can help it. Instead I'm here, wandering around the Louvre, staring at Picassos and Matisses. Every time I visit, I imagine my stuff hanging up there beside them. Maybe that sounds like skiting, if so I don't care!

Of course, I'll never forget my time with the Group. Despite the way it ended, those years were diamonds to me. Do you see the others at all? What about Val — how is she? I still find myself thinking about her — though towards the end, it was becoming too much of a distraction. I took my eye off the ball. Now I can focus on the real business: painting.

Wish your old mate luck, Johnno. I really feel the next six months will make me or break me. The chance is here if I'm good enough to grab it.

Au revoir mate,

Jimmy

6 March '51

Dear Johnno,

Just came home from a walk by the Seine to find your latest letter. Only got time for a quick reply — I've been working like a maniac and there's bugger-all time for anything else. This is the chance of a lifetime and I'm not going to blow it. You can spend your life getting swept along with the current, or you can try your damnedest to fight your way upstream, like a salmon. You ask me when I'll be coming back, Johnno — but the answer could be never. I'm not the person I used to be. I know the old days were important, but the past is the past, the Group don't exist anymore and you have to accept that, mate. You sound a bit down about things — chin up! You should do what you've always dreamed of, throw in your job, bugger off and see a bit of life.

You'll be sorry to hear I had some bad news about my old man — apparently he's only got a few months left. All the old bloke wanted was a few more years to tend his roses, now he won't even have that. Feel terrible that I'll be out of the country. God knows we never had much in common — his interest in art being equivalent to mine in the trots — but he's still my father, and every son wants his dad to be proud of him. It just makes me all the more determined to put Yarraville behind me and forge my own path.

So I'm pressing on with work. It gets a bit dispiriting sometimes — I'm not good at working on my own, miss the camaraderie of the Group. And sometimes it feels like every painter in the world is here. Most of 'em give up after a while, run out of money and piss off home. Determined that won't happen to me, but how do you break through? There's an old drunk who sits outside the Notre Dame, selling sketches to tourists for a few francs. They say twenty years ago he was the most promising painter in the city.

Surprised by your news about Val. She writes occasionally, but she hasn't told me about it. Frankly, Johnno, I wouldn't believe what Bill tells you. He never forgave me about Val — since then he's been full of jealousy and bile. Wouldn't be surprised if this story's just more of the same. God, thinking about it makes me even gladder to be gone!

Anyway, it's back to work for me now. Got to keep going.

Take care,

Jimmy

18 March '51

Johnno,

Great news! The other night I was invited to a reception at the embassy. Had to borrow a jacket from the crazy Bulgarian upstairs, with a carnation in the buttonhole — you'd have pissed yourself to see me. Met some nice people there — among 'em a chap from the delegation who's keen to put on an exhibition of new Aussie painting. Next day he came to the studio, spent half an hour here looking at pictures. The upshot is he's promised to include some of my stuff! Contacts, that's what this game's all about. Some people have talent, a few of them work hard, but if you don't know the right people, you're stuffed. I've got big plans. One good show here will mean more than a hundred back home.

Can hardly wait to start work. My head is bursting with a thousand images — bustling cafés, the light on the river, the beauty of the buildings, the marvellous exotic creatures I see around me. They'll be different to my old style, but pretty good I reckon. Tomorrow I get down to it.

Jimmy

16 April '51

Dear Johnno,

Bad day yesterday. Have spent weeks working on a series of paintings, trying to capture my impressions of Paris. But nothing worked. In the end it all looked like trash. Everything was competently done, but there was no spark in them, no life. The thought suddenly hit me: what if I'm not good enough? To have come to Paris, to call myself a painter, seemed absurd, the act of a lunatic. Very depressed about the whole thing, drank a couple of jugs of red and crashed on the studio floor. Never felt so low in my life. Felt like coming home. Woke up stiff and cold at dawn. Went for a walk by the river, bought coffee in little café. That's when I found your letter in my pocket, Johnno, with your encouraging words. It cheered me up no end. Realised I have to go on — I have no choice — would be letting down not just myself but everyone at home.

Your letter set me to thinking about Yarraville again. That's when it dawned on me, Johnno — *that's* what I should be painting. I remembered the smoke, the stink, the screaming of the animals in the slaughterhouse — and I started to paint again, a completely new picture. Does it sound barmy, surrounded by all this beauty, to be painting my home town? But that's what I have in my bones, my blood, my lungs — that's what I have to give to the world. An artist's job is to say: *I was a man at this time, in this place, and this is what I saw.* Art's not about beauty and sublimity, it's about telling the truth, without lies or evasions, no matter how ugly it is. I suppose you think I'm mad, but it's how I feel. And when I looked at the picture, it had all the vigour and energy that the others had been lacking. Thank Christ — just in time!

So maybe I'm not finished after all. No time to write more now, but I wanted to tell you how important your letters are.

Au revoir mate,

Jimmy

21 June '51

Johnno,

Hope you like the little *fillette* on the reverse. Not bad is she! Too busy, though — working hard. A doz or so paintings ready for show opening Sat'y week. Some damn good stuff — hope so, anyway. Will write properly later.

Au revoir mate,

Jimmy

30 July '51

Dear Johnno,

Thanks for all the letters, mate — sorry I haven't been in touch for so long. Things have been crazy here. The exhibition's a tremendous success — sold half-a-dozen paintings — one to the ambassador's wife — even the snobby Paris critics liked it! Made enough dough to keep me here another six months. Keep having to pinch myself.

Last night a bloody strange thing happened. A group of us had gone out to celebrate, and around midnight we headed for a club in the Latin Quarter. I saw a woman across the street, and for a second I could have sworn it was Val standing there in a white top and brown slacks. Unsettling! But despite what happened between us, I have only the tenderest feelings for Val. If you ever see her, give her my best.

All the best to you, too, Johnno. I hope you are in great shape. As for me, I'm heading to London next month. There have been some amazing changes in my life. Will tell you more next time.

Jim

16 August '51

Dear Johnno,

What awful news. I had no idea it was so serious. I suppose Val was too proud to tell me. Everything was over between us, but I feel rotten about never having the chance to say goodbye. She could have been a damned fine artist. After I got your letter, I headed for the Museum of Modern Art and found myself looking at Picasso's *Weeping Woman*. Came back to the studio and started messing around, trying to paint my own version. Funny, they all kept turning out like Val.

Johnno, I'm leaving Paris soon. I'm off to London with Pam. She has chums there, who it'll be useful to get to know. Since the exhibition, I'm confident enough to show my stuff anywhere. Have I told you about Pam? She's marvellous, a real thoroughbred. She started off modelling for Dior. I met her at a party a few months ago. She absolutely believes in my work. She knows everybody in London — artists, writers, critics, gallery types — they were all at Cambridge together. Sometimes I look at myself and think, Christ, this is funny. Bloody marvellous, though.

I've crated some of the pictures and I'm sending them back to Oz. Too many to keep carting around with me. Could you look after 'em for me? There's plenty of space in that big house of yours. Just till I get back — it'd be a big help.

Keep in touch, old chum. If you want to reach me in London, write c/o Pam's family at 149 Grosvenor Square.

Cheerio,

Jim

8

Several weeks passed. Winter arrived. Philip went through his routine: work, pub, sleep, work, pub, sleep, forgetting every day as soon as it was over. Mornings found him scraping ice off his windscreen; often the car refused to start at all. He bought extra blankets but shivered through the nights in his unheated flat. As he lay awake police helicopters swept overhead, shining huge spotlights into suburban backyards. Sometimes he heard the horn of the express approaching the station: it came through every night at 11.05.

Philip had let the Michael story go. He needed his job, and if that meant keeping his head down, so be it. There had been no further contact from Sally Maher. Ron had decided to wage war with the council over rate increases, and every other issue had been subordinated to that.

The anaesthetic of habit wasn't completely effective. He hadn't seen Nina since the funeral, but on a couple of occasions he'd spotted a woman with red hair and his mind had given her Nina's features. Each time, though, he had caught up with her and realised his mistake. He thought about her more often than he would have expected, and was troubled by dreams in which her face and Valerie's portrait were superimposed.

And then Maureen appeared again. Philip stepped out of the office one lunchtime, cigarette to his lips, and saw her walking towards him with her big smile. He took her to a Vietnamese place nearby.

'Is this your local?' she asked, as they edged their way down the long, narrow room. 'It makes a change from Bonetti's.'

The place was crowded. There were families with children in strollers; a group of shaven-headed Buddhists in orange–brown robes, their books on the table in front of them; young guys doing business on mobiles; and old men and women silently watching a Vietnamese opera on tiny televisions. Maureen and Philip sat at a small table. She took off her leather jacket but left her scarf on.

A young man appeared instantly and placed a thermos and a small cup on the table.

'You wouldn't get this at Bonetti's,' Philip said, unscrewing the top of the thermos and filling the cup with scalding liquid. 'Want tea?'

'No thanks. Where's the menu?'

'Forget about menus.' Philip glanced up at the waiter. 'Two chicken-noodle soups. It's the best in the city,' he added, for Maureen's benefit.

'Are you a restaurant critic now?'

'The sports reporter does that. 'He only goes to places owned by footballers. *Dick Domenico is kicking goals with his new pizzeria* – that's his usual style. What brings you here?'

'Had a job interview this morning,' she said. 'PR for AusFuel.'

'Any luck?'

'I told them if they wanted some good press, they should cut down on their carbon emissions. They didn't like that.'

'You and your fine ideals.'

She shrugged. 'Anyway, I wanted to catch up. I want to hear more about that story.'

'You could have saved yourself the trip. There's no story.'

'How come?'

'Callum Mackenzie blasted my editor.'

Maureen whistled. 'Callum, eh? So what did you do?'

'I did as I was told.'

'Seriously?' She stared at him.

Philip fumbled for a cigarette, then remembered smoking wasn't allowed. 'I'm not putting my neck on the line again, Maureen.'

'You've changed, Phil.'

'Yeah.'

The waiter laid before them two steaming bowls of soup stuffed with chicken and noodles, a plate of basil and beanshoots, and a small dish of chillis. Philip grabbed some basil, ripped it apart and scattered it liberally on top of the soup.

'Have you found Nina yet?' Maureen said. He wasn't surprised she'd remembered the name — she had always had a lethal memory for facts.

Philip shook his head.

'That's suss. Where could she go?'

'Forget it, Maureen.'

'What's happened to you, Phil?'

'You know what.'

'I'm sorry.' She touched his hand.

He jerked his arm away. 'It's over, and I'm getting on with life.'

'I still can't believe you work out here.'

'When I came out of Castlemaine, employers weren't exactly queuing up. A publisher wanted me to write a book about Stevenson, but then he started shitting himself about getting sued.'

'Gutless prick.'

'I didn't blame him,' Philip said. 'Anyway, I bumped into Ron one day and we got talking. Turns out he's an old mate of Graeme's from way back — before Graeme was at *The Biz & Fin*. He asked me to cover for someone on maternity leave. After she had the baby, she decided not to come back, so here I am. Anything you want to know about flashers or zoning, I'm your man.'

'That's not real journalism.'

'I've realised something about journalism, Maureen. Its fatal flaw: it just doesn't matter.'

Philip didn't add that when Ron had made his offer of work in the western suburbs — *Pretty basic stuff I'm afraid mate, but you'd be helping me out of a spot* — it had seemed an ideal place to disappear. The moment you crossed the bridge, which supposedly connected the two halves of the city but in reality divided them, you were far from the world of power and wealth. The Zegna-suited men from the towers of glass hardly knew the existence of most of these suburbs. They were more familiar with beach resorts three hours down the coast than with places ten minutes from their offices. Until Philip had got a job there, he had hardly known of them himself. But the remoteness was ideal. He had planned to stay with *The Messenger* for a few months, until he found his feet. Over a year later, he was still there. But few of his former colleagues and acquaintances knew where he was.

Maureen was eyeing him with scepticism. 'Bullshit, Phil. What about that Walkley?'

'Ancient history.'

'Then what were you doing in the city?' Philip didn't answer. She pressed her advantage. 'Or is there something else? Is there some chick involved?'

'There's been no one for ages.'

She looked at him. 'Yeah right. You've become a monk. Shave your head and get some robes.' She glanced at his left hand. 'What happened to Sarah?'

Philip's ring finger was circled by pale skin, a ghost ring that marked where his wedding band had once been. 'She's moved to Queensland with her artist,' he said. 'He's built them a house in the bush, with his own bare hands.' He chased a piece of chicken around the bowl with his chopsticks, gave up and reached for a spoon. 'We'd been in trouble for a while. The hours I wasted on that Stevenson story didn't help.'

'You exposed him.'

'He's still running companies. And I'm here.' Philip upended the thermos and shook out the last few drops of tea. 'From now on, it's road accidents and council meetings for me. Talking of which, I have to go.' Philip pushed away his bowl, still half full.

'Don't go yet.' Maureen leaned forward. 'How did Nina know the kid?'

'I don't know, and I don't care. The kid's dead and Nina's disappeared. I'm still here and I've got a meeting to attend. So —'

'But something connects Stefan to the kid, right?'

Philip sighed. She was as good as ever. 'Yeah, a photo. I found it on Michael's wall.'

'And?' She raised her eyebrows at him.

He pulled the photo from his pocket. 'That one there is James West — Stefan's father.'

'Where would the kid get a photo like this?'

'Nina, I guess.'

'And why would he put it on his wall? Unusual kid.'

Philip didn't answer. Michael had hardly existed for him when he wrote the original story. He had attributed qualities to him from the grab-bag of popular virtues — *good at footy, community-minded, popular with his mates* — and had missed everything that mattered.

'Say he was interested in photography and Nina was teaching him,' Philip said. 'He rides to her place late one night, catches the last train to the afterlife. He's dead, she's vanished, Stefan's not talking. No story.' Philip wiped his mouth with a paper napkin. 'Now I really must —'

'How did you get the photo, Phil?'

'I borrowed it.'

'Borrowed?'

'Took it, then. So what?'

'You cared enough to steal a picture.'

'OK, I was curious. And Ron had told me to write a follow-up. But it's not worth it, Maureen. I'm not hassling Stefan anymore.'

'But Stefan doesn't know *me*, does he?' Maureen said.

'Drop it, Maureen.'

'I could go to the gallery. Chat to him. Anything wrong with that? Come on, Phil,' Maureen leaned forward and touched his hand. 'We were a good team. What about it?'

He felt his resolve weaken. She was right – he wasn't a suburban hack. He was Philip Trudeau, Walkley winner! The scourge of corporate crime! And this girl sitting opposite him, her cheeks flushed, her lips slightly parted, she *cared* about him. It could be like the old days at *The Biz & Fin*, when they'd sit together planning how to bring Stevenson's rotten empire crashing down.

'Listen, Maureen. It's not the old days anymore. There could be something suss, I agree. But Callum, Stefan West ... these are powerful people. When I was talking to Stefan, Roger Sterling strolled in to have lunch with him. They could destroy me, or you, any time they felt like it. Once upon a time, that didn't bother me. But now ... I can't do it anymore.'

'That is so not true, Phil. When I was a cadet, you were the one I looked up to. Remember how you dug up the truth about Stevenson.'

'And look where it got me.'

'I'm not doing much at the moment. How about I talk to West? He wouldn't know it had anything to do with you. What do you reckon?'

Philip sighed. 'I can't really stop you, can I?'

She got to her feet decisively, flashing him her familiar grin. 'Nup.'

That night Philip found it harder than usual to sleep. *What about that Walkley? What's happened to you, Phil?*

He tried watching TV but nothing interested him. He turned it off and sat in the darkness. In the distance he heard the horn of the approaching express, and his thoughts turned to Michael. What had Nina said about him? *Mike was just curious. Too curious.* The same had been said of Philip when he was a boy. He had always been driven by the desire to know. As a young boy he'd been obsessed with taking machinery apart to see how it worked. Later on he'd applied the same intelligence to business and had quickly learned that human machinery didn't operate with the same regularity. It was driven by things that were harder to see and measure – influence, ego, hidden agendas. Still, the desire to look inside and see the hidden workings had grown more acute, and brought him plenty of trouble over the years, as well as the odd moment of glory. But curiosity could go too far. Like any addiction it could make you reckless, sweep you over the edge of what was reasonable, disregarding warning bells, into the path of forces as powerful as a train. It had led Philip to a narrow cell, six metres by five, where it had been worn away by the drip of boredom, and battered against the walls, leaving him permanently deaf in one ear. That had cured him. No addiction was worth that kind of punishment.

But Michael had only been thirteen, and curiosity had still burned brightly inside him. He had been looking for something – maybe something related to the photograph he had kept by his bed.

Maybe he had even found it. But what?

Go back to the accident. Philip tried to visualise the scene: rain, the passengers on the platform, the waiting train, the kid riding towards the tracks, the clanging bells, the express bearing down. The kid had paid no attention to the bells and the boom gate. Why hadn't he stopped? A smart, streetwise kid, didn't he know that you never cut behind a stationary train? But he'd been in too much of a hurry, too scared, too distracted, as he rushed towards Nina's flat. Something was missing from the picture. The witnesses had seen a kid on a bike, felt the rush of the train, seen the bike fly through the air. What hadn't they seen?

Then the answer was there, like the cards lined up in a game of solitaire. They'd all been looking at the boy, not at whatever was behind him. They had focused, naturally, on the horror in front of them. *They hadn't seen what he was riding away from.*

Who could Philip ask? Not the witnesses – they had already told all they knew. Not Nina – she had disappeared. But there were others, Philip knew, who hung around the station, and not because they wanted a train. They would not have been on the platform, but a short distance away, in the shelter of the toilet block and the bus shelter, on the scrubby patch of ground where deals were done. From there they would have had an uninterrupted view of the whole street. But nobody had asked them what they had seen, and they were hardly likely to volunteer.

Philip extinguished his cigarette and got to his feet. The horn of the express sounded again, closer now. The red figures on the clock glowed 11.05. Philip felt a sensation that he recognised. He had experienced it, momentarily, when told about Callum's phone call. Now it surged again, like the blood rushing back into a sleeping limb. The need to know. Maureen was right – once you had it, it never went away. He walked to the door and stepped out into the night.

9

Outside the wind whipped at his jacket. A white streak of cat blazed across the road, coming to rest under a car parked opposite. Low clouds threatened rain.

His car started at the fourth turn of the ignition and he drove along empty roads. He parked outside an old factory, newly converted into ultra-modern apartments. Turning up his collar, he walked towards the deserted station. No staff had been on duty since the last were Jeffed in the mid '90s, and there were no passengers on the exposed platform. Opposite were the bus shelter and the brick toilet block, behind which a few scrubby trees struggled for survival. Beside the building was a flagpole, erected by some civic patriot. A metallic clanging came from the top as the cable fretted against the pole.

Below the flagpole, his back against the toilet block wall, a man sat, his tracksuit hooding him like a monk. He had his knees drawn up in front of him, his arms folded. A pair of white runners provided the only spot of brightness. Philip walked past, then returned and stood in front of him.

'How's it going?'

No answer. Philip repeated the question, and after a long pause there was a muttered reply.

'Shit.'

'Cold?'

There was a slight movement from inside the hood. 'What the fuck do you think?'

'Here.' Philip held out a cigarette and a wiry hand took it. Philip lit one and passed it over so the monk could light his.

'You often hang around here?' Philip asked. This drew no response: the monk clearly belonged to a silent order. Philip tried again. 'A kid was killed a few weeks ago. D'ja hear about it?'

'People die all the time.'

The voice was familiar – where had he met this guy before? 'This one was hit by a train.'

'So?'

'Were you here?'

'Nah.'

'Know anyone who was?'

'Nah.'

'There are always people here. Someone must have seen it.'

'Fuck off.'

Philip stared down into the gloom. A car swept past, its headlights momentarily illuminating the guy's face, his sharp nose, straggly beard and the tattoo on his neck. 'Snake?'

The guy looked at him for the first time. 'Fuck, it's you. What are you doing here, man?'

'I could ask the same question. When did you get out?'

'Three months ago.'

The lights flashed and the bells rang as the boom gates descended. The tracks began to hum, and there was a long, gathering, rushing sound as the train approached. Then with a whoosh and a blast of its horn it came bullocking through the station.

When the noise had died away, Snake spoke. 'There's a girl. She said something about it.'

'Where is she?'

'Refuge, maybe.'

'Can you find her for me?'

'Maybe, for a hundred bucks.'

Philip hesitated, dragged on the cigarette. He'd come this far. 'OK. Bring her here tomorrow night.'

'I dunno if she'll come, man.'

'Try. I'll be here.'

Snake grunted. Whether in assent or not, Philip wasn't sure. He handed the guy more smokes and went back to his car.

He returned the next night and waited, parked in the same spot, from which he could see the station and the toilet block. Through the windscreen he looked across the tracks and up the wet black ribbon of the street. Once this suburb had belonged to the industrial working class. Its factories, railways, quarries and slaughterhouses had been engines driving the whole city. Philip had interviewed elderly local residents who had told him about the stink that used to fill the air, the window-shaking explosions, the regular Saturday night brawls. But the abattoirs and factories had long gone, and in their place were fashionable apartments, restaurants and boutiques – though in recent times a few developments had failed when it was discovered the land they were built on still oozed toxic chemicals. Four-wheel drives now forced their way up and down the narrow streets of Yarraville, people flocked to sip lattes in the cafés, and every weekend sharply suited real-estate agents auctioned workers' cottages for prices that would have astonished their original occupants.

Snake failed to show. By twelve the street was completely

empty. When the last train had arrived and its few passengers had scattered, Philip abandoned his post and drove home.

It was the same the next night, and the next. He decided that Snake had either been unable to find the girl, or had been bullshitting. Even if the girl existed she was probably a junkie worded up to spin him a yarn in exchange for the dough. On the fourth night he returned unwillingly, and sat with the radio tuned to the late-night quiz. *'Now we have Glenda on the line. Which local businessman was named this week at number three in Australia's rich list?' 'Was it David Stevenson?' 'That's correct, Glenda — not everyone's favourite person, but there's no denying he runs a very successful empire ...'* Philip hit the 'off' button and sat in silence. Unanswered questions of his own buzzed in his brain. Someone discarded a half-eaten burger in a bin; a rat came out of nowhere, retrieved the morsel and ran off with it. A scavenger for other people's rubbish, just like him.

At 11.20 a suburban train pulled in and among the few disembarking passengers he saw Snake. With him was a teenage girl. Philip got out of his car and walked towards them.

'Hi, I'm Philip.'

The girl muttered something. She wouldn't look at him. She was fourteen or fifteen, dressed in grey tracksuit pants and an ancient coat.

'Are you the girl who saw the accident?'

'Yeah,' she said almost inaudibly.

'A hundred bucks, man,' Snake said.

'Afterwards.'

'Hey, don't bullshit me. You said —'

'Let's see how real this is first. We'll talk in my car,' Philip told the girl. Snake backed off and resumed his trademark slump against the wall. Philip led the way to his car, opened the passenger door for the girl and got in the driver's seat. She got in reluctantly.

'What's your name?' he asked.

'Zayley.' She stared straight ahead through the windscreen. She had a round pale face, heavy-lidded eyes and a resentful look.

'Want a cigarette?'

She nodded.

He handed her one and lit it. 'So, tell me what happened.'

'I saw that kid get hit.'

'Where were you?'

She pointed towards a bench among the trees behind the toilet block.

'What were you doing there?'

She shrugged.

He tried again. 'Where was the kid?'

She indicated over her shoulder, back down Anderson Street.

'Right down the end?'

'Nah.'

'Then where?' Philip had to be patient.

'Out of that side street. He was going really fast, he was flying. Then I heard the train coming.'

'You heard the horn?'

'Yeah.'

'How come he didn't hear it?'

'He was yelling into his mobile.'

'Yelling what?'

'Dunno.'

'Then what happened?'

'I thought he'd stop,' she said. 'But he didn't. He just kept going, and ...'

'What?'

'I'm gonna be sick,' the girl said.

She opened the car door and Philip heard her vomit splatter

onto the wet road. He smoked and looked ahead down the deserted street. It would be hard to fake that, he thought.

When she had finished she closed the door, wiping her mouth. 'Sorry.'

'It's all right. Take your time. Did you see the train hit?'

She shook her head. 'Just saw it go through. Afterwards, I heard people shouting.'

'Shouting what?'

'Call an ambulance. Someone's been hit. Stuff like that.' She inhaled deeply, filling her mouth with the smoke, screwing up her face. 'There were people everywhere. It was, like, chaos. Then I saw this guy.'

'What guy?'

'In a car behind.'

'Chasing the kid?'

'I dunno. He was really close.'

'What was the car?'

'Big black one.'

Philip felt his heart rate increase. 'Four-wheel drive?'

'Yeah.'

'What did the guy look like?'

'Couldn't see much. Think he had a leather jacket. Runners.'

Philip realised that his hands were trembling. 'What did the guy do?' he asked, his voice slightly unsteady.

'He stopped at the level crossing. Then he walked onto the tracks.'

'What was he doing?'

'Looking for something, I reckon.'

'What happened then?'

'Dunno. I didn't hang around.'

If this was true, Stefan had lied about the accident. Michael had been riding away from him. What could the kid have had that Stefan West wanted?

'Did you tell anyone what you saw?'

'The pigs? Yeah, right.'

Philip half smiled. 'I don't blame you. Look, I might need to contact you again. Got a place to sleep?'

She shrugged. 'The refuge, or the Blue Moon.'

'That shithole?' Philip said incredulously. The Blue Moon was a caravan park, notorious for violence and drugs. Journalists, social workers, council officers, even the police rarely ventured there.

'Nothing ever happens to me.'

'How come you're homeless?' Philip asked. She looked incredibly young.

'My parents split up and my mum got a new boyfriend. He's a bastard.'

'Why?'

'He belts her up. And he's tried it on with me. I won't have it though. So I moved out.'

'Do you ever see your Dad?'

'Nah. He's interstate.' She stared at him. 'What's wrong?'

'Nothing.'

'Thought you were crying.'

Philip shook his head. 'Just a cold.'

'Are we done?

'Yeah, we're finished.'

'Give me the money then.'

Philip opened his wallet and handed her some notes. She took the cash, opened the door quickly and got out. 'Wait,' Philip said. He fished in his pocket for a card and handed it to her. 'This is my number. If you see that guy again, or there's anything else you remember, give me a call.'

She nodded reluctantly and took the card from his outstretched hand.

'You take care, OK?' Philip said. She didn't answer.

He watched her walk up to Snake. The two of them headed up the ramp and onto the platform. Perhaps she'd look back? She didn't. Philip turned the ignition and drove away.

Once home, Philip hurried up the concrete steps to his flat, reaching for his key. The porch-light globe had long since died, so he stood in a pool of blackness, fumbling for the keyhole, while with his left hand he pressed against the thin wood of the door. It swung open.

He stood motionless and stared into the black interior. Had he failed to close the door? He thought he remembered slamming it, but the latch was unreliable. Maybe it had given way. Either that, or someone had been here in his absence.

As he hesitated, a memory flashed into his head from the height of the Stevenson investigation. Receiving an urgent telephone message he had rushed home to find their house trashed, filing cabinets ransacked, drawers pulled open and emptied onto the floor, furniture overturned, shit smeared across the walls and a message scrawled on the front door: LEAVE IT OR YOUR DEAD. And Sarah standing in the doorway with wide-eyed Amy clutching her hand, looking at the wreck of their home. That night they had fought like never before: she had accused him of risking their safety with his obsessive pursuit of a story. Not long after that, she had delivered the deathknock to their marriage. Was it all happening again? It couldn't be: he had bothered no one, kept his head down. He cautiously stepped inside and fumbled for the light switch. The place seemed just as he had left it, but he sensed an unfamiliar presence.

He stopped and listened, hearing only the drip of the dodgy tap in the bathroom and bursts of sitcom laughter from the flat upstairs. Closing the door behind him, switching on the lights, he checked every room, finding no damage, no intruders. He made himself breathe slowly to bring his heart rate back to normal. *Christ, you're getting past it, mate.* He would have to get that latch replaced. He went into the kitchen, took down the bottle of Jameson's and poured himself half a tumbler.

Then he saw it.

On the table, between an empty cigarette packet and the morning's leftover toast, there was a small yellow envelope. He picked it up: a packet of photos. Outside, he heard a car engine start. He dashed to the door. By the time he had flung it open, stumbled down the steps and run to the end of the driveway, the tail-lights were turning out of the street into the main road. He looked across at the newly empty parking space opposite, and the white cat froze for a moment and stared at him, its eyes two stars in the night. Then it turned and trotted into the darkness.

10

Philip ripped open the envelope and took out the shiny bundle. *Trust Your Memories to Us*, said the slogan on the packet. Someone was trusting him with these images – but who, and why?

Quickly he flipped through the pile. The photos had been taken in and around Yarraville. One showed the station on a wet morning: some passengers huddling under cover and a woman hurrying over the level crossing. Among the other photos he recognised the main street, the new apartments, the church, the place where Nina had lived – he remembered the geraniums and wind chimes. Sometimes the photographer had failed to fit the subject into the frame, and a few were out of focus. They couldn't be the work of a professional like Nina. More likely a kid – such as Michael. And yes, there was Nina standing on her balcony, looking down towards the camera, a hand half raised to discourage the photographer. Philip had only seen her face full of grief and anger, but here she was smiling, despite her reluctance to be in front of the camera.

He put the picture of Nina next to the print from Michael's wall. Yes, there was some physical resemblance, and Nina's taste for retro clothes added to the similarity. But there was something missing. Whatever quality their faces had seemed to share before, it wasn't there now.

The last few pictures showed a wealthier area with wider streets and bigger houses: Williamstown. Among them were photos of a solid but neglected house. Philip looked closely. An untidy, overgrown garden. A couple of nymphs, green with moss and lichen, on plinths beside a stagnant pond. Trees with fruit gone rotten on the branch. He could see a pair of French windows, and beyond them were bookcases and piles of boxes. It was John Price's home.

Why would Michael have been there? And why would he take photos? Philip studied them more closely, seeing nothing remarkable. Some pictures had been taken from outside the gates; in others, the photographer had become bolder, entering the garden and shooting from the lawn. One had been taken through an open window. Inside the dark room – no flash had been used – Philip could make out a figure, a silhouette. Was it Price? No, too tall. Stefan, perhaps?

Philip laid the photos aside. He could not unravel their mysteries yet. Perhaps a return visit to Price's house would help.

The next day, a Saturday, Philip drove to Price's place again. On arrival, he found a crowd had gathered in the genteel back street. People were congregating in the garden and spilling onto the verge outside, while others were trooping in and out of the house itself. Men in suits were handing out brochures. The place was about to be auctioned. A huge board by the front gate advertised its virtues.

Philip walked into the house and discovered a radical transformation. Every square centimetre had been painted, primped and polished. The old carpets had been ripped out, and the wooden boards beneath now gleamed. The walls had been stripped of their ancient wallpaper and painted in bright shades of lemon and white. Light poured in through newly installed windows. Philip walked into the library. Every sign of Price's presence had been erased — the shelves had gone, along with the books, cabinets, boxes, the piles of papers and albums and records. Philip was amazed by the space. The musty smell had been chased away by fresh paint and flowers. Reynolds' words crossed Philip's mind: *Smells terrible ... dead for several days.* The heavy velvet curtains had been replaced by a venetian blind that opened and closed with a discreet hiss.

Philip stood at the window and looked out at the magazine-perfect garden. The lawn was green despite the dry spell, the magnolia showed signs of professional care. He remembered the expression on Price's face as the old man had stared out of his windows. It was the look of a man afraid of something that he couldn't talk about. What was it he had feared? Whatever it was, had it come for him in the end, as he lay pinned under the boxes, with the darkness closing in?

Philip walked into the garden and leaned against the tree. Nearby, two suited men were talking. 'Let's roll,' one said, and headed towards the gate. The other saw Philip and called: 'Can I help you, sir? We're just about to start.'

'I was just thinking how much this place has changed.'

'Local are you?'

'I knew the previous owner.'

The agent looked at Philip warily. 'Not the old guy?'

'Yeah. Who's selling it?'

'His daughter.'

'Is she here?'

'Confidential, mate,' the agent said with a smile.

'I'm not a buyer.'

'Doesn't matter. Still can't tell you.'

'Pity.' Philip glanced at the crowd, which had now swelled to several dozen. Judging by the cars they drove, they were a well-heeled bunch. 'I suppose everybody knows the house's history.'

'Over a hundred years of elegant living.'

Philip almost smiled to hear Price's lifestyle described as 'elegant'. 'I'm talking about the previous owner. He died here.'

'Oh, that,' the agent said. 'It was in the papers.'

'The local papers, yeah. But some of these people might be out-of-towners. Of course, you're legally obliged to tell them, aren't you?'

'Tell them what?'

'Anything that might influence their decision. Rotten stumps. Structural problems. Unpleasant deaths.'

The agent didn't answer.

'Funny, I don't see any mention of it here.' Philip read from the flyer: '*This splendid Victorian mansion ... full of tradition ... magnificent fireplace* ... No, no mention.'

'We don't dwell on that kind of thing,' the agent said, relieving the pressure on his collar with one finger.

'Course not. You buy a new house, you want to feel positive about it. You don't want to think about an old man lying here dead for a week. Might drop the price, eh?'

'Maybe.'

'Definitely, I'd say. He was chewed by rats, did you know that? Right there, in the front room. Kind of creepy, isn't it?'

'Look, mate –'

'Who's the vendor? That's all I want to know.'

The young agent looked around desperately for one of his colleagues. Philip guessed he was new at this. 'I'll need to ask my –'

'You've got five seconds,' Philip said. 'After which I start talking to people. Then you can explain to your boss why it was passed in.'

The young guy hesitated, sweat beading his lip. Then he nodded across the road. 'The blonde in the dark suit. Over there.'

Philip smiled. 'You've got a great future in real estate.'

'Was he really chewed by rats?' the young guy asked.

The auctioneer was launching into his introductory spiel. A short distance back from the crowd, resting against a Range Rover, a woman was watching the proceedings intently.

Philip took up a position close by. 'The place is looking amazing,' he said conversationally. 'What a brilliant job.'

She accepted the compliment with a microscopic smile. She was dressed in a navy suit, ears and throat glinting with gold. 'It was a challenge. The house had gone to rack and ruin. It's beautiful now though – a good investment for some lucky person.' She weighed Philip up, assessing whether he might fall into that category, but his appearance suggested otherwise.

'Actually I'm not a buyer. I'm an old friend of your father's.'

'Oh.'

'It was tragic. You must be devastated.'

'I'm not sure I can place you ...'

'Philip Trudeau.' He saw with relief his name meant nothing to her. 'It all looks so empty now. What happened to his collection?'

She laughed. 'Is that what you call it?'

'I mean all the papers and –'

'Oh, I know *exactly* what you mean. Don't worry, we found appropriate homes for it.'

'The museum?'

'The tip, more likely.'

'What about the paintings?'

'Gave them to junk shops. Who in their right mind would want that rubbish? It's a miracle the place didn't burn down years ago.' Her tone of voice suggested an opportunity missed.

'He thought they were valuable.'

'He was in la-la land,' she snapped back, eyes on the crowd.

The auctioneer, strutting and preening, had worked them into a frenzy of property lust. Bidding was brisk.

So Price's prized collection, built up over seventy years, had been disposed of in a few hours, divided between charity shops and landfill. Philip wasn't surprised that Price's daughter had acted smartly – it must have taken great patience to keep her hands off the house while her father dawdled to the age of eighty. At least now that patience was about to pay off.

'Come on sir, say a million – it'll sound better when you tell your friends,' cried the auctioneer. There was a ripple of applause as the bidding broke through the seven figure barrier, showing no sign of slowing its upward progress.

'But the James West painting,' Philip said. 'Surely that was worth something.'

Finally she looked at him. 'What?'

'The portrait of the woman with red hair. John showed it to me.'

'I have no idea what you're talking about.'

The bidding had now come down to only two serious contenders. The auctioneer was working hard, turning his attention first to one, then the other.

'I'd like to see it again,' Philip said, coming up close. 'Your father asked me to help him. Now he's passed away, I feel a responsibility to complete the work. John was a fine man, with a lot of fascinating experiences, and –'

'In his dreams,' she cut in.

'That's harsh. He –'

'Going for the third and final time ... Sold!' There was a second, louder burst of applause, and the successful bidder was surrounded by backslappers.

Price's daughter turned on Philip. 'You're the ghostwriter, aren't you? You visited him once, took his money, then he never saw you again. Now you're sniffing after his paintings. Well, you're too late.' Her small eyes glittered. 'Excuse me, I've got an auction to deal with.' Turning her immaculate back on him she strutted away.

As the crowd dispersed, Philip wandered back into the garden and looked up at the house. Who had come and gone through those rooms, fifty years before?

There was a woman at an upstairs window. A familiar woman. White blouse, red hair. Philip watched her carefully for a few seconds. She yawned, turned towards him, smiled. He felt his hair prickle. He remembered Price staring into the garden, the ice rattling in his glass.

'Having a last look, mate?' It was the young estate agent. Now that the house had successfully been sold, he had recovered his good mood.

'There's someone up there,' Philip said, not moving his eyes.

'Excuse me?' The agent turned and looked. 'Where?'

'Right there. The top right window.'

She was close enough for Philip to see the hollows of her cheeks and the hair falling over her forehead. She looked back at him with a slight smile, rested her elbow on the window sill, lifted her face up to catch the light. Any young woman on a sunny day.

'Can't see anyone, mate.' The young guy turned back to Philip, hiding his mistrust under professional bonhomie. 'Big place though, isn't it? Much too big for an old bloke to live in alone.'

'If he was.'

'Sorry?'

'Alone. If he was alone.'

'Yeah, the papers said he was. Buried alive in a tomb of his own ... whatever. By the way, did you find her?'

'Find who?'

'Your friend. The one from the flat.' Then it clicked with

Philip — this was the prick with the clipboard he had met in Nina's apartment.

'No, I didn't.'

'That's women for you. Here one minute, gone the next. Way of the world, mate.'

Philip glanced up. The window was empty. 'Sure is.'

Philip drove back towards Yarraville. Like Price's house, these inner western suburbs of Melbourne — grouped together under the name Maribyrnong — were undergoing a process of transformation. Evidence of a grittier past was there if you looked — the shells of old factories were visible in the facades of apartment blocks, and here and there faded signage proclaimed that a café or boutique had once been a workshop or tannery.

Philip drove past a large brick building, once a religious hall, now a bazaar in which antique and junk dealers peddled their wares. *We gave them to junk shops.* This place was large, close, convenient. Could some of the old man's paintings have ended up here? He pulled over.

The hall was crammed with furniture and bric-a-brac. While some of it might qualify as antiques, much of it was trash. Philip wandered from stall to stall, occasionally stopping to make an enquiry. He received blank looks and shakes of the head. He was getting hungry and he needed a drink. He turned towards the door.

As he did so he noticed reddish hair on the far side of the room. A woman, medium height, in a leather jacket and jeans, was browsing among the stalls. He paused. It had happened several times before that he had seen someone he thought was Nina, only to be mistaken. He moved cautiously closer. It was her. She didn't seem to be shopping. She had a preoccupied air, as if she was expecting to meet someone.

He took a circuitous route, ducking behind tallboys and display cases, and was almost beside her before she saw him.

'Hi, Nina.' She immediately tried to walk away, but he blocked her path. 'Nina, I want to apologise. About the funeral, it was unforgivable. I'm sorry.'

She paused, looked at him. Her eyes were pale green. 'Are you following me?'

'No. I came here for something else – I just noticed you. How are you?' She turned away in contempt. He pressed on: 'Are you into this retro stuff?'

Her way was clear to pass him, but she stood still for a moment. Her hair was falling over her face – he wanted to reach out and brush it aside, but she pushed it back herself. 'I came here with Mike,' she said finally.

'Really?' It seemed a weird place for a teenage kid.

'Just once,' she said. 'I thought maybe if I came back, I'd remember something.'

'Like what?'

'I dunno. A clue, or something.'

Philip watched her face. He was struck again by her resemblance to the painting – but rather than any physical trait, it was her expression that reminded him of Valerie. The same sense of loss and despair. She's telling the truth, he thought. The tabloid fantasies he'd been lazily constructing were just that – fantasies. The truth was becoming altogether more complicated.

'So, you have no idea why he was coming to see you?' he asked.

'No. We used to hang out during the day.'

'Why here?'

'We found some photos.'

Philip remembered the picture from Michael's wall. The two men and the woman in a car. The painting trip. 'The Maribyrnong

Group?' he said.

'Who?'

'It was a group of artists. James West. And Valerie. Did you find pictures of Valerie?'

She stared at him. 'What are you talking about?' She began edging away.

Perhaps, Philip thought, some of Price's collection did end up at the bazaar even before he died. Nina and Michael could have found the photo here. Philip remembered him saying: *I've been sorting my collection, getting rid of a few non-essentials.*

He followed her. 'Did you ever meet John Price?'

She shook her head in frustration. 'You keep asking me about people I don't know. What do you want anyway?'

'Same as you. To find out what happened to Michael.'

'But I don't know.' She stared at him for a moment. 'Look, I've got to go.'

'Wait ... Can I ... Can I call you?'

She almost laughed. 'Yeah, right.'

'OK, OK. I don't blame you.' She was heading for the door now. He couldn't let her go: he needed something to get her attention. He took a gamble. 'Are you seeing Stefan?'

She turned. 'Stefan? What about him?'

'Your pictures are in his gallery.'

'So you *have* been following me.'

'No, but listen. Stefan —'

'Why are you talking about Stefan?' she was almost shouting. 'He had nothing to do with it. I didn't even meet him until after Mike ...' She couldn't finish the sentence. She put her hand to her eyes. 'Just leave me alone, will you?'

For a moment she was a silhouette in the doorway, then she was gone.

11

At eight that evening Philip sat alone at Phoney O'Riley's. That, at least, was Philip's name for the place. Once a traditional working-class pub, it had been bought by an international chain and Irish-ised by the addition of Dublin posters and Guinness on tap. This had paid off commercially – you could hardly move in there now. Why did people like fakes so much? Even the band was a fake – a bunch of suburban kids pretending to be The Pogues. Philip chose a table as far away from them as possible. With his crook ear, conversation was hard enough already. Besides, he preferred to sit in a place where he could see the whole pub. It was an old habit: never have your back to the room.

Someone had left behind an old copy of *The Biz & Fin* that Philip flipped through, unable to concentrate. He kept replaying the conversation he'd had with Nina. He could have followed her out of the bazaar, but what would have been the point? He'd stuffed up again. There was no chance of her talking to him now. Anyway, he doubted she had much to tell – she had no idea why Michael had been riding to her house, and she knew nothing of Price, Valerie and the Maribyrnong Group. So who *did* know why Michael was out that night? There was one obvious candidate – the guy who'd chased him onto the train tracks. Stefan had been pretty keen to cut short Philip's interest in the subject, even coming to his flat and making threats. Maybe it was time for a change of tack. Maybe he should turn his attention back to Stefan. As he was thinking this, he looked up and saw Maureen making her way across the room.

'Hiding in the corner, Phil? I almost didn't see you.'

'What are you doing here?'

'Had a hunch I might find you,' she said, flopping into the seat opposite him. 'Wanna buy me a Guinness?'

'Can't we go somewhere else? I can't stand Irish music.'

'I thought you'd been to Ireland.'

'Once. Hated it.'

'Well, I love it. Have another drink and relax, you grumpy bastard.'

Philip fought his way to the bar and returned with two beers, plus a chaser for himself.

Maureen delved into her bag, took out a notebook and flipped it open. 'Don't you want to hear what I've found out?' She crossed her legs, clad in emerald tights. 'I've been digging the dirt on Stefan West.'

'Go ahead,' Philip said.

'He's forty-two. He was born in England, where his parents lived for years. He went to some fancy English school first, then they sent him back here to Grammar.'

'Very Map 58.'

'Totally Map 58. Finished school, uni – but he left after a term. Our Stefan's not the academic type. He played in bands, messed around with painting, didn't get anywhere. After that he disappeared for a while, then he resurfaced as an art dealer. It was the '80s – remember all those entrepreneurs with sudden wealth syndrome? He had contacts through his family. Mummy and daddy owned some good pieces, and he persuaded them to sell at inflated prices. Pretty soon he had his own gallery, and was buying and selling other people's pictures. When Lady Pam died, he inherited the lot. He knows his stuff and he does a lot of business.'

'How'd you find all this out?'

She grinned. 'I'm a newly qualified freelance journo, green but enthusiastic, profiling leading arts identities for an online magazine.'

'Don't tell me he fell for that wide-eyed crap.'

'Never fails, Phil. Remember Stevenson?'

He nodded. 'I'd spent weeks hammering on his door, then you flashed your legs and got straight in.'

'Then I hit him with "What happened to the missing $15 million from the Regency deal?" and watched him go purple.'

'I remember. What did you get from Stefan?'

'He's pretty excited. He's planning an exhibition of James West paintings. He mentioned some "exciting recent discoveries".'

'Business will boom.'

'Right. Which is very nice for him.' She closed her notebook, began to roll a smoke. 'Well, I reckon I've done pretty well. What about you?'

'I've got something, too.' Philip told Maureen about his conversation with Zayley.

Maureen whistled. 'Is she reliable?'

'I think so.'

'What a bastard. We've got to nail him.'

'For what?'

'Chasing Michael when he was killed. That could be manslaughter.'

'Did you ask Stefan about Nina?'

'Yeah, I suggested an interview with her, but he got cagey. Told me she's had bad experiences with unscrupulous journalists.' Maureen grinned. 'Your fatal charm, Philip. Don't worry, I'll find her. Same again?'

'You've twisted my arm.'

She laid a couple of notes on the table. 'Could you get them for me? It's mayhem up there.'

Philip took the money and went up to the bar. As he waited for the Guinness to settle, he tried to clear his thoughts and close out the noise. *Dirty old town, dirty old town,* ranted the singer, in an accent so broad it verged on parody. Philip's head felt heavy and slow; his tolerance wasn't what it used to be. Turning around, he thought he saw a figure watching him among the dancing crowd, but when he tried to focus it withdrew into the darkness.

'Are you all right, Phil?' Maureen said, as he sank back into his chair.

'It's nothing.'

'You don't look well. You're pale.'

A curious phenomenon had tipped the pub onto an angle. Philip waited for it to right itself before he answered. 'It's just that some weird things have been happening.'

'Weird?'

'I've got a feeling someone's watching me. And someone was in my flat the other night.' He described the photos he had found. But when he told her about visiting Price's place that morning, and the woman in the window, his voice faltered. Here, in the warmth of the pub, the story sounded ridiculous and he could see the doubt in her face. 'I'm not kidding, Maureen. I saw someone up there. But the next moment she was gone.'

'Phil, be serious. What was she – a ghost?'

If Philip had ever thought about ghosts, he'd assumed they were insubstantial things. The woman in the window hadn't been like that. 'No. I dunno. But she was there, that's all. Don't look at me like that.'

Maureen tried unsuccessfully to suppress a grin. 'Some kind of wispy maiden, was she? All dressed in white?'

'No. She was solid. She was there. And then she wasn't.'

'But Phil ... she could have been anyone. You said the place was open for inspection.'

'She was there,' Philip repeated. He tried to take his mind back: the feeble afternoon sun, the crunch of wheels on gravel as the house-hunters departed, and the girl in the window looking out. Then he remembered John Price's terrified face as he stared into his garden.

'Phil, have you thought of seeing someone?'

'Like who?'

'Y'know, like a counsellor.'

'You think I'm cracking up? Is that what you mean?'

'Calm down, Phil. I'm just saying, you've been through some hard times, and a counsellor could help you work through –'

'I don't need to *work through* anything. There's nothing wrong with me,' Philip said, fumbling with Drum and Rizlas.

'OK, be strong and silent then. Sorry I spoke.'

'I'm sorry.' He drew smoke into his lungs. 'I s'pose you're right. Must have been someone looking round the house. Gave me a shock though.'

'Yeah.' She managed a smile. 'You had me going there for a minute, Phil.'

'Relax. It was nothing.'

They both sat quietly for a few moments. Then Maureen said: 'So what do we do next?'

'Do we have to do anything?' Philip didn't like the turn the conversation was taking. He would have preferred to let the story, if it was a story, quietly fade away. He wanted to sit with Maureen, sharing gossip and jokes like regular people. But she wouldn't drop it.

'Oh, come *onnnnn*, Phil. You can't opt out now. Tell me, what was Stefan doing at Price's place?'

‘Valuing his collection, supposedly. But I guess Price had something he wanted.’

‘Such as?’

‘Maybe a painting.’ Philip described the portrait of Valerie. ‘I saw it the first time I interviewed him. When I went back, it had gone. Stefan said it wasn’t worth anything, but ...’

‘I wonder if it’s one of his “exciting recent discoveries”?’

‘Could be. I haven’t a clue about stuff like that.’

‘We need some help,’ she said. ‘Hey – what about Richard?’.

‘Nah, lost touch.’

‘Wasn’t he a mate of yours?’

‘I thought so, but he ran for cover like everyone else.’

‘That was more than three years ago, Phil. Don’t you think you should let it go?’

‘Don’t give me that crap.’

‘OK, great. Stay bitter forever. Richard could help.’ Taking his hand, Maureen went on: ‘Phil, you can’t keep avoiding everyone. And Richard knows heaps about art.’

‘Yeah, yeah, I’ll think about it.’ Philip’s head was starting to spin, his vision was blurred. It would be a good idea to stop drinking now. Instead he lifted the glass to his lips.

She twined her fingers into his, leaned towards him. ‘What about a dance?’

‘Oh no. You know I’m a terrible dancer. Especially to this.’ The singer was bawling: *and a roving a roving a roving I’ll go, for a pair of brown eyes.*

‘No arguments, Phil,’ she said, dragging him to his feet. ‘I love this song.’

As he shuffled awkwardly from foot to foot in a lame imitation of dancing, Philip looked down into her face. She smiled up at him. He could smell her perfume. Her body was firm and pressed against him. Was it possible that in spite of everything she still liked him? Her cheek brushed his, smooth and cool. At that moment his guts began to send urgent distress signals. The floor was tilting, the lights a blur, the music overpowering. His balance deserted him and he staggered.

'Phil! You OK?'

'Just a minute ... I've gotta ...'

Breaking away from her, he barged to the toilets, crashed into a cubicle and threw up. Oh, Christ. His hand groped for the button, and flushed. He slumped on the floor, gripping the rim of the toilet, waiting for everything to stop lurching.

'You're a dead man, Trudeau.'

He froze. The voice had come from the adjacent cubicle – a man's voice, low, almost conversational, but unmistakably menacing.

'What?'

'I said you're a dead man. You're finished.' There was a pause, then a hoarse laugh. 'We're gonna cut you into pieces and feed you to our dogs, you cunt.'

The toilet flushed next door, the bolt shot back and footsteps walked away. Philip heard the squeak as the main door closed. Shaking, he got to his feet. He stood at the washbasins, sluiced his face and stared at himself in the mirror. Behind him the door opened again and a man walked in. Philip recognised Ted, the photographer.

When Ted saw Philip he grinned and slapped his shoulder. 'Phil! I saw everything.'

'What?'

'Those moves on the dance floor. Like Travolta on tranquillisers. You on the pull tonight, or what?'

'Ted. Did you pass anyone walking out just now?'

Ted shook his head. 'Why?'

'Doesn't matter.'

'Are you OK? You look fucking awful.'

Not answering, Philip pushed past.

'Hey, I've got some beaut new photos to show you,' Ted called after him. 'Truck cleaned up a Kawasaki on Ballarat Road. Monday, OK?'

Philip walked back out and headed for their table. There were two people sitting there, a man and a woman.

'You've taken our seats,' Philip said.

The man bristled, Saturday-night machismo barely in check.

'There was no one here,' the woman said quickly.

'Yeah, she was ...' Philip looked for Maureen's jacket on the chair, her bag on the floor, but they were gone, and the glasses had been cleared.

'You've been dumped, mate,' the man said with a grin. The two resumed their conversation.

Philip turned away. No sign of her. Well, he wasn't surprised. Who had he been kidding anyway? Why would she want to spend her time with a drunk – a middle-aged drunk to boot? Still, a pang of emptiness ripped through him. Another night alone in his flat, with only the box and the neighbours' fights for company. He scanned the pub again. Hundreds of people drinking, laughing, shouting, flirting. Was the guy who had threatened him among this crowd?

He stood outside, checking up and down the street. Perhaps she'd come running up. *Hi Phil, I had to get out of the smoke, let's go somewhere else* ... Nothing. He began walking back to his car. Halfway there he stopped, checked his wallet, turned back to the bottle shop and spent the last of his dough on the cheapest Scotch they had. Lonely nights were the longest and he'd be needing something to see him through.

12

Several days later, at lunchtime, Philip sat in a small Italian restaurant in the city, trying to forget the price of his drink. La Dolce Vita wasn't top of the range, but it was good enough to attract a smart business clientele. In places like this the waiters judged you by your shoes, and the expression on the maitre d's face when he saw Philip's footwear had implied that their owner belonged in a caravan park. Philip had ordered the most expensive beer to prove a point – a gesture as stupid as it was costly.

The beer was almost gone by the time Richard rolled in. He looked much as Philip remembered: nice suit, silk tie, pink complexion beneath thinning hair. He was a little thicker round the middle, but this only added to his boundless self-confidence. Wherever he was, Richard gave the impression that if he didn't own the place he was on close terms with the person who did. Philip must have changed more than he'd realised, for Richard stood staring around the room until Philip raised his arm. Then he walked across, shook Philip's hand briskly and sank into a chair.

'Long time no see. It was a pleasant surprise to get your call. Greetings, Marco.' The waiter materialised – clearly Richard had passed the shoe test. Richard ordered a mineral water as the man dispensed menus. 'Where are you working these days?'

Philip told him.

'I haven't heard of it.'

'You wouldn't. It's a suburban paper.'

'Stopgap measure?'

'Stopgap measure.' Philip noticed spots of perspiration on Richard's upper lip.

'Tell me, how's your lovely wife?'

'Fine, but no longer my wife.'

'Ah. I'm sorry to hear that.' Richard fiddled with his knife and fork, unusually ill at ease. 'And little — was it Emily?'

'Amy. She's in Queensland, with Sarah.'

The waiter reappeared, simper at the ready. Richard asked if the Tasmanian oysters were freshly shucked and, on being assured that they were, ordered a dozen followed by duck. Philip asked for pasta and allowed Richard to select a bottle of South Australian red that cost at least four times what Philip could afford. At least it would be good: Richard prided himself on his knowledge of wine. And on his knowledge of art.

'So how's *The Biz & Fin*?' Philip said.

'Not too bad. Graeme finally made me arts editor.' Richard's cheeks darkened slightly. 'Philip, I thought it was very unjust, what happened to you.'

'Thanks Richard. Water under the bridge.' If Philip could have a beer for every colleague who had expressed support in private, he'd never need to buy another drink. Few, if any, had done so publicly.

'And young Maureen, too. Just awful.'

'These things happen. I've put it behind me.'

'Good. Good.' The waiter poured a small amount of cabernet sauvignon into Richard's glass. Richard held it to the light, swirled it, sniffed, tasted and nodded. The waiter filled their glasses.

'Still a young pup, but drinkable.' Richard had recovered his good spirits. 'Cheers.'

The waiter placed the meals before them. To accompany Philip's spaghetti, he proffered a pepper grinder the size of a ballistic missile. Philip wasn't particularly keen on pepper, but made the man stand and grind.

'So, you're interested in James West?' Richard said. 'I hadn't pegged you as an art lover.'

'No, but I've met some interesting characters lately.'

'Such as?'

'Stefan West.'

'Ah.'

'Know him?'

'We just profiled him in the paper. But I first ran across him twenty-five years ago.'

'Of course, you went to Grammar, didn't you?'

'He was in my class for a couple of years, but I don't remember much about him.'

Philip nodded. He could hardly remember himself what Stefan looked like. What came to mind instead was the photo of James West – tall, bohemian, charismatic.

'I seem to remember he got bullied a fair bit,' Richard went on. 'It can be hard having a famous father, especially if you don't have any talents yourself.'

'He hasn't changed much.'

'Well, we might have underestimated him. I was surprised when he surfaced a few years later as a gallery owner. I didn't think he'd make a success of it.'

'And has he?'

Richard nodded. 'Of course the family connections helped. But he's made some smart moves, too. His first big break came with

Bradley Black – you know of him?'

'Even I've heard of *him*.'

'A few years ago Black was just starting to make his name. He had a show in a North Shore gallery that sold out in days. It transpired that all the paintings had been bought by a single person – a mystery buyer. Well, the show selling out was great for Black's reputation. He became the artist *du jour*, and his prices went through the roof. Unfortunately he celebrated with some dodgy heroin, and bingo, he's history.'

'What's Stefan got to do with that?'

'Soon after, when the papers were full of the young genius and his tragic death, Stefan held an exhibition of twenty of Black's paintings. The prices, needless to say, were outrageous. He sold the lot.'

'So he was the mystery buyer.'

'Exactly.'

'But he couldn't know that Black would die.'

'He could see Black's star was rising and he knew that selling-out an exhibition would make prices shoot up, if you'll pardon the expression. Black's death was a bonus. It's a high-risk strategy, but it paid off big time.' Richard finished his first goblet of wine and recharged both his and Philip's. 'Funny how an average red gets better, the more you drink. So what's young Stefan up to now?'

'He's planning an exhibition of his father's work.'

'I heard about that. Some unknown works have surfaced, apparently.'

'What do you know about James West?'

'Big-name painter. Made his reputation in the '50s, same generation as Tucker and Nolan. But he was clever enough to keep in with the younger generation as well. Peter McKendrick wrote a biography in the '80s, which gave a fillip to his reputation. His later work's not so good, though. Reworked the same ideas too many times.'

'Are his paintings worth much?'

'They vary. Collectors like the early ones, when he was young and angry. Social realism with a surrealist twist.'

'Say I wanted one. How much would I need?'

'Oh, at least $100,000 for a good one. Stefan doesn't let them come up for sale very often. If someone else sells one, he buys it himself to keep it off the market.'

'So he's hoarding them?'

'Yes, waiting for the value to appreciate.'

'How? James West can't OD on heroin. He's dead already.'

Richard smiled. 'Well, maybe Stefan's thought of something.'

'An exhibition will make the prices rise, won't it?'

'If it's a good one, yes. So why are you interested?'

Philip explained about the picture he had seen at Price's house, then mentioned the railway accident and Nina. 'Stefan keeps turning up – first with John Price, then Nina Fletcher. I'm looking for the connection.'

'Who's Nina Fletcher?'

'A photographer. Stefan's showing her work in his gallery.'

'He doesn't usually do contemporary stuff.'

'Then why now?'

'Australian photography is hot right now. Maybe he thinks he can make some quick money. Is she good looking?'

'Not bad. Why?'

Richard laughed. 'Perhaps he's not thinking with his brain.'

Maybe, Philip thought. Or maybe there was some other reason that Stefan wanted Nina onside. But what?

The waiter cleared the empty dishes and placed a plate of duck in front of Richard. Proclaiming his own appetite satisfied, Philip watched as the steam rose gently from the moist slices that Richard lifted to his mouth.

'What about the rest of the Maribyrnong Group?'

Richard shook his head. 'No big names among them. One of them might have become a cartoonist, from memory. I think Vic Smith had something to do with them, too. He's one of the old Communist realist school – heroic factory workers and the like. He had a show a couple of years ago at Trades Hall.'

'Where can I see West's paintings?'

'The State Gallery. The NGA. A few of the regionals. Stefan has some, obviously. The rest would be in private collections or bank vaults. He's a good investment.'

'Can the owners be traced?'

'Dealers guard their clients' anonymity with their lives.'

'There's no way of finding his work?'

'Go to the State Library and see what you can dig up.'

Richard mentioned the titles of some reference books, which Philip scribbled down.

'When I did my Masters, I spent months looking for Streetons,' Richard went on. 'You wouldn't believe the places I visited. Regional galleries in Woop Woop. I've never drunk so much instant coffee.' He rolled his eyes. 'Talking of investments, there's something I wanted to ask you, confidentially.' Dropping his voice, he leaned forward slightly. 'I was thinking of buying into Alitex – good move?'

Philip hesitated. 'I'm not up with all that these days.'

'Come on, Phil.' Richard smiled incredulously. 'You used to read the market better than anyone.'

Philip needed to show that he still had something to offer. 'Well, they've got a strong asset base, and with Michael Sheeney in charge it's a good bet. But don't get in too deep. Their operations in PNG are shaky as hell.'

They talked business for a while, but investments no longer excited Philip. The stock market, with its hunches, manias and panics, left him cold. It struck him that the art market functioned the same way. You found a stock you liked – a Bradley Black – and went in hard. If your gamble paid off, you made a killing. But there were always those for whom the odds weren't good enough. The free market was a little too free for their liking. They wanted to give things a nudge in the right direction. The David Stevensons of the world. The Stefan Wests.

Richard lifted the bottle of wine and emptied the dregs into their two glasses. 'By the way, Phil, a chum of mine has just set up a strategic communications consultancy. They're doing pretty well and they're on the look out for good people – I could put in a word if you're interested.'

'You mean spin?'

'They call it reputation management, public education and issues containment. It's good money, and easy for someone of your experience.'

Philip smiled. 'With my record?'

'Ancient history. You don't belong at a suburban paper.'

Maybe not – but did he belong in the world of spin? He looked at Richard, flushed with oysters, duck and cab sav.

'Thanks for the offer, Richard. But it wouldn't suit me. I guess I'm too much of a journo.'

'You can't tell me life in the suburbs suits you.'

'Not exactly, no.'

'Then what *do* you want?'

An insane thought: Nina Fletcher turning towards him at the bazaar, her freckled skin, her tousled red hair falling over her face.

'I'll let you know when I find out,' Philip said.

Richard signalled to the waiter for the bill. They rose. Richard tossed a gold card onto the table. 'My shout this time, Phil.'

'No, no, Richard,' Philip said, not particularly forcefully, making a show of reaching for his own wallet.

'Next time. It's good to see you again, Phil. Don't be a stranger.'

Philip winced as a pain speared through his guts. 'Are you all right?'

'Yeah ... it's nothing, it's OK.'

They emerged into the sunlight. 'If I can help at all,' Richard said.

'Well, if you happened to hear anything about Stefan ...'

'I'll pass it your way.' Richard hesitated. 'But be careful, Phil. Maybe I'm being over cautious, but don't get on the wrong side of Stefan West.'

'Why?'

'Let's say I've heard a few things. Stefan has some powerful friends.'

'I know that.' Philip told Richard about Callum's phone call.

'Well that's not all. Another one of his pals is David Stevenson.'

Philip took his time to respond, rolling a cigarette and lighting it. 'Oh yeah? How do they know each other?'

'Not sure. But a little bird tells me Stevenson's keen to be the next chairman of AMOMA.'

'AMOMA?'

'Australian Museum of Modern Art.'

'Since when did Stevenson give a shit about modern art?'

'He doesn't – but he's cosying up to the new government and he wants to look public-spirited. The point is, I don't recommend tangling with Stefan.'

'Thanks Richard. I only swim between the flags these days.'

'Ah, here's a cab. Need to go anywhere?'

'You take this one. I'll walk.'

'Bye, Phil. Love your work.'

Philip watched the taxi disappear and began walking slowly in the direction of the tram stop, his guts aching. *I don't recommend tangling with Stefan.* Well, he wouldn't let it bother him for now.

Another sharp pain. He stopped at the lights and looked around him. Suited men with post-lunch faces, berating their mobiles. Harried mothers with strollers. Truanting teenagers with skateboards. And a red-haired woman walking towards him across the road, in a white blouse and retro corduroy trousers. Briefly their eyes met, then she was gone. Philip took a long breath. People pushed past, giving him odd looks. He closed his eyes and leaned against the streetlight, waiting for the pain to clear. When he opened his eyes, nothing had changed. The city flowed on around him. *Pull yourself together.* He made his way to the tram stop and jumped on the first one that came.

13

Philip sat in the State Library Reading Room in a pleasantly drowsy cab-sav haze. Fellow scholars surrounded him: teenage computer geniuses, Japanese kids in cartoon t-shirts, and assorted eccentrics, sociopaths and chess fanatics.

Philip disliked libraries. He'd never been one for formal research. At uni he'd cajoled mates and girlfriends to lend him their assignments so he could be free to run the student newspaper. In his final year he'd scored a cadetship and chucked in his degree. Working at *The Biz & Fin* didn't change his view. Journalism wasn't about books. It was about hanging around the bars where the players gathered, your ears open, your antennae quivering. That's what the young kids with their media and comms degrees didn't understand. It was about sensing an evasive answer, noticing a misplaced word, picking up an unexplained fluctuation in a share price. That had been Philip's trade, and he'd been good at it – the best.

Now here he was with books spread around him: Peter McKendrick's biography of James West, an encyclopaedia of Australian art, a guide to sale prices, a catalogue from an exhibition, and a folder containing miscellaneous articles and an obituary. Richard had recommended some; the girl at the information desk had found the rest by searching under James West and the

Maribyrnong Group. When he'd given his name she'd looked up with sudden interest, her lips slightly parted showing white teeth.

'Philip Trudeau, the journalist?'

'Yeah.'

'I did media studies at uni. The tutor gave us your stuff to read.'

Philip shifted uncomfortably. He was anonymous these days, and that was the way he liked it. There'd been a time when it wasn't so unusual for girls to offer him more than smiles. Like that guest lecture in '97. His exaggerated stories of unmasking corporate crime had drawn laughter and applause. Afterwards the fearless crusader and his admirers had kicked on to the pub, and then ...

But those days were long gone. Pushing his reminiscences away, he took up the encyclopedia.

Sir James Frederick West. 1926–1996. Born in the industrial suburb of Yarraville, West trained as a draughtsman but was largely self-taught as a painter. His early paintings fused social realism with surrealism resulting in vigorous and original paintings of urban life. In 1951 he won a Travelling Scholarship and moved to Paris. After exhibiting in Paris and London he became known as one of the best young Australian painters. In 1952 he married Pamela Flett, the English socialite. During the 1960s and 1970s he achieved great commercial success, and he represented his country at the Venice Biennale in 1964. He was knighted for services to the arts in 1980. His work is represented in many national, state and private collections.

Next Philip took up the guide to prices. Artists were listed in alphabetical order next to graphs plotting the prices each had achieved at public auctions. Philip understood this kind of analysis. No subjective opinion, no debate about artistic merit: here was the unfettered market in action. James West wobbled through the

1980s and 1990s, rose in 2000 and spiked in 2001. The average price was $80,000; the best was $310,000. Who'd pay that kind of money? Philip had his suspicions.

He opened the catalogue of West's works published by the State Gallery in 1982. It was a slim book with a dozen reproductions. The owner's name was recorded next to each picture. *Collection of M. Martin. Collection of Dr M. Vandenberg. Collection of K. Matthews.* He noted these and studied the images; none portrayed Valerie. They were strongly painted in a style that, to Philip's eye, looked similar to the portrait he had seen in Price's house, but they lacked its compelling quality.

Philip turned to the biography, *A Truthful Eye: The Life And Painting of James West* by Peter McKendrick, and flipped through the pages. After a brief description of his early life in Yarraville – the Maribyrnong Group was disposed of in less than a page – McKendrick took up West's career in Paris, in a chapter titled '*Au revoir*, mate': *It was in Paris that West took his first steps towards becoming one of the major painters of the twentieth century...*

A London chapter followed:

Pamela provided invaluable, unfailing support to her husband. Her extensive acquaintance with dealers, critics and other painters ensured that James' work was exhibited, reviewed and widely discussed. Her beauty and vivacity, coupled with James' talent, soon made them one of the most sought-after couples in London. Equally at home at a royal reception or a Chelsea loft party, their list of friends read like a Who's Who of the contemporary art scene. As James' fame grew, his prices rose. Collectors squabbled over his work and celebrities queued up to be painted by him. Pamela managed all of this with skill and aplomb.

At times, Pamela exerted a significant influence on the directions

West took with his art. 'His series of slaughterhouse paintings came directly from a suggestion I made to him,' she once told me. 'Now, of course, they are known all over the world.'

In the feminist era, it has become unfashionable for a woman to devote herself to furthering her husband's career. Lady Pamela does not see it that way. 'I see it as a partnership. He has the vision; I have the business skills and the contacts. I regard myself as fortunate to be the wife of a man who is not only a great genius, but a loving, loyal husband.'

Philip skimmed the rest of the book, making occasional notes, then turned to the collection of articles. Soon after returning to Australia, James had fallen ill. He'd moved to a nursing home in the mid-1990s, where he'd died a couple of years later. Lady Pamela was killed in a car accident not long after. Philip was searching for references to Stefan, when the girl from the information desk appeared beside him.

He caught a trace of her perfume as she bent down and whispered: 'I ordered this up for you from special collections. It's a catalogue from his first exhibition.' She placed a small grey pamphlet in front of Philip — no more than a folded sheet of card with a piece of paper stapled inside. On the cover was printed:

The Maribyrnong Painters' Group
Catalogue
1st Annual Exhibition
Salvation Hall, Yarraville
13–24 September, 1950
Price: Two Shillings

Inside, on the sheet of paper, was a list of some two dozen

pictures. Philip scanned the artists' names. The most frequent was J. West – ten times. He recognised W. Shearwood and T. Zylinski. The others were unknown to him: F. Hall, N. Redfern, K. McConville, V. Elliott, M. O'Keeffe, K. Taylor, B. Cockram, P. Race, V. Smith. James West had made the journey from Yarraville to Venice in a few short years; his fellow Group members had sunk into oblivion.

Philip stared at the list. V. Elliott. V. Smith. 'V' for Valerie? He checked the Australian art encyclopedia for both names: there was a two-line reference to a Victor Smith (b.1920), but no V. Elliott. He was still frustratingly far away. He could hardly ring every Elliott in the telephone book asking after a red-haired woman who went on painting excursions fifty years ago.

'Anything interesting?' the librarian asked.

He was conscious of her bare arm close to him, and felt a flicker of desire. Better not go there. He shook his head and tossed the pamphlet aside. Without speaking she returned to her desk.

Philip pushed the books away. He'd found out as much as he could in here. He needed to talk to people now. People who'd known James West. And there were some obvious places to start.

'Is that Mr Zylinski?'

'What are you selling? Timeshare?' A man's voice, loud and beery.

'Nothing.'

'Market research, is it? What do I drink? What do I wipe my arse with?'

'Nothing like that. I'm a writer, my name's Philip Trudeau. I'm researching a group of artists from the 1950s called the Maribyrnong Group. I'd like to know if you're related to Tom Zylinski.'

'No one of that name here.'

Philip sighed and started to put a line through the last Zylinski in the phone book. This was number eight — he had already drawn a blank with the other seven.

'You didn't have any relatives of that name then? Father? Grandfather?'

There was a pause. 'Why d'you want to know?'

'Tom Zylinski was one of the group. He was a painter.'

'I had an uncle used to paint,' the man said.

'What?' Philip had been on the point of hanging up.

'Yeah. Died ages ago though. I was just a little tacker.'

Philip heard an unsuppressed belch. 'Could you tell me something about him?'

'I doubt it. Whaddya want to know?'

Philip kept his patience. 'I was wondering if he left any papers, letters, paintings even, or if he told you anything about a painter called James West who lived in England.'

'James who? Nah. Don't know anything about that.'

'Well is there anyone else? Other family members?'

'His daughter's in California, if you want to go that far. Got a mobile dog-washing service.'

'That's great, but I'd like to know about Tom.'

'He died when I was little. Dodgy ticker.'

'When was that?'

'Look, mate, what's this about? Are you paying anything?'

'Please try to think, Mr Zylinski. Did he ever say anything about a girl, a girl with dark red hair?'

'Is this a wind up?' The man was half mystified, half belligerent. 'About the only thing I know about my uncle is that he was a commercial artist. And he barracked for Fitzroy. Now I'm going to finish my dinner.' Click.

'Mr Shearwood?'

'Yes.' A diffident male voice. Philip launched into his spiel. This was the twenty-sixth call he had made, not including messages left on answering machines and phones ringing out in empty houses. The present number was on the opposite side of town in a leafy suburb about as far from Yarraville, socially and geographically, as you could get. Halfway through his question, a second voice came on the line, a woman saying: 'Who is this?'

Philip repeated himself.

'Do you mean my husband's father, William Shearwood? He was a cartoonist.'

'Is he still alive?'

'No, he died years ago.'

'Did he happen to leave anything? Paintings, letters ...?'

'We do have some of his things, but most of it is packed away I'm afraid. However, in the case of genuine research ...'

'This research is very significant,' Philip said. 'I'm re-evaluating the importance of the Maribyrnong Group and Bill Shearwood was a leading member of it.' She sounded unsure; he tried another tack. 'His works could increase in value.'

'I see.' He sensed a nibble at the bait. 'Are you from a university?'

Philip named his *alma mater.*

'Art history department?'

'That's right.'

'Very interesting. If it would help your research, perhaps you'd like to come and look, Mr ... what did you say your name was?'

'Philip Trudeau.'

In the silence that followed he realised his mistake. 'You're not that ghastly journalist, are you?'

'No, no, that's a different Philip Trudeau ...' Philip began desperately. What were the chances, after all these years, that she'd recognise his name?

'I have no intention of talking to you.' The woman's voice shook. 'You wrote terrible things about friends of mine and you got exactly what you deserved. Now you ring here, pretending to be a university lecturer. You're a disgrace.'

'But —'

'If you contact me again, I shall call the police.' Click.

Philip put the phone down wearily. He reached for a bottle and splashed its dregs into a chipped mug. He noticed his hand was trembling. There were times, especially late at night, when he wondered if he was losing it. He remembered the look Maureen had given him at the pub — one-third disbelief, one-third pity, one-third wondering why she was hanging out with him. He would end up like John Price: an old recluse, alone with the phantoms of his brain. Philip cursed himself for not making better use of Price when he had been alive. Somewhere among those boxes and papers had been everything he wanted to know. Now it all lay rotting on a tip ... Except Price's paintings. They wouldn't have been thrown out. Hadn't Price talked about bequeathing them to somebody?

His will! A collector like Price must have made one. Wills were public documents. Philip had once spent days scouring the estate of a dead banker for missing shares. First thing Monday he would contact the Probate Office and request a copy.

Philip looked again through the notes he had taken in the library. He had failed with Shearwood and Zylinski. *Died 1996 — Holmesdale Nursing Home.* Perhaps someone at the home would remember Mr West, the famous painter. Maybe he'd talked to them about the old days. Philip consulted the phone book, then picked up the phone again.

'Holmesdale Nursing Home.' An antiseptic voice.

'A relative of mine was a patient at Holmesdale in 1996. I'm researching his life and I'd like to contact anyone who knew him.'

'None of our current staff was here then.'

'Could you check your records? His name was James West.'

'The database only goes back to 1998.'

'What about paper records?'

'Lost them. Floods.'

'Look, are you sure no one would remember him? It's rather important.'

She sighed. 'Hold on.'

Bored, Philip gazed out of his window into the dark, empty street. No, it wasn't quite empty — a solitary figure, muffled against the cold, stood in the shadows. He couldn't tell if it was a man or a woman. The figure looked up, noticed him, then turned and walked quickly away. Philip considered following, but calculated that while he was running downstairs to the street, the person would turn the corner out of sight.

The antiseptic voice was back. 'Our former matron might remember Mr West. She retired last November, but she'd been here twenty years. Leave me your details and I'll pass them on to her.'

Without much hope, Philip gave his name and number, then grimaced as pain lanced from his abdomen to his back. These spasms were getting worse, and more frequent. He needed a doctor. He knew what they'd say, and he wasn't ready to hear it. But maybe they could give him something to kill the pain.

Philip winced and clutched his guts. As he did so, his mobile rang. Bent almost double, he answered it.

'Philip Trudeau?' A young, female voice.

'Yeah.'

Without further warning she unleashed a torrent of abuse. When she paused for breath, Philip interrupted. 'Who is this?'

'It's me, Zayley. You said you wouldn't tell anyone.'

‘Tell anyone what?’

‘That you’d been talking to me.’ Her anger was mingled with something else: distress, fear.

‘Will you just tell me what happened?’

‘You told that guy that I’d seen him.’

‘No, of course I didn’t.’

‘Well someone did,’ she shouted. ‘They found me tonight. I’ve got bruises. They knew what I told you.’

‘I didn’t tell him, I swear it.’

‘Then who did?’ she demanded. ‘I’ll have to leave the refuge now, they know where I am. I should never have talked to you. Well, I take it all back, right? I never saw him there. Don’t write anything, I’ll deny it all.’ She was about to hang up.

‘Wait – that guy at the station, Snake. Did you tell him what you told me?’

‘Snake’s OK.’

‘He’d sell his mother for ten bucks,’ said Philip wincing from pain. This was bad news for him, too. He could see Ron’s face whitening as another blast came down the phone from Callum, rapidly followed by Philip’s marching orders. And with his only witness about to disappear, the story was in ruins.

‘Tell me exactly what they said.’

‘They said no one would notice another dead junkie.’ Though she spoke with bravado there was no concealing the fear.

‘They won’t do anything. It’s bullshit.’ Philip spoke with difficulty, gripping his side. He realised he had no idea what Stefan might be capable of. The man had probably contributed to the death of one kid already. He recalled Richard’s advice: *Be careful, Phil … don’t get on the wrong side of Stefan West.*

‘Meet me somewhere,’ Philip said.

‘No way! I’m getting out. Don’t try to contact me, right?’

'Zayley, wait –'

But the line was dead. Philip stared at the phone in his hand. His heart hammered painfully. What had he started? He remembered the voice in the pub: *We're gonna cut you in pieces and feed you to our dogs* ... Just who and what was he dealing with here? What had he got Zayley into? How could he protect her?

Then his guts heaved and he ran for the bathroom.

14

‘I’m looking for Victor Smith.’

‘You’ve found him. Who are you?’

‘My name’s Philip Trudeau. I’d like to talk to you about the Maribyrnong Group.’

The man at the door stared aggressively at Philip. ‘How’d you find me?’

‘Trades Hall gave me your address. Are you the painter, Vic Smith?’

‘I just told you, didn’t I?’

‘It’s just that I was expecting someone older.’

‘Nah, that’s me. Vic Smith, OBE.’

‘OBE?’

‘Over bloody eighty.’

The nuggety little man didn’t look sixty, let alone eighty, standing at the doorway of an un-renovated worker’s cottage in Yarraville. He was completely bald and wearing a paint-splashed singlet. His muscular torso and pugnacious manner gave him the appearance of a lightweight boxer. He looked much fitter than Philip felt.

‘Bit old to be a student, aren’t you?’ Smith said.

‘I’m a journalist.’

‘Who d’you work for?’

‘*The Messenger.*’

Smith snorted. ‘A lackey in Mackenzie’s empire.’ But he let Philip in and stomped off down the hall, calling over his shoulder: ‘Come through to the studio. I can’t give you more than ten minutes, I’ve got work to do.’

Philip followed him through the house and into a bright studio out the back. Vic Smith was clearly not a man who believed retirement was a time for taking things easy. The studio was cluttered with pictures in various stages of completion. On an easel a painting of a nude woman was in progress. The model, now in a dressing-gown, was smoking a cigarette.

‘Take a break pet, while I talk to this representative of the capitalist press,’ Smith said. Blowing him a kiss, the woman left the room.

‘Keeping busy, I see.’ Philip tried to keep the admiration out of his voice.

‘Course I am. I have to put food on the table. You don’t mind if I carry on, do you?’ He took up his brush and resumed work, continuing to talk as he did so. ‘If I charged more I’d be a rich man by now, but I insist on keeping the prices low so working people can afford ’em. That’s why the critics don’t rate me. Some kid out of art school asks five grand, old Vic Smith with sixty years’ experience asks five hundred, so they say I’m no good. But I’ve got two paintings hanging at the State Gallery, six at the MUA, another three at Trades Hall. One of the banks tried to buy one but I told them where they could stick it. Course, my gallery wasn’t impressed. Now, what can I do for you?’

Philip began to explain, but Smith interrupted. ‘I know your name from somewhere. Trudeau, Trudeau. Who’d you work for before?’

'The *Business and Financial Review*. Now, about the –'

'Of course, the capitalist's friend. I remember now.'

'I assume you don't read it.'

Smith grinned. 'Never assume. It's useful to know your enemies. Besides, you were famous. Didn't you expose Stevenson?'

'I tried to.'

'One day that bastard'll get what's coming to him. So, a troublemaker like myself, eh?'

Philip didn't want to waste time. 'I'm trying to find out about the Maribyrnong Group. I believe you were a member?'

Smith didn't answer for a few moments, stepping back to examine his work. 'For a while, yeah. I grew up in Yarraville when it was working class, not full of yuppie scum like it is today.'

'So you knew James West, Bill Shearwood ...'

'Knew 'em all, yeah. They were training at the tech, I was a bit older, but I'd already been bitten by the painting bug. So when I heard about a group of young painters, I joined like a shot. I thought art was going to change the world.' He glanced at Philip, then at the canvas in front of him. 'I know, I know, there's nothing revolutionary about this. But I'm an old man, I reckon I can indulge myself a bit.'

'And John Price – you knew him?'

Smith puckered his forehead, thoughtfully dabbing white paint onto the curve of a breast. 'Little Johnny Price? Haven't thought about him for years. He wouldn't say boo to a goose. Always trotting round with his camera.'

'How well did you know James West?'

Smith smiled. 'Well enough to know he was a show pony. Fancy jacket, tie, that little beard. His old man worked for Murphys, but Jim couldn't wait to leave all that behind. I never liked his art, neither. Decadent surrealist rubbish.'

'And what about Valerie?'

Smith paused. His expression became more guarded. 'Well, fancy you mentioning her.'

'You did know her then?'

'Yeah, but not well — I don't think anyone did.'

'Could you have a look at this?' Philip handed Smith the photograph from Michael's room.

'Well, I'll be buggered. Yeah, that's Valerie, with Jimmy and Bill. She was a good-looking sheila.' He turned back to his painting. 'Not as good as this one, but not bad.'

'Was she West's girlfriend?'

'She took up with Bill first. Bill was a good bloke, come from the country. He was working at a printer's shop and doing evening classes, that's where he met her. But as soon as she met Jimmy, she gave Bill the arse. When she saw something she wanted, she didn't let anything stand in her way. The Group broke up pretty soon after that.'

'Wasn't there an exhibition?'

'Yeah, that's right. A dozen of us got together and hired Salvation Hall, where the bazaar is now. Art shows were pretty rare round here in those days, so we got a lot of attention. Jimmy called the papers and they sent a reporter. He was always skiting.'

'Have you got anything from those days — photos, letters ...?'

'Nah. The future's what matters to me, not the past.'

'I heard there was some kind of fight,' Philip said.

'Who told you that?'

'John Price.'

Smith put down his brushes and wiped his hands on a rag. 'I do remember that. It happened the day the exhibition opened. I came outside for a smoke and saw Bill and Jimmy having a blue. It started off with shouting, then there was a bit of push and shove and soon they were throwing punches. We pulled them off each other. There wasn't much in it. I saw much worse at sea, I can tell you.'

'What were they fighting about — Valerie?'

Smith laughed. 'Poor bloody Bill never had a chance — he was just a hick to her. She had an education, she liked Jimmy and the way he talked. I told Bill to forget about it, but he took it pretty hard.'

Philip looked again at the photograph. He knew enough about these three now to see the tensions that would later erupt in violence. John Price believed that fight had broken up the Group. Could a simple punch-up be so significant?

'What happened after that?' Philip asked.

'Pretty soon I did a pier-head jump and went to sea for six months. By the time I came back everyone had gone their separate ways. But I'd changed, too — I'd joined the Seamen's Union, I was committed to the Party, and that took up all my time.'

'Did you hear what happened to Valerie?'

Smith shook his head. 'Lost touch with everyone. I saw Bill once, years later. He came to my exhibition. I never saw Jimmy, except in the papers of course, with that ritzy wife of his. Can't say I was surprised, I always thought he'd turn out a class traitor.'

'Do you want me again, Vic?' It was the model, reappearing in her dressing-gown.

'You bet, love, this fella's just leaving.'

He led Philip to the studio door, where he paused. 'You know, Valerie was a good painter, I'll give her that. But too obsessed with death for my taste. Realism, yes, but with her it got morbid. Socialist art focuses on life, not death. Like her, for example.' He nodded towards the model. 'Plenty of life in Mona. You can find your own way out, can't you?'

'I felt sorry for the poor old bugger,' said Kathleen O'Regan. She set two steaming mugs of tea on the tiny kitchen table and eased herself into a chair opposite Philip. Close by, a very old man was immobile in an armchair, his eyes fixed on a quiz girl spinning a wheel. From the wall above the TV, Jesus stared down from his cross. Not much company. Philip guessed Kathleen had responded to the message he'd left with Holmesdale Nursing Home out of loneliness as much as anything. He'd told her the same story he'd used with Mrs Shearwood: he was an art historian working on a biography. But now that he was here in her seventh-floor flat she seemed nervous, spilling tea and fidgeting. Her anxiety made him unwilling to take out his tape recorder or notebook. It was better to keep it casual. For a short time at *The Biz & Fin* he'd had a regular column: *Lunch with Trudeau.* He'd often persuaded prudent businessmen to loosen up over a good steak. *Look Phil, I'll tell you what the score really is ...* Make it a chat and they'd forget it was an interview.

He raised his mug, marked with the insignia of the Victorian Nursing Federation, and drank. 'Great tea. Irish?'

She smiled broadly. 'That's right.' Her accent was unaltered by nearly forty years away from her country of birth. She was a small, indomitable-looking woman, her face still youthful despite her grey hair.

'Lovely stuff,' Philip said. 'I had this in Galway once.'

'Are your people Irish?'

'My wife's people. We travelled around a few years ago, visiting the ancestral haunts. Gorgeous place.'

'It is.' Her eyes roamed up to a bottle on the kitchen shelf. 'You don't fancy a little drop of Irish whiskey?'

'Perhaps just a small one.'

'That's the way.' She took down the bottle and poured them both a glass.

'*Slainte,*' Philip said. 'Where are you from?'

'Enniskillen. Haven't been back in twenty years ...'

As she talked, Philip drifted off into memories of his trip to Ireland. It had been a last ditch attempt to save the marriage, and it had ended in miserable failure, although it had been another year or so before Sarah walked out. They had travelled from one bunch of relatives to the next, Sarah singing the praises of the warm-hearted, loveable Irish, while Philip became more and more resentful. He forced himself back to the present.

'You've always been a nurse?'

'It was all I ever wanted to do. Ten years in Ireland, thirty out here.'

'My mother was a nurse at the Alfred,' Philip said. 'Very hard work.'

'It surely is.'

'Is Holmesdale a good place?'

'I've seen worse. It wasn't cheap, mind you.'

'How long did Mr West live there?'

'Eighteen months, two years maybe.'

'I heard he had some health problems.'

'He was in a bad way. Heart, kidneys, the works. But at least he could communicate, in the early days at least. Later on he developed dementia. Then he had a stroke, and he was practically a vegetable after that.' She glanced at the old man in the chair. 'It's the same with Dad – he doesn't know who I am half the time.'

Philip nodded. He'd been introduced to Dad on his arrival. The old man had peered up from a high-backed armchair, his scrawny neck and bald head giving him the appearance of a tortoise flipped onto its back. He'd shaken Philip's hand in puzzlement.

'Paddy, it's been a long time ...'

'This isn't Paddy, Dad. It's the writer I told you about.'

The old man had nodded, trying in vain to place Philip, then turned his attention back to the TV. As Kathleen and Philip had sat down at the table, she'd said: 'He lives in the past. Paddy was his brother – he died thirty years ago.'

'It must be hard work looking after him.'

'Who'd do it if I didn't? I'm his daughter.'

Philip nodded, reflecting that when he, Philip, was old and mad, there'd be no one to look after him. He wouldn't have the energy of Vic Smith. He couldn't afford a nursing home. Amy would have too much sense to waste her life on an old fossil. He'd end up on his own in a flat like this, if he was lucky. Christ, no. He'd drink himself to death first.

'Did Mr West have any visitors?'

'Not many. He was a lonely old man.'

'What about Lady Pamela?'

'A real piece of work she was.'

'Really?'

'She expected us to fetch and carry for her. Treated us like servants. Nothing was good enough for her, you know. Bed too hard. Room too hot or too cold. Food not good enough. I felt like saying, well if that's how you feel, you look after him. No danger of that, of course. She couldn't wait for him to pop off.'

Philip half smiled. This was a new angle on the devoted wife and noted philanthropist.

'Could you look at this?' Philip showed her the photograph from Michael's room, now crumpled from being carried in his pocket. 'Do you recognise any of them?'

She reached for her glasses. 'Who are they?'

'The middle one is James West.'

'Really? Not a bad looking chap, was he?' She shook her head and handed the picture back. 'I've never seen the other two.'

'Did any women visit him in the home?'

'Apart from Pamela, no.'

Disappointed, Philip gave up on that line of questioning. Even in old age, a woman as striking as Valerie would be remembered.

'You say he never painted?'

'Sometimes a wee bit. It wasn't what you'd call art, just shapes and squiggles. But Vandenberg was happy.'

'Vandenberg?' The name sounded familiar.

'The doctor. He encouraged Mr West to paint again.'

He had it now. Vandenberg had been one of the collectors listed in the catalogue that Philip had seen in the library. Why had he wanted West to paint? It could be worth following up.

'Would Dr Vandenberg still be at Holmesdale?'

'No, but he'd be in the phone book. Anyway, nothing helped. The poor old bugger just got worse and worse.'

'In what way?'

'He hardly spoke, he was paralysed, seemed scared all the time. Jumpy. He'd sit there in his chair, muttering away to himself – nothing you could recognise, just nonsense – his hands shaking. It was a terrible thing to see. It wasn't so bad when other people were with him, but he hated being alone. Night was the worst time. The girls said he'd often cry out. It's not unusual.' She glanced across at her father, who was staring open-mouthed at the screen while a beaming young woman invited him to guess the identity of a mystery celebrity. 'They get the past and present all mixed up. They dwell on things that happened long ago.'

'Bad memories?'

'There was something terrible on his mind, that's for sure. I remember one time towards the end. It was nearly dusk, the end of a beautiful sunny day. He was sitting on the lawn in his chair. There were rosellas in the pear trees; he liked to watch them. It was nearly dinner time, so I went out to fetch him. Suddenly he said: "Get away!" It was the first time he'd spoken for weeks. "Come on Sir Jim," I said, "time for your dinner" – but when I touched him, his hand was freezing. He was holding onto the frame of the wheelchair, like this, tight' – she gripped Philip's hand – 'as if his life depended on it. He was staring, but there was nothing to stare at. "Get her away from me!" he said. "Get her away from me!"'

'Who did he mean?'

'God only knows. I turned him round and wheeled him in. As soon as we got inside he calmed down.'

'Do you think he really did see someone?'

'I'm sure he thought he did. And that's what matters, isn't it?'

Despite the heat of the room, Philip shivered. He thought of John Price staring into his garden, the ice rattling in his glass. *Don't go yet, Mr Trudeau. ... The curtains ... please ...* Like West, he had ended his days alone and terrified. Why?

Kathleen took another sip from her glass, and twisted her handkerchief between arthritic fingers. Something was making her deeply uncomfortable.

'Take your time, Kathleen,' Philip said gently. 'Would you like another cuppa?' He reached for the teapot.

'I was just remembering that last evening. It was autumn. It had been a nice warm afternoon, so I'd taken him outside for an airing. I had a lot to do inside. One of the girls hadn't turned up, and a couple of patients were in a bad way.' She looked at him. 'People don't realise ...'

Philip nodded. 'You were terribly busy.'

'And what with everything I had to do ...' She hesitated. 'As soon as I remembered I rushed out. It was dark by then. And he ...' She had tears in her eyes.

'He'd passed away?'

She nodded.

'What was the cause?'

'Heart failure.'

'It would have happened anyway. You told me how sick he was.'

She turned to look at Philip, her eyes brimming. 'But he was on his own out there. And it was getting dark. Something might have scared him.'

'I wouldn't worry, love. It was probably a mercy.'

Shortly afterwards Philip rose to leave. On the way out to his car, he clasped her father's hand again. 'Paddy. It's been a long time,' the old man said. Mad old men. They were everywhere. James West paralysed in his wheelchair, John Price trapped on the floor. Both of them terrified. *The curtains ... please ...* What were they scared of? The certainty of approaching death – not rapidly, like the train that smashed the life out of Michael, but the inevitable glide into the dark? Or something else – something worse? *His hand was freezing* ... He remembered the woman watching him from the window. Had James West seen something similar, as the shadows lengthened across the lawn and the dusk settled over Holmesdale Nursing Home? A young woman in a white blouse, a light smile on her lips, advancing towards him? *Get her away from me!* But James West had been an old, sick, demented man; John Price half crazy. Philip looked at himself in the rear-view mirror. Was he going mad too?

Philip watched as Dr Martin Vandenberg walked out of his house and paused to breathe in the smell of the forest, damp from the rain that was falling in a fine curtain over the valley. He glanced at the old Holden parked on the road at the end of his drive. Philip knew that he'd been aware all morning of his presence and had ignored it, just as he had ignored the persistent rings at the doorbell. As the doctor approached his Mercedes, Philip got out of his car and hurried towards him, holding a newspaper over his head.

'Dr Vandenberg? I'm Philip Trudeau. We spoke on the phone.'

Vandenberg pressed his car key, unlocking the doors with a soft hiss. 'As I said, I can't help you.'

'It won't take long.' Philip positioned himself beside the Merc.

'Get out of my way.'

'Just five minutes. I need to ask you about James West.'

'James West?' Vandenberg was six inches taller than Philip, and frowned down at him. 'How did you get my name?'

'I understand you were West's doctor?'

'I don't discuss my patients with journalists.'

'It will only take five minutes.'

'I don't have five minutes.' The car door was open, the doctor was in the driver's seat.

'I've found a painting by James West. I think it would interest you.'

Vandenberg paused, looked at Philip. Eventually curiosity won out over impatience. 'All right, five minutes. After that, I'm throwing you out.'

The house was constructed of giant concrete and glass cubes stacked together among the trees. Vandenberg opened the front door and led the way inside. Light fell through vast windows onto polished wooden floors, illuminating the sculptures that stood on pedestals and the pictures hung three deep on the walls.

'Beautiful house,' Philip said.

'It's by Kapinski.' Vandenberg led the way to a pair of black leather and aluminium chairs. 'Ever heard of him?'

'Can't say I have.'

'One of the best.' He sat down, a window at his back, and motioned Philip to sit opposite. 'Five minutes, then.' He took a gold watch from the pocket of his vest, rested it on the glass table in front of him, and looked at Philip with unblinking eyes.

Facing Vandenberg's silhouette, Philip felt as if he was about to be questioned himself. A memory flashed into his head of another room, another interrogation. *You're in deep shit, Phil. You're in it up to your neck. Tell us who you've been talking to, and tell us now.*

'What was West's health like?' Start with the easy questions.

'I won't go into details, but he needed constant care.'

'You're a specialist in dementia. Is that what was wrong with him?'

'Among other things.'

'How did it show itself?'

'Confusion. Forgetfulness. The symptoms of dementia are pretty well known, even to journalists. What is the point of this?'

'Did you discuss art with him?'

'A man in his condition? No, I did not.'

'What paintings do you have by West?' Philip asked.

'What makes you think I have any?'

'You loaned them to the State Gallery.'

Vandenberg looked at him. 'If you say so.'

'Can I see them?'

'No.'

'Why did you encourage West to keep painting?'

A momentary hesitation. 'Who told you that?'

'Confidential. What was the reason?'

'It's good for patients with dementia to practise creative arts. It keeps their minds active.'

'And what happened to those paintings?'

'Why?'

'I've been told you collected them. How do you respond to that?'

'They were gifts.'

'Very generous gifts, don't you think?' Philip was gaining momentum. 'They'd be worth a small fortune.'

Vandenberg slid his chair back and stood up with a sigh. 'Your suggestion is absurd.'

'Then tell me what happened.'

'I'm not explaining myself to you,' Vandenberg said. 'Don't get too wet on the way back to your car.'

It was stalemate. Philip cast around for another shot, but was unable to come up with one. He got to his feet. But as he touched the door handle, Vandenberg spoke, affecting casualness.

'You mentioned a painting by James West.'

Collectors. They couldn't control themselves. Vandenberg fancied himself an expert on West. He couldn't bear the idea of a painting that he didn't know about. You should never love anything too much, it leaves your weaknesses exposed. Philip turned.

'You haven't exactly been forthcoming, Dr Vandenberg.'

'All right. You tell me about your painting, and I'll explain about mine.'

They resumed their seats.

'Well?' Vandenberg said.

'There's a portrait of a woman called Valerie. Red hair, dark eyes. Striking.'

'Where is it?'

'John Price showed it to me.'

'Who?'

'A collector. Know him?'

'Never heard of him – and I know most of the collectors in this town.'

'He was a mate of West's when they were young.'

'So Price has this painting?'

'Had. He's dead.'

'How old is it?'

'Price said it was done before West went overseas.'

Vandenberg shook his head. ‘I doubt it’s genuine.’

‘Why shouldn’t it be?’

‘Very little work from that period has survived. If it really were by West ...’

‘Yes?’

‘It would be extremely interesting,’ Vandenberg said softly. For a split second his expression had become hungry, the face of a hunter. Immediately he resumed his mask of detachment, but Philip knew he had not been mistaken. Doubtful or not, Vandenberg wanted the painting.

‘So, is that all you’re going to tell me?’ Vandenberg said. ‘Who has the painting now?’

‘Try Stefan West.’

‘Stefan West?’ There was contempt in Vandenberg’s voice.

‘You know him?’

Vandenberg stood up, walked to the window and stared out across the valley. ‘Unfortunately, yes. I bought some paintings from him a few years ago. Cash sales, no receipts. Everything on a handshake. He can be charming, when he wants to be. Anyway, it turned out the provenance wasn’t what he claimed.’

‘What happened?’

‘He’d tried the same trick with a number of people, and the police became involved. But the charges were dropped.’

‘Why?’

‘No one wants to stand up in court and say “my pictures are worthless”. Collectors hate publicity. If you’ve been conned, you keep quiet about it.’

‘Well, that’s all I know,’ said Philip. ‘Your turn.’

Vandenberg turned as if he had made a decision. ’Come this way.’

He led Philip into another, smaller room, which was kept

in semi-darkness. There were several large cabinets inside. Vandenberg unlocked one, sliding out a drawer that contained dozens of artworks on paper. He laid several out on a table. These paintings were no more than ribbony lines, streaks and dribbles of paint.

Philip looked at him. ‘Kids’ pictures?’

Vandenberg shook his head. ‘These were painted by James West, in the last few weeks of his life.’

‘Dementia?’

‘Exactly. That was all he could do.’

Philip leafed through the pictures. This was what was left when the discipline of a lifetime had been peeled away like the shell from an egg. If obtaining relics had been Vandenberg’s master plan, it was doubtful he’d profited from it.

‘Are they worth anything?’

‘Commercially, no. Anyway, I would never sell them.’

‘Then why *did* you want them?’

‘For my research.’

‘Research?’

‘I specialise in brain disorders, Mr Trudeau. I’m also interested in art. It’s true, I have a personal collection, including a couple of quite good Wests from the ’70s. They were the ones I loaned to the State Gallery. In the ’90s, West was admitted to the nursing home where I was a consulting neurologist. It occurred to me that work produced by an artist suffering from dementia could provide an insight into the disease. I have published a number of articles on the subject. Lady West was quite aware of what I was doing.’

‘Go on.’

‘I gave him paper and paints, and suggested he use them whenever he felt like it.’

‘How did he react?’

'He didn't touch them for months. Zero interest. Then he had a stroke, lost the power of speech, was immobilised. I'd given up on the idea by that time. But a strange thing happened. One day I found him with the paper in front of him, a brush in his hand.' Vandenberg leafed through the pictures. 'As you can see, all his expertise and training had gone. But what was left was interesting. It was completely instinctive. He painted them, and tossed them away. Sometimes the same shapes, over and over again.'

'But they don't look like anything.'

'Many of them, no.' Vandenberg opened a second drawer and took out another batch. 'But you may find these interesting.' He handed the pictures to Philip.

Philip saw crude paintings of a face. Dozens of them. Some only a few streaks of paint, some no more than two eyes filling the page. Despite their childishness, they were unmistakeable. A woman, red-haired, dark-eyed.

'Well?' said Vandenberg.

Philip examined the pictures, feeling once again that familiar prickle at the back of his neck. The small room seemed unbearably close. *The girl in the painting. And the girl in the window. Valerie.* 'So many,' he forced himself to say.

'Exactly. He was obsessed.'

'He only painted this one face?'

'As you see.'

'He never said who she was?'

'He'd lost the power of speech.'

Philip picked up one of the paintings, held it to the light. Valerie, painted by James West, forty years after he had first painted her. Why had she stayed in his memory all that time? Was it, as with Kathleen O'Regan's father, a case of figures from the past coming alive in a ruined mind? Or was there something else involved? He thought of the girl standing in the bright window at John Price's house. And James West's words: *Get her away from me!* There were things here that Philip did not understand, could not accept.

He forced his mind back to something more familiar – human greed. He turned to Vandenberg. 'Suppose there was an unknown painting by James West. A painting that was so rare, it was worth a small fortune. If Stefan West found out about that, he'd want to get his hands on it, wouldn't he?'

'Oh yes. He'd kill for it.'

15

‘Jeez, Phil, how long are you intending to live?’ Maureen said. ‘I can’t believe you might actually eat that.’

She had appeared beside him one lunchtime as he pondered the offerings of his local café. The bain-marie was a nightmare of deep-fried pornography.

‘You having anything?’ Philip said.

‘I’m on the Pritikin diet. Low fat, high carbs. Don’t look at me like that.’

Philip ordered for himself and they took a seat at a small table, where they were almost deafened by the crash of tureens, the hiss of steam and the waitresses’ shouts. Outside, a strumming busker, off his head on some stimulant, broke off from his rendition of ‘Mister Tambourine Man’ to abuse the queue at the ATM.

‘Listen, sorry about the other night,’ Philip said. ‘I got crook all of a sudden.’

‘Can’t hold your grog anymore?’

‘There’s something wrong with my guts.’

‘I had to go anyway. Somewhere to be.’

Philip considered this, and decided to let it pass. Nearly two weeks had gone by since the night at Phoney O’Riley’s, and he’d thought Maureen had abandoned him for good.

'Whatcha been doing?' he asked.

'Not much.'

'Any sign of Nina yet?'

'Nup – exhibition's over.' She tossed the *Urban Images* postcard onto the table. 'What have you been up to?'

'Researching James West.'

'Why?'

'Last year someone bought a painting of West's for $310,000. My guess is it was Stefan. He's a sharp operator.'

'Well, duh. He wouldn't be where he is if he wasn't. Any more brilliant analysis?'

The waitress laid a plate in front of Philip. It was his usual order – a castle of lasagne encircled by a moat of bolognese sauce – but now he was confronted with it he had no appetite. He tried a couple of mouthfuls and pushed it away.

'How's work going?' he asked.

'What work?'

'I thought you were doing something with Amnesty.'

'Oh, that,' she said vaguely. 'It fell through.'

'Maybe you should get back into journalism.'

'Are you trying to give me advice, Phil?'

'I'm just saying ...'

'You're lecturing me on my career? That's pretty hilarious.' She lit a cigarette and puffed on it. 'It's a mess. I wish I'd stayed overseas. There's nothing for me here.'

'You been overseas?'

'Didn't you get my cards?'

'Yeah, of course.' He vaguely remembered bright pictures of mountains, messages on the back in her slapdash handwriting.

'You never replied.'

'I was in prison, Sarah was divorcing me ...'

‘Did it ever cross your mind to wonder how *I* was?’

‘I often thought about you.’

‘Yeah, right.’

‘It was hard to write.’

‘Not a word in two years.’

How could he explain that the daily business of surviving had taken all his energy – coping with the boredom, the hatred, the humiliation, the violence? ‘While I was in there, I had a … I got sick, couldn’t function. It wasn’t that I didn’t want to.’

‘A line would have been enough. *Hi Maureen. How are you going? Phil.* Seven words, not War and fucking Peace.’

‘Where did you go?’

She blew out a cloud of smoke, as she stared out the front window of the café. ‘Tibet.’

‘What was it like?’

‘Awesome.’

‘How long did you stay there?’

‘A few weeks. I had some decisions to make.’

‘What decisions?’

She looked at him. ‘I’ll tell you one day, Phil. Not now.’

‘Fine.’ Philip checked his watch. ‘Well, I’ve got work to do. See ya.’ He gathered his newspaper and cigarettes, and stood up. At that moment his mobile went off. It was the office.

‘Phil. There’s been a shooting in Yarraville. Some street kid. She’s critical, in the Western. Ron says get over there now.’

He made it to the hospital in seven minutes, running red lights and overtaking in the path of oncoming trucks. He double-parked and sprinted to the entrance. The word EMERGENCY was written in huge red letters along the wall. A girl in a silver jacket was slumped there, tears streaming down her face, hugging herself tightly. A knot of teenagers was hanging around her. They stared at him as he approached.

'Hey guys – what's this about a shooting?'

'Who are you?'

'Phil. Did someone get shot?'

'Some psycho went crazy.'

'Who's been shot?'

'You a cop?' a boy said.

'No, I'm a friend.' But their faces were hard with suspicion. 'Please, I just want to know –'

'Piss off!' one of the girls screamed. Her face distorted by grief, she flung herself at him, and her nails raked across his cheek. Clutching his face, Philip backed away and stumbled into the hospital.

In the waiting area small groups sat silent or quietly whispering, as though sealed in private booths of anxiety. He walked to the admissions desk. A large sign on the glass read: *Aggressive and abusive behaviour will not be tolerated.* Another, on the receptionist's side, read: *Just call Security. Don't even think about it.*

'I heard a kid's been shot. Can you tell me who it is?' Philip said.

The receptionist looked at him. 'Who are you?'

'Philip Trudeau from *The Messenger.*'

'I can't give you any information. Stand aside, other people are waiting.'

'Will she be all right?'

'It's too early to say.'

'Don't tell him anything,' said a voice behind Philip. Turning, he saw the burly figure of Gary Fennelly. Fennelly, an ex-footballer, was a youth worker who ran the centre for street kids.

'Who is she, Gary?' Philip said.

‘Keep out of it. There’s nothing for you here.’

‘I think I know her.’

Fennelly smiled without humour. ‘I didn’t come down in the last shower you know.’

‘It’s not for a story. I just want to know.’

‘You’ve been writing some lovely stuff lately. *Kids out of control. Junkies. Thieves.* I’ve invited you blokes to the centre a dozen times to see what’s really going on, but I never get a reply. The moment something like this happens —’

‘Just tell me — has Zayley been shot?’

Fennelly stared at him. ‘Zayley? What’s she got to do with it?’

‘It wasn’t her?’ Hope and relief leaped inside him.

Fennelly shook his head, mystified. ‘Nothing to do with her.’

‘Mr Fennelly, the police are here to see you,’ the receptionist interrupted. Behind her Philip saw Reynolds and another detective.

‘Crawl back under your rock, Phil,’ Fennelly said.

Philip walked unsteadily outside, leaned against the wall and lit a cigarette with trembling fingers. Relief had drained his strength. So it wasn’t Zayley. He’d been so certain that Stefan had acted on his threat. But he hadn’t been thinking straight. He’d leapt to conclusions. Zayley was OK. Maybe cold, hungry, sleeping rough, but alive.

He knew what Ron would expect him to do now. Go back inside and get a name. Talk to the kids until he found out what had happened. He could already see the reporter from the *Post* entering the car park. In the staff canteen he glimpsed a couple of ambulance drivers on a smoko; the Philip Trudeau of old would have been in there before you could say ‘the public’s right to know’. But he couldn’t face it now. Not with his heart still pounding, the blood barely dry on his cheek. Slowly, he walked back to his car.

Ron was unimpressed. 'I told you to get the story.'

'They wouldn't talk to me.'

'Oh, that's all right then. Jesus, Phil! Some fucking professional.'

'Ron, the kid was critical. I couldn't ...' He stopped.

'Couldn't what?'

'I just couldn't, that's all.'

Ron gave him a long look. 'OK. Get back to your desk.' As Philip started to move, Ron said: 'This isn't a sheltered workshop, Phil. Either piss, or get off the pot. Shit, what's the matter?'

Philip had suddenly doubled over, as an atrocious pain speared from his guts to his back. For several seconds he was unable to speak. Still doubled up, he whispered: 'I've been ...getting ... these ... pains ...'

'Christ. Don't die in my fucking office, the cleaners don't come till Friday.' Ron walked into the newsroom shouting: 'Sal, get down to the Western and find out about this shooting. Phil's feeling too delicate at the moment.'

Eight hours later Philip was back at the Western, this time horizontal on a hospital trolley. He'd been there most of the afternoon. At least, thank Christ, the worst of the pain had gone. But it was now ten in the evening, and he was gagging for a drink.

The curtains around his trolley parted and a new doctor walked in.

'Philip Trudeau? I'm Dr Paul O'Day.' He sat down beside Philip, shuffling a clipboard and papers. 'So — acute abdominal pain?'

'Yeah.'

'Ever had it before?'

'For about two weeks. Today was the worst.'

'How bad was it?'

'Excruciating.'

'Any nausea and vomiting?'

'Yeah. Look, I've already told –'

'When did you last see a doctor, before today?'

'About five years ago.' Philip wasn't going to mention his trips to the prison hospital – much less his sessions with the psychologist.

'I've got your test results here,' O'Day said, unfolding a piece of paper as if about to announce the winner of an award. 'They show a high level of amylase in your blood.'

'What's that mean?'

'You have acute pancreatitis.'

'What can you do about it?'

'Give you some painkillers.'

'About bloody time. What about my pancreas?'

'It'll heal itself in time. Of course, you'll have to lay off the grog – I emphasise that strongly – or you'll get it worse next time. Just how much do you drink, Mr Trudeau?'

'A few beers most nights. Scotch. Vodka. Occasionally wine.'

'How much Scotch?'

'Half a bottle. A bottle. I don't keep track.'

'Every day?'

Philip nodded.

'How long have you been drinking that much?'

'About a year maybe. Before that, I didn't drink at all for two years.'

'And before that?'

'A lot.' How many reservoirs would it fill, Philip wondered, if you added up all the grog he had consumed while schmoozing and coaxing, pouring it into himself and his contacts in the hope that, in return, a few precious drops of information would come trickling out?

'What made you start again?'

‘A few life changes.’

O’Day tapped his pencil on his clipboard. ‘Well, you’ve certainly made up for lost time. Who was the doctor you saw when you first came in?’

‘I dunno. She was about twelve.’

‘Who else has seen you?’

‘I can’t remember. Lots of people.’

‘Remember any names?’

‘No. Why?’

‘Have you been forgetting things recently?’

‘Maybe. I dunno.’

‘All the doctors you saw today introduced themselves, didn’t they?’

‘I suppose so. I was in pain.’

‘How’s your coordination and balance?’

‘OK.’

‘Nothing wrong with your vision?’

‘No.’

‘Not been seeing anything unusual?’

Philip hesitated. ‘No,’ he said, as firmly as he could.

‘Well, that’s positive. But excessive consumption can cause neurological damage.’

‘There’s nothing wrong with my brain.’ The doctor’s questions were evoking uncomfortable memories of previous consultations. ‘Just give me the painkillers — I want to get out of here.’

‘OK. But you can’t go on as you have been. Pancreatitis is a severe condition. In the long run, you’ve got to cut down, and in the short-term, cut it out completely.’

‘That’s easier said than done.’

‘You have no choice.’ The doctor got to his feet. ‘Tell me, do all journalists drink as much as you?’

'They used to. These days, the young ones are more moderate.'

O'Day smiled. 'Like young doctors. When I remember my student days ...' He shook his head. 'You can stay here tonight. We'll give you a drip to get some fluids into you. Tomorrow, you're a free man.'

16

He was running, running, running. Behind him dogs barked, lights swept the ground. He stumbled, tripped. *We're gonna cut you up and feed you to our dogs.* A searchlight picked him out, the reluctant star frozen centrestage. *There he is, down there!* He crashed to his knees. Then, ahead of him, a figure. A woman. She beckoned him into the darkness. He followed, low branches slashing his face. Ahead, a shape slipped away. *Stop no stop wait stop ...* He caught up and touched her shoulder. When she turned, he saw red hair, dark eyes. Who was she? Nina? Valerie? *Come on,* she said, *it's this way.* They entered a wide, exposed area, where a shallow grave had been dug into the earth. A wooden cross was ready to be knocked in. People waited, still and silent: Stefan, Maureen, Richard, Ron. *I don't understand. Who's dead? Did you know him? Do you feel numbed by his death?* No one replied, and he realised the grave was his own. He lay in the soft, cold stench. The priest intoned the words: *O God, in whose presence the spirits of the dead have life ...* Dark silhouettes began shovelling above him. He tasted dirt and stones. The clods of earth became boxes. He was John Price. Boxes rained down. He tried to open his mouth, but his lips wouldn't move. *Nonononononono ...*

Philip woke, blanket-shrouded. It was the morning after his return from hospital. It must have been the painkillers and sleeping tablets that had caused the dream.

He phoned the office and returned to bed. The cadet would have to cover the council's new recycling policy and interview octogenarians Madge and Don on the secrets of a happy marriage. He spent the morning drifting between sleep and semi-consciousness. Some time in the afternoon he heard the postman's motorbike and saw him stuff a couple of envelopes into the letterbox. Philip groaned: another threat from his wife's lawyers. But when he stumbled down to collect them he found that the thicker of the two was from the Probate Office. It was the copy of John Price's will he had requested.

Price's house, fittings and furniture were disposed of on the first page, bequeathed to his daughter. On the next ten pages Price had listed in loving detail his books, paintings, catalogues, albums, correspondence. Beneficiaries included the State Gallery, libraries and universities. At the end of the will came the words: *The rest and residue of my estate I leave to my friend, Stefan West.* At the bottom of each page was his signature: *John Price.*

Propped up in bed, Philip went through the will line by line. In the list of paintings he found a few names he recognised – Shearwood, Zylinski – but there were none by James West. The titles didn't help: *View of the Maribyrnong, Bay by twilight, Nautical scene* – nothing that sounded like the portrait of Valerie. It didn't make sense. The James West paintings that Price had boasted about were not listed. *I was right first time. The old bugger was as mad as a snake.* Still, he would call on the State Gallery and ask about the paintings.

He reached the end of the document and stared at Price's signature. The executor was named as Gordon Parker.

He'd heard the name somewhere. Christ, his memory these days. Maybe the doctor was right, his brain cells were dying in their millions, plunging like lemmings into a sea of grog. He reached for his notebook, flipped through the pages. There it was: the place Stefan had visited in Williamstown the day Philip had followed him. He had copied the name from the sign out the front. Mr Parker could be worth a visit.

He had almost forgotten the second envelope. Inside was a brief note: *Found this in the files – thought it might be of interest – Richard.* Stapled to it was an old cutting from *The Biz & Fin*. Philip read it quickly, and as he did so the reasons for visiting Parker multiplied tenfold. Ignoring the doctor's prescription of a week in bed, he reached for his clothes. Parker was high on his 'to do' list, but first he would find out whether anyone at the State Gallery remembered John Price and his generous gift.

'I remember him all right,' said Lloyd Carter, Manager of Donations and Bequests, with a groan. He glanced at his watch. 'I can't give you much time. I have to raise ten million dollars by June 30.' A sign was taped to his desk bearing the slogan: *Triumph is just Umph added to Try.*

'When did you meet Price?' Philip asked.

'He walked in off the street about six months ago. Sat in that chair, talking his head off. I couldn't get him out of here.'

'What did he want?'

'He was rambling all over the place. The war, his friends, some argument with the council. It took me ages to find out what he wanted. Eventually I got out of him that he had an important collection of books and paintings he wanted to donate to us. Everyone thinks their own collection is important, so I treat these claims with caution.' Carter smiled. 'This place attracts some peculiar people. We get the DIY taxidermists who want us to take their stuffed wombats, and the people who think we'd like their granny's watercolours. They get offended when we refuse, but what can we do? We've got a small staff, a limited budget. There's insurance, storage and maintenance. And it has to fit in with our collections policy. A few weeks ago someone offered us a Streeton. But it wasn't a particularly good one, we already have a lot of Streetons and it would never be displayed, so what would be the point? The owner wouldn't let us sell it, so we said take it to a regional gallery instead.'

'So you didn't believe Price?'

'Well, he did seem rather eccentric. Besides, I think I know most of the significant people' – Philip supposed this was code for 'rich people' – 'in this town, but I'd never heard of him. And then he told me he had forty paintings by James West! Now, *one* I might have believed, but forty? I don't think so! Still, the old fella was very keen that we send "an expert" to his house, so I promised him one of our curators would take a look. After that I kept getting phone calls asking when "the expert" was coming.'

'Did anyone go?'

'One of our junior curators checked it out. She reported back there was nothing of value.'

'What did she see there?'

'Let me ask her,' Carter said, picking up the phone. 'Kirsten, remember that old man in Williamstown, who said he had a collection of James Wests ...?'

After a brief conversation he put the phone down. 'She didn't actually see Price. She talked to another guy – a friend of the old man. He showed her the paintings and they weren't Wests, so she left it at that.'

'Did you hear from Price again?'

'He rang up several times, but I never called him back. After a few weeks the calls stopped, and I forgot all about it. Then a solicitor contacted us. Said John Price had passed on and left us some artworks. When we checked them out, it was as we thought – just minor artists, nothing of value.'

'Could I see the pictures?'

Carter shook his head. 'They were no use to us, so we returned them.'

'What happened to them?'

'I suppose the executors auctioned them.'

'Was there a portrait of a woman with red hair and dark eyes?'

Carter frowned. 'Can't remember anything like that. They were landscapes, pretty awful ones. Why?'

'I saw a painting at his house. He said it was by West.'

'And was it?'

'I'm no expert, but it could have been.'

'Our curator didn't think so.'

'Funny, that,' Philip said. 'Do you know who I think she met at Price's place?'

'Who?'

'I'd put money on it being Stefan West.'

'The dealer?' Carter's eyes widened. 'What would he be doing there?'

'What do you think?'

Carter tapped his pencil on the desk, watching the rubber end bounce up and down. 'Do you mean that John Price may have had the things he said he had?'

'It's possible. But Stefan wasn't about to tell you that.'

'Then what happened to them?'

'That's what I'm trying to find out.'

'Let me know, if you do. It may be that we could challenge the will,' Carter said. He examined his pink fingernails. 'A West sold recently for over a quarter of a million, didn't it?'

'So I believe.'

Carter spun his chair round and stared out of the window. He had a look Philip had seen before on the faces of men who had unloaded all their stock from a company the week before its share price skyrocketed.

'Surely the executors would know?' Carter said. 'Perhaps you should talk to them.'

'That's exactly what I'm going to do.'

When he entered the tiny waiting room of Parker's suburban office, Philip found a well-groomed woman at a desk, sorting files. She turned and stared at him.

'I'd like to see Mr Parker.'

'He's on the phone.' She glanced towards an inner office.

'I'll wait.'

'Do you have an appointment?' Her voice dripped disapproval.

'There's nobody else here.'

'But he's very –'

'I think he'll want to see me,' Philip said, and forestalled further conversation by taking the only seat. There were a couple of small pictures on the wall. He looked closely at one: a caricature of Menzies, signed W. Shearwood. He picked up a magazine and flipped through it. The receptionist watched him as if he were a bug she longed to Mortein.

She finished filing, closed the drawer of the filing cabinet and dropped the keys into her desk drawer. There was a jar of multicoloured jelly beans on the desk: she popped her hand in and took a few, not offering the jar to Philip.

'Do you know Stefan West?' Philip asked.

'I should do.'

'Does he come here often?'

‘At least once a week.’

‘Would that be about John Price?’

He’d overstepped the mark now. ‘Couldn’t tell you.’ She dabbed her lips with a handkerchief.

After a few minutes the door opened and a man appeared, presumably Parker, an unlit cigarette between his lips. He was thin, nervous-looking, as insubstantial as a coat on a hanger. ‘I’m just popping out to lunch, Jan.’

‘There’s a gentleman here to see you,’ the receptionist said. Parker turned a startled expression on Philip, who offered his hand and gave his name.

‘You’d better come into my office.’

Philip followed Parker into a room as tiny as the one they’d left. ‘How can I help?’ Parker said.

‘I’m an old friend of John Price.’ Philip watched Parker to see how much the name meant to him. The lawyer fidgeted, keen to get outside for his cigarette. ‘Ah yes, Mr Price,’ he said. ‘Tragic.’

‘He certainly was,’ Philip said. ‘I’m trying to trace his paintings.’

‘He left them to the State Gallery.’

‘All of them?’

‘Yes. Look, I can’t discuss —’

‘Bear with me for a moment. Do you know if he had any James Wests?’

‘Not off the top of my head.’

‘Let me jog your memory. The Gallery wasn’t offered any Wests. The pictures they got were worthless.’

‘There’s your answer.’

‘Not really, Mr Parker. As his executor, it was your duty to ensure that the estate was properly disposed of.’

‘And of course we did. When the Gallery returned the pictures, we auctioned them. They certainly weren’t James Wests.’

‘The question that’s bugging me is this: John told the State Gallery he had some paintings by James West. But in his will there’s no mention of them, even though he listed everything — even the program from the Gilbert and Sullivan Club. Bit of an oversight don’t you think, Gordon? As his executor, I’d have thought you’d be a teensy bit curious?’

Parker smiled. ‘Don’t believe everything you hear. John had some funny ideas.’

‘You mean he was crazy?’

‘Let’s say eccentric.’

‘Oh, I agree with you there,’ Philip said. ‘He was mad as a snake. But I’m certain he had at least one painting by James West.’

‘And how would you know that?’

‘Because I saw it.’

Philip’s eyes locked onto Parker’s, and though the other man met his gaze Philip saw a pulse flicker in his cheek. Neither spoke. Then the door burst open.

‘Gordon, look.’ The receptionist, flustered, had hurried into the office with a copy of *The Messenger*, which she held under Parker’s nose.

Parker looked at the newspaper, then at Philip. ‘You didn’t say you were a journalist.’

‘You didn’t ask.’

‘Get out.’ Parker stood up abruptly.

‘Just a moment, Gordon.’ Philip reached inside his jacket. ‘I came across an interesting article — I wonder if you remember it?’ He unfolded the cutting that Richard had sent him. ‘It’s from the *Business and Financial Review*, 3 May 1999. The headline is: *Art fraud charge dropped. “Art dealer Stefan West and his co-accused, solicitor Gordon Parker, walked from court today after fraud charges against them were dismissed. The case collapsed when key witnesses refused to give evidence.*"' Philip refolded the cutting. 'Care to comment?'

'That's ancient history. There was no foundation to it at all.'

'OK, Gordon, if that's what you want. But the story's three-quarters written, and I thought you'd like the chance to put your side.' Philip stood up.

'Wait. What story?'

'Come on, Gordon. I've seen the will. I've talked to the Gallery. I interviewed John Price before he died, and I know that his paintings went missing. Stefan took care of the pictures and you handled the legals – that's how it worked, isn't it?'

It was an old tactic – pretend to know more than you did, and let people incriminate themselves. But Parker, though rattled, tried to brazen it out.

'I don't know what you're talking about. Everything was accounted for and the beneficiaries were happy. If you want to pretend otherwise, that's up to you, but if you print a word we'll sue. Now get out.'

Philip shrugged. 'OK, Gordon. Enjoy the paper on Thursday.'

He walked out to his car. Maybe he'd been reckless, but he'd enjoyed seeing the look on Parker's face. Just like the old days. He was getting close now, no question. Philip could picture the scene: John Price slumped in his armchair in a whisky-sodden doze, while Stefan loaded the four-wheel drive with paintings. Then, with Parker's assistance, he'd fixed the will to conceal their existence. So where were they now?

There could only be one answer. With Stefan. They made up a part, perhaps, of the exhibition he was planning of 'exciting recent discoveries'. But how to prove it?

This might persuade Ron that the story was worth investigating. *In the months leading up to his death, a vulnerable old man was defrauded of his priceless art collection by a well-known art dealer ...*

It might even convince him that Philip was doing a good job. He could almost hear the editor's words: *Phil, you were right all along. It's a great story! Follow it up, mate. Do whatever it takes ...*

'Phil, there's a problem.'

The moment he'd walked into the newsroom, Philip had been summoned to Ron's office. The editor had closed the door, a sure sign that something was up. Usually the whole office listened in on his rages and the telephone calls to his ex-wives. This time he kept his voice down. His face was flushed and his hand trembling, though whether from emotion or grog Philip was unsure.

'What's happened?'

'I've been told to cut back.'

'What?'

'Economics mate. Sales are panicking. Word's come down from the mountain, we've gotta do more with less, all that crap. Jeez, Phil, I hate to do it, but –'

'Bullshit, Ron. What's this really about? Has Callum been leaning on you again?'

Ron swore, sighed, fumbled for Winfields. 'I told you to lay off Stefan West, didn't I?'

'I haven't been near him.'

'You've been hanging shit on him.'

'Who says?'

'Gordon Parker's a well-respected solicitor. You can't march into his office spouting wild allegations.'

Philip flung himself into a chair. So he was going to pay for his outburst in Parker's office. He'd known it was rash, but he hadn't expected such instant consequences.

'They're not wild. West and Parker were charged with fraud.'

He handed Ron the cutting from *The Biz & Fin*.

Ron skimmed the article. 'It says here the charges were dropped.'

'Because no one would testify. Now they're at it again. Valuable paintings have gone missing, and the will's dodgy.'

'You can prove this, can you?'

'Ron, you got me into this in the first place. You told me to follow up the death of Michael Maher.'

Ron stared. 'What's he got to do with this?'

'Stefan West was chasing him when he died.'

'There you go again. Where's your proof?'

'I've got a witness – a homeless girl.'

'Who'd believe her? She's probably a junkie.'

'Zayley's not a ... OK, Ron, maybe I don't have the proof yet. But I'll get it, if you give me another chance.'

'I already did, Phil. But you haven't learned.'

'Let me get this straight – you're sacking me?'

'I can keep you on as a casual if you promise to drop all this shit with West and Parker. There's no story, and we couldn't run it if there was.'

Philip walked to the window and looked out over the street. Just outside, a drug deal was going on involving a young guy and a mother with a baby. Ron was right: Philip had been lucky the first time. It wouldn't happen again. Get the sack now, and he'd be out in the cold for good. Jobless. How would he live? He thought of Amy up in Queensland. With no dough, he might never see her again. But to take Ron's path – what did that involve? Biting his own tongue off? Thinking only of filling the paper with something – anything – every week? It was a choice between death and live burial. He turned back to Ron.

'You know what really pisses me off about this paper? It's not that it's small and suburban. There are plenty of real stories around here, if we bothered to look for them. But we don't. It's a five-finger exercise. Eighty per cent of the paper is press releases. We might as well give the media officers a direct link to the subs and have done with it.' He picked up their most recent edition and leafed through it. 'Weddings. Press release. Sport. Another press release. Cars, cars, cars. Impotency cures. Real estate, real estate, real estate, real estate. Why do trees have to die for this?'

Ron sat down at his desk, took off his glasses and rubbed his forehead. He looked much older than his sixty-odd years. 'We give people what they want, Phil. And it's a living – which I can't afford to lose, with three women bleeding me dry.'

'I've had enough, Ron. I can't do it anymore.'

'Then no one's forcing you to. Clear out your desk. I've got a newspaper to run.'

17

A few days later, on a grey, wintry morning, Philip sat struggling with the word puzzle in the daily paper. Since his sacking, apathy had taken over. He spent most of the day in bed for the sake of warmth, listening to old tapes, drinking gallons of tea – since grog was off limits – his only pursuit the puzzle, to which he'd become addicted. It consisted of nine letters, out of which you had to make as many words as you could. There was always one nine-letter anagram. It took hours sometimes, but that was OK. He had little else to do.

He had attempted to find Nina again, but with no luck. Australia Post had no forwarding address. He'd called photography schools, galleries, local Fletchers in the phone book ('Hi, I'm an old friend of Nina's. Are you related by any chance?'). Zilch. Maureen hadn't been in contact with him, and there was no reply on her mobile. Zayley had disappeared, too – he'd dropped by the refuge and the Blue Moon, but had been met with blank looks when he asked after her.

What was the point, anyway? Even if he got to the bottom of it all – how Stefan had taken the paintings, why he was chasing Michael, how Nina was involved – there was no one to print the story. His career had been dealt the deathknock. He should get himself a job bartending or labouring and forget the world of newspapers for good. But he wasn't quite ready for that. For one thing, he felt too crook to go job-hunting. For another, curiosity still flickered inside him. He couldn't lay the puzzle down: he hadn't solved it yet. And, of course, there was Nina. Coltrane was playing it now: that melancholy riff that always made him think of her, standing by the railway lines, her hair in her eyes. To give it away completely ... no, he wasn't ready to do that.

Taking a break from the puzzle, he looked out the window. A removal van had parked across the road and furniture was being carried out while a woman stood watching with a baby squalling on her shoulder. Removalists were never short of work, Philip thought. Soon he'd be needing them himself. No one stayed put for long. People upgrading, downsizing, getting together, splitting up, moving in, moving out, moving on. Removalists knew all about it. They knew when your business folded or your marriage failed. They knew when you got promoted or retrenched. They knew where you lived.

They knew where *everybody* lived.

He lunged for the phone book. Maureen had mentioned Nina's exhibition closing. Someone had moved her pictures, then. Who, and where had they taken them? He flipped to 'R' and discovered that removal firms were listed under 'relocation consultants'. He scanned the list. There was a small box: Michael Portelli, Art Transport Services. *We handle your treasures with care.* Portelli! That was the one. He'd seen them outside Stefan's gallery. He picked up the phone and dialled.

'*PortelliTransportServicesthisisAmyhowcanIhelpyou*?' said the receptionist in one rapid breath.

'I'm calling from the Stefan West Gallery,' Philip said. 'We need you to do a job for us.'

He heard a keyboard being tapped. 'What are we picking up?'

'Remember the pictures you delivered to Nina Fletcher last week?'

'The photographs?'

'That's right. We have a few more. We need you to come back and get them.'

There was a pause, during which his heart performed a drum solo worthy of Art Blakey. He waited for the suspicious questions, the demands for proof of identity, the recital of the company's confidentiality policy. Lord, let this girl be a temp. 'We're flat chat today,' she said. 'How's Wednesday?'

'Fine.'

'Same address as last time?'

'Yeah.' He took a breath. 'Could I check you have the correct details?'

'Let me look,' she said. Another long pause. 'The screen's frozen. Can you tell me the address again?'

Shit! 'I'm not sure I have it handy ...' Philip began.

'Wait a minute, here we go: Nina Fletcher, Flat 2, 17 Andrews Street, St Kilda. That the one?'

'That's right,' Philip said, scribbling. 'Exactly right. Thank you so much.'

'And you'll make sure someone's there to let the guys in?'

'I'll be in touch with Nina personally.'

Philip sat in his car outside an anonymous block of apartments on Andrews Street. It was a 1960s brick block flung up by a hungry developer between two genteel mansions. He'd been there for hours, having received no answer when he'd knocked. The flat was unlit, but it was definitely the right place: he'd checked the mailbox. He just had to wait. He couldn't turn the heater on and run down the battery, so he pulled his St Vinnie's jacket tight. He rested his knees on the steering wheel. The tip of his cigarette glowed intermittently. Several streetwalkers had accosted him, but after a few rejections they left him alone. Likewise the dealers. It had been a long time since he cared enough about anything to stake out a place like this, but the situation was desperate. Only Nina could help him now.

Finally, he saw her walking up the street. She disappeared into the driveway. Philip didn't follow immediately. After a few moments lights came on in the flat and he watched her take off her jacket, unpack her Safeway bag and unwrap a chocolate bar. Why didn't he move now? Philip was reluctant to get out of the car. Now she was relaxed, off her guard, but the moment she saw him she would be suspicious and hostile. He liked watching her move around her flat She'd had her hair cut short and it looked good. He saw her pick up the phone and smile. He'd never seen her smile before. Not surprising, given the circumstances in which they'd met. He found himself envying whoever was on the other end of the phone. *Oh, get real and get up those stairs.*

The entrance was unlocked and he walked up ill-lit concrete steps. Outside flat two he paused. Outside flat two he paused. Strains of Latin jazz, her voice in harmony with the singer's. Well, this would shut her up. He rapped on the door.

It opened on a chain. 'Hi Nina,' Philip said, and it was as if a shutter slammed down on her face. She tried to close the door, but he wedged his foot in.

'Nina, we've got to talk.'

'Leave me alone.'

'I've found out some things you ought to know.'

'I'm not interested!' She tried to force the door shut. He winced but kept his foot there.

'Stefan was there when Michael died,' he shouted.

'What?' She stared at him through the crack.

'He was at the station. He was chasing him.'

'That's impossible.'

'There's a witness. She saw the whole thing, recognised his car.'

'But the police said –'

'She didn't tell anyone. She's scared of the cops.'

'Stefan didn't even know Mike.'

'Yes he did. Listen, Michael knew about train tracks. Why would he cross, unless he was scared?'

'Boys take stupid risks,' she said. 'Why are you telling me this?' But she wasn't trying to shut the door anymore. Cautiously he moved his foot and flexed it.

'I only want to find out the truth. We owe it to Michael.'

'You don't care about him. You just want the story.'

'I've lost my job. There's no one to write a story for.' Seeing her expression he went on: 'OK, so you think I deserve it. The reason they sacked me is I've been investigating Stefan. He's got powerful friends, Nina. I don't know how well you know him.' He was taking a risk, but there was nothing to lose.

'Hardly at all. I haven't seen him for weeks.'

'Because he doesn't need you.'

'I don't understand,' she said. 'Why would he ever have *needed* me? And why are you following me?'

'Same answer to both questions. Because you were Michael's friend.'

She looked at him for five long seconds. Finally she said: 'You'd better come in.' She unhooked the chain, turned and padded down the hall. He limped after her.

It was a small apartment with little furniture except a bookshelf, a couple of chairs and a table. He glanced around. Discarded chocolate wrappers, rented videos, books, CDs. The indicators of a single life. A poster with a clenched fist and words in Spanish. A stink of chemicals. Photographic equipment all over the place and hundreds of photos taped to the walls: grinning Aboriginal kids in the outback; old men playing cards in a café; a woman in some South American country, with a baby in her arms and a machine gun over one shoulder.

'Did you take these photos?' he asked.

'Yeah.' She turned the music off.

'They're great.'

'What do you want?'

Philip turfed a snarling cat and sank into a chair, nursing his ankle. 'I think you've broken my foot.'

'You shouldn't stick it in doors, then.'

OK, cut the pleasantries. 'You and Michael were friends?'

'Yes.'

'What was he up to?'

'I don't know. He used to ride around all day, God knows where.'

'But sometimes to your place.'

She nodded. She didn't look in good shape: dark rings round her eyes, ragged fingernails, angry red patches on her skin. Maybe she was allergic to him. She sat in a chair, arms folded, avoiding eye contact, closing him out. He watched her face.

She glanced up reluctantly. 'Why are you looking at me like that?'

'You remind me of someone.'

'Who?'

'Why was Michael coming to see you that night?'

'For the hundredth time, I don't know.'

'He often visited you?'

'Yeah, but usually in the afternoons, or on weekends.'

'What did you do together?'

'I was teaching him photography.'

'That night I saw you by the tracks. Why were you there?'

'I knew something was wrong.'

'How?'

She rubbed her forehead. 'He phoned me, just before it happened.'

Of course. Philip remembered Zayley's words: *He was yelling into his mobile.*

'What made you think something was wrong?'

'He sounded terrified.'

'What did you say to him?'

'Nothing.'

'But you just said ...'

'I was in bed. It went through to my machine.'

It took a second for this to sink in. 'It was recorded?'

She nodded.

'I've got to — please let me listen to it, Nina.'

'No.'

'You've wiped it?'

She hesitated. 'No ... but I can't play it. I just can't.'

'It could be important.'

'I've been trying to forget about it.'

'Then why have you kept it?'

She stood up and stared out of the window. 'Why are you asking me this now? It's too late. You should go.'

'Listen, Nina. A couple of days after Michael's accident, Stefan's round at your place. Doesn't that strike you as a coincidence?'

She turned on him, almost shouting. 'I keep telling you, that was nothing to do with it. We were talking about the exhibition.'

'He didn't mention the accident?'

She hesitated. 'He could see I was upset. He asked what had happened.'

‘He was chasing Mike when he got killed.’

‘Bullshit.’

‘Then prove it. Play me the message.’

She looked at him. Then she opened a drawer and took out a small tape. ‘Listen if you have to. There’s nothing about Stefan on there.’

Philip slotted the tape into the machine and pressed the button. At first he heard nothing. Then there was a series of gulping breaths, followed by a kid’s voice, high and panicky. ‘Nina! Nina, are you there? Answer the phone if you are.’ Cars hissed past. He was gasping between words. Philip imagined his legs pumping, muscles burning. In the distance, the faint sound of a horn. A truck went past, drowning out the kid’s voice. Then: ‘Mr Loony’s place. I saw him there ... I’m coming over, Nina. ... Are you there? ... Please pick up the phone ... oh shit, he’s behind me ... Are you there?’ Another long pause, filled with gasping breaths. ‘Are you there?’ Suddenly he sounded joyful. ‘Oh Neen! I can see –’ but he was cut off by the clamour of the bells. Then another blast from a horn, incredibly loud, and then the train, going on and on, until at last the roar diminished. The bells were still ringing, and in the background vague shouts had started. Then the line went dead.

Philip turned off the machine and looked at Nina. He realised his hand was trembling. She stood by the window, biting her nails. He waited. She grabbed tissues, blew her nose. She was only just keeping it together.

‘You heard what he said. “He’s behind me”.’

‘That doesn’t mean it was Stefan.’

‘My witness said it was.’ Philip reached for cigarettes, lit two from the gas ring and handed her one. ‘Who’s Mr Loony?’

She dragged deeply on the cigarette, recovered a little of her composure. ‘That’s what we called him. An old man. Big house in Williamstown.’

'Whereabouts?'

'Clarke Street.'

'John Price?'

'I don't know his name.'

'Big brick place, statues in the garden, iron railings, full of boxes and books?'

'Yes. But how ...'

'I know him. Good name, by the way.' Mike must have been at Price's place. He'd seen Stefan there. He'd ridden away, heading for Nina's flat. But Stefan had chased him. Why? Because there was something Mike wanted to tell Nina, that Stefan didn't want her to hear.

'Why did you go there?' Philip asked.

'We found some photos at the bazaar. We wanted to know about them.'

'Have you still got them?'

She opened another drawer and tossed a few prints onto the table. They were black and whites, like the picture from Michael's wall. Philip leafed through them. As he did so he remembered seeing something fluttering down onto Michael's coffin, and he realised what Nina had dropped into the grave. It must have been one of these prints. The pictures showed small groups of people picnicking in the bush or standing painting at their easels. He reached inside his jacket and took out the photo of the group in the car.

'Was this one of them?'

She looked at the picture, then at Philip. 'Yeah. But how did you ...'

'Mike had it on his wall.'

'You've been in his room?'

'It's my job ... *was* my job.' He ignored her look. 'So, what about the pictures?'

'We wanted to know what they were. Then Mike found the

house in the photo. So we went round there, and …' She stopped. Her face was pale.

'And?'

'Stefan was there.' She looked at Philip. He sensed another sliver of doubt in her mind.

'Listen, Nina. I think Stefan chased Michael because he didn't want him to talk.'

'Talk about what?'

'Maybe Mike saw something.'

'It doesn't make sense. Say Stefan was chasing Mike. How could he know Mike had been talking to *me*?'

Philip hesitated. She was right. As far as Stefan knew, Michael could have been going anywhere, talking to anyone.

'I don't know. But you're the only person who knew them all. Stefan. Mike. John Price. I know they're connected, but I don't know how. Please help me.'

The prowling cat leaped onto Nina's lap and glared at Philip. Her hand moved automatically on its fur, igniting the throb of its purr.

'If I agree,' she said finally, 'if I tell you everything I know, will you leave me alone?'

Did she really hate him that much? In general, Philip didn't care whether people liked him. Since his first day on the job he'd specialised in getting information out of people who didn't want to talk. But Nina was different. She was the phrase in Coltrane he couldn't quite get. At the thought of not seeing her again a black hole opened up inside him, and something fluttered away.

'Yeah, no worries,' he said, and glanced at his watch. 'I've wasted enough time already. Let's get on with it.'

So Nina told him everything.

18

She raised her head to look at the clock through eyes blurry with sleep. The red digits stood at 11.05. She'd been in bed an hour, hoping an early night would stop her headache from turning into one of the star-studded migraines that hit her every few weeks. The phone had put paid to that, ripping her out of sleep. She scrambled up, turned on the light, and replayed the message a couple of times. She walked into the bathroom and splashed water on her face. Then she opened the balcony window, letting in cold air and spits of rain.

When she stepped onto the balcony she heard a distant horn and the faint sound of bells. The street was deserted. She looked in the direction from which he had come many times, a grin splitting his face as he looked up and waved. But there'd been no joy in his voice this time. She couldn't make sense of what she'd heard: *Mr Loony's place. I saw him there ... I'm coming over, Nina. ... Are you there? ... Please pick up the phone ... oh shit, he's behind me ...*

Dread swelled inside her. She breathed as slowly as she could to bring her heart rate down. She was grasping the edge of the balcony so hard that the metal imprinted on her palms. She squinted down the street, looking for him in pools of light. He should be here by now, the speed he rides. Still nothing.

What was he doing at the old man's place, especially at this hour? She had tried to discourage him, but when he wanted to know something he was like a terrier. And now he had dug something up. Whatever it was, it wasn't good. And he would never have been out there, fleeing from God knows what, if it hadn't been for her.

Click. The first time she'd seen him was on a summer morning, not long after six – her favourite time, when the morning sky was peach and blue. She was outside the electricity substation, all pylons and girders and signs saying *Keep Out, Danger, High Voltage*. She was there to photograph its ugliness, but the sunlight on the metal made it oddly beautiful. She was up an embankment, pointing her camera over the wire fence. He appeared from nowhere on a patch of waste ground below, watching silently, straddling his bike, one foot on the gravel. She ignored him – she knew how to close out unwelcome intruders – but ten minutes later, when she had taken her shots and slithered down the embankment, he was still there. She swung the camera towards him, and pressed the shutter.

'Dja doing here?' he asked, unfazed.

'Taking pictures.'

'Why?'

'What's it to you?'

He grinned, took a drag from a cigarette and threw it away. She busied herself changing the lens, glancing up at the sky. A dark cloud was encroaching onto the peach and blue, and soon her perfect light would be gone. The kid watched her.

'Seen you heaps of times,' he said. 'Last week in Barkly Street. Before that, the station. 'Nother time down the refinery.'

'Smart, aren't you?'

'Bet you didn't see me.'

'Are you a spy?'

'Nah, a detective.' He rode casually in a circle, no hands. The bike was about three sizes too small for him. His hair was very short and had a home-cut look.

'Why are you up so early?'

'Mum has to get up for the bakery. Why are you?'

'The light's better. And I don't usually get disturbed.'

'Can I see your camera?'

'No.'

'I won't nick it. Just interested.'

She sighed. 'All right.' She held the Pentax out.

'Is it digital?'

'No.'

'Why not?'

'I've had this one for years. I like it.'

He accepted this with raised eyebrows. 'Never seen one like this.'

She explained the camera's workings to him, surprised by the intent look that came over his face.

'I've got to go,' she said eventually. 'I've lost the light.'

'What's your name?'

'What's yours, stickybeak?'

'Michael.'

'Nina.'

'Can I come with you sometimes?'

'I need quiet when I'm working.'

'I'll just watch.'

'I start early.'

'Me, too.'

'I don't always plan where I'm going.'

'I'll find you.'

'Don't give up, do you?'

He grinned again. 'See ya.' He stood up on his pedals and, pumping his legs furiously, accelerated towards the road just as a car appeared. 'Look out!' she shouted. He cut across in front of the car, swerving easily out of its way, then flipped up onto his back wheel. He rode along like that for a while, circus-style, down the middle of the road, then, tiring of it, he dropped the front wheel down, turned his head and laughed at her. Wheeling from left to right he rode rapidly out of sight, one arm raised in farewell.

The next time she saw him she was surfing the sales crowds, snapping people as they fought over bargains. An old man with darting eyes – *click*. A hassled mother battling through the throng with a stroller – *click*. A teenager in shoes like spaceships, repeating the same skateboard trick over and over – *click*. Gradually she became aware of the bike boy following her. She lifted the camera – *click*. He went on circling like a seagull, so she took a few more, expecting him to take off. Instead he followed her. She noticed him, smiled, but he kept his distance. She raised her camera again but this time he was out of range. So it became a game. The station, the market, the skatepark, the mall: wherever she went he'd turn up. She'd feign indifference, then pounce. Mostly, she missed: he was a wheeled centaur, his stringy thirteen-year-old legs fused to the bike, and he was out of shot too quickly. She could set the fastest shutter speed she liked: he was still a blur. But when he got careless she would spin on a ten cent piece and gotcha! He acknowledged the hit with a wry grin.

She saw him often in the weeks that followed. Sometimes she heard the scrunch of his bike approaching, other times he seemed simply to materialise. She looked up and there he was. He never had any problem finding her. After a while she started to miss him if he didn't turn up. Gradually she let him hold the camera and showed him how to use it. In return he brought her croissants from the bakery, still warm.

She allowed him to visit her flat, and showed him her darkroom. He had never seen anyone develop and print their own pictures. She taught him the techniques, smiling at his amazement as the picture appeared. He learned how to crop the pictures and manipulate light and shade. He was a quick learner and had a good eye. Soon he was printing his own pictures. On his birthday she gave him a camera. When he looked into it his face became tense with concentration, the way another kid's might when lining up a kick at goal.

She shivered. Going back inside she grabbed her coat and put it on, then went back to the balcony, pulling it tight around herself. Still no sign of him. Perhaps he'd changed his mind when she didn't answer, decided to go home instead. That was the most likely reason, she told herself. Then she heard the siren. The hospital was only a mile away, and overdoses and fights were common. But the sound scared her, it was too close. She tried to contain her rising panic. Should she go and look for him? No, they might miss each other in the dark. Who was yelling? She could see flashing lights from the direction of the station. She lit her last cigarette, told herself that she wouldn't move until she'd smoked it. If she moved now, it was bad luck. As she waited, forcing herself to stay fixed to the spot, she ransacked her memory for anything that might explain why he was coming over, and what his message had meant.

One afternoon as she was getting into her car he appeared on her driveway, his grin as wide as the bridge.

'Shouldn't you be at school?'

He pulled a face. 'It's sport today. Can we take some pics?'

'I'm going shopping.'

'Can I come?'

'It's only the bazaar.'

'All right.' She knew there was no point in arguing. 'Come if you want.'

'Cool! Bet I beat you there.' And he'd taken off.

It had been that afternoon, as she browsed and Michael wandered among the stalls, that she had made her discovery: a small cardboard box, stowed under a table beside a pile of old musical scores and some tatty books. She'd pulled the box from its resting place and looked inside. About fifty glass slides, dusty, scratched in places, but in reasonable condition. How old were they? How long was it since anyone had looked at them? The images were beautifully clear – she hardly needed to hold them to the light. She stared at the transparent figures. Among them was a close-up of a young woman's face. Her eyes met Nina's. Nina shivered as if she felt a sudden cold draught.

'Whatcha looking at?' Mike appeared by her shoulder, craning his neck.

'Look.' She lifted the fragile squares one after the other out of the box, studying them. 'I love them.'

He stared. 'Why?'

'They're so beautiful. Look at the detail.' She held it so he could see.

'Are you gunna buy 'em?' Michael asked.

'Can't afford it.' *$40 the lot* was written on the box in texta. After bills she would only have about twenty bucks in her pocket, enough to eat for five days if she was careful. She lived her life according to these microscopic numbers. But still she held the slide between her fingers and gazed at it. How hard would it be to make a print?

'We could nick 'em,' he said casually.

'Mike!'

But she looked up from her kneeling position. The woman in charge was sitting at a counter beside the door, deep in her knitting, radio tuned to the nostalgia station. Beside her the open door led to the street. The other customers were absorbed in their browsing. She cautiously judged the weight of the box: not as heavy as she'd expected.

'Watch this,' he said, and got to his feet.

'No, Mike!'

His winked and strolled between the tables towards the back of the hall, out of sight behind tallboys and mirrors, bedsteads, mannequins, cabinets. What was he up to? The hall drowsed in the mid-afternoon heat. Murmurs of conversation. Someone on the radio sang: *I did what I did for Maria.* Then from the farthest corner of the hall came a spectacular crash. All heads swivelled. The woman at the counter raised hers like a dog on the scent. 'What on earth was that?' she asked the room. No one answered. Reluctantly she got to her feet. There was a second outrageous crash, as if a bottle recycling truck was disgorging its load. The woman broke into a stately cardiganed trot. 'What's going on over there?' She hurried towards the scene of the catastrophe, leaving Nina's way clear to the bright rectangle of sunlight.

She couldn't do it. Someone would see, bells would ring, alarms go off. But there was the exit, unguarded, and here was the box, small, discreet, full of treasures. And who else could want them, except for her?

She stood up with the box, her heart hammering. No one paid any attention. She began walking towards the door, her face advertising guilt. She foresaw the box slipping through her fingers, and her slides – already they were hers – in smithereens on the floor. Ten more steps – then five – then two, and she was stepping into the sun. Somehow she managed the fifty yards to her car, fumbled for her keys, and climbed in with her treasure. Then Michael was there, grinning triumphantly.

'How did you ...'

'Back door,' he said. 'Easy peasy.'

'You shouldn't have.'

He was offended. 'I thought you wanted 'em.'

'I did. I do. But we'd better go.' She looked around.

'Nobody saw you, OK?' he said, and took off. She watched him go. When he was nearly at the corner, she shouted 'Hey, Mike!' He turned. She gave him the thumbs up out of the window. He grinned, swooped round in a circle and sped back to her.

'Whatcha gonna do with 'em?' he asked through the window.

'Print them, of course.'

Nina loved her darkroom, with its sharp, familiar stink. The old enlarger she'd picked up for a song in the *Trading Post*. The three trays in a row: develop, stop, fix. Boxes of virgin paper, only to be opened under cover of darkness. The hose in the bath with the constant flow of water. She worked methodically: light, dark, develop, stop, fix, wash, hang to dry. Hand dodging under the beam of light. It was hard making the magic happen: she liked that. She worked for hours, unconscious of the passing of time. Light, dark, develop, stop, fix, wash, dry. The collection built up. When she finally looked at the clock it was four in the morning. She crawled to bed and fell asleep without undressing.

At seven she woke to a knocking at the door. Michael, with warm bread rolls. She made coffee and they ate. Then he joined her in the darkroom and worked alongside her. Usually she couldn't abide intruders in her space, but he was quick and deft, like a sorcerer's apprentice, his unseen hands passing things when she needed them.

She got her second wind as the caffeine kicked in. She'd got the hang of it now: slides were trickier than film, but the reward was the depth, the detail. She'd never seen such clarity. Finally it was done, and they emerged, blinking, into the light. Fifty prints hung around the room on lines she had strung up. They ducked their heads in the forest of sticky leaves, careful not to touch. Till then she had focused on the technical challenge; now she realised the pictures were beautiful. It was no ordinary collection of family snaps.

'Who are they?' she wondered aloud.

'We could ask at the bazaar.'

'No way, Mike!' she said, with a horrified laugh. The theft made that impossible. All they had to go on were the pictures themselves.

'They were taken round here, anyway,' he muttered.

'How can you tell?'

'Whaddaya *mean*? This is the old mill. You *blind*, or what?'

'Is it?' she said doubtfully. She thought of the mill as it was now, windows smashed, the walls a gallery for taggers, floors strewn with needles and condoms.

'Course it is. I've been past it heaps. That one's Yarraville Gardens. And that's the station.' He was in his element now, walking from picture to picture. 'I'm a detective, remember? I don't need a camera, I've got these.' He pointed at his eyes.

'What about that one, smartarse?' She pointed to a picture of gum trees and a creek.

'Dunno,' he admitted, crestfallen.

'That one then?'

The picture showed a woman and two men in a car. One of the men had his head on the woman's shoulder and was staring up at her. He was good-looking; fair-haired with a little beard. The woman's arm was around his shoulder. The other man, on her left, was gazing into the distance, smiling awkwardly. The woman was looking straight into the camera with the hint of a smile. She knows exactly what's going on, Nina thought: knows they both want her.

'I bet I could find it,' Michael said, regaining his confidence. He pointed. 'Look at that house – there's a statue in the garden.' She hadn't even noticed the house, focusing on the people in the foreground. 'I could find the house, ask about the photos. Can I take one of these?'

'OK, Sherlock. You really think you can find the place?'

He nodded seriously. 'Leave it to me.'

Left alone, Nina stared at her copy of the print, studying the three people. It was easy to characterise the men: one of them was diffident and uncertain, with more than a trace, Nina thought, of the clumsy country boys of her youth; the other, the bearded one, was smarter, better dressed, but a bit too sure of himself. They were both in love with the woman, Nina felt sure, though the position of her arm marked the bearded guy as the one in favour.

The woman was harder to figure out. She was guarded, yes, but self-assured. Nina liked the cool way she looked into the camera. She was the strongest of the three, despite the young man's bravado. She had her hair pulled back and pinned behind her ears; her eyebrows, pencilled in, were two long, graceful curves above eyes that may not have been particularly big, but the smallness of her face made them seem so. Dark lipstick accentuated the shape of her lips, curved in a smile that was more knowing than amused.

Nina turned and looked at herself in the mirror. She never wore make-up, and she never put her hair back, just brushed it impatiently and let it fall as it wanted. Uncertainly she tucked her hair behind her ears, scrabbled around for a clip and pinned it behind her ears. The shape of her own face was not dissimilar to the woman in the photo. She rummaged around for an eyebrow pencil, and drew in two slender lines over her own faint eyebrows. Finally she hunted for a lipstick, unearthing one she had been given as a sample months ago. Not bad, she thought, but the Ramones t-shirt would have to go. She replaced it with a simple white blouse, like the one the woman was wearing. It completed the effect. She looked at the photo, looked at herself, and smiled. It was a good feeling. As if in taking on the unknown woman's appearance she had gained some of her coolness, her assurance.

Michael didn't return for several days, so she kept up her normal activities without him. Early morning excursions, late sessions in the darkroom, without the presence she'd become used to. She missed him. One evening she heard her name, ran out to the balcony and saw him down below, face red and sweaty.

'Find anything?' she called.

He shook his head in disgust. 'Nah.' He looked at her. 'You look different.' He raised his camera – *click*.

'Hey,' she said, trying to console him, 'if you can't find the house, it really doesn't –'

A mistake. His face darkened, he spun his bike round and pedalled off without a word. He made no contact for days, and she wondered if his pride was so hurt that she wouldn't see him again. Then a few days later her phone rang and his voice was at the other end.

'Hey, Nina. It's Mike.' He was deliberately cool. 'I've found that place you were looking for. It's near Williamstown Gardens. Meet you there in fifteen minutes, OK?'

She pulled her coat on and drove straight there. He was waiting at the park gates. As soon as he saw her approaching he took off, and she followed him into the tangle of streets. He led her down an old, posh avenue. He halted before a two-storey brick place, secluded from the street by a wall and iron railings. A four-wheel drive was parked outside. She pulled her Mazda over to the kerb and got out. So quiet. A few gulls mewing overhead, somewhere the sacred ritual of lawn mowing. The garden beyond the railings was thick and overgrown. A bed of roses had gone feral. Rotten pears carpeted the grass.

'There you go,' he said.

'Where?'

'*Look*,' he said, impatient with her lack of observation. 'It's the same house.'

'Is it?'

He held the photograph in front of her nose. 'That's the tree. Those railings. And the statue. Sooooo obvious.'

She looked from the picture to the garden, and back. He was right. It had changed, of course: a pear tree stood slap in the middle of what was once a proudly kept lawn. The statue was mottled with lichen. Other trees and bushes had gone, new ones been added. But the oak was the clincher. It was the same one, several decades older. She raised her Pentax, focused and shot.

'Maybe they still live here,' he said.

'I don't think so.' The place will have been bought and sold a dozen times, she thought.

'But they might know something. Let's ask.'

Reluctantly she tried the gate, expecting it to be locked, but the bolt disengaged and he shoved it open. 'C'mon,' he said, and they walked up the overgrown drive. Though the place looked uncared for, it wasn't boarded up, there were curtains in the windows, and they could hear classical music at high volume. Stone steps, an antique doorbell that Michael pressed firmly, drawing a chime from inside. What were they doing there? she wondered. She tried to compose an explanation for their presence. But she didn't need her speech, because no one answered the door.

'Let's look round,' Michael said.

He was down the side before she could object. She hesitated on the steps for a moment, then took a few more photos: the tree, the ivy climbing the brickwork, the statue, the roses. Then she followed him. He'd stopped at a window, begrimed by dirt and spider webs, cupped his hands to his face and was staring inside. She peered, too, into a dim room piled high with boxes, papers, furniture, pictures. It could be a tomb, she thought. They continued around the back, where there was a second garden, as neglected as the front, and a choked fish-pond. She could see orange corpses glinting among the leaves. They reached a pair of French windows and looked inside.

It was a library. That was how she thought of it, because of the high, crammed bookcases – though the word library suggested order, and there wasn't much system here. The music was building to a crescendo – somewhere out of sight there must be a stereo. Michael carried on, but she stayed, and as her eyes adjusted she saw the old man in the corner. He was half obscured by the armchair in which he was sunk, his eyes closed, his head back, lost in the music. His lap was covered with papers and there was an empty decanter beside him on the table. She watched him. As the music came to a climax his eyes opened and he saw her.

She didn't move, and neither did he. His pale eyes blinked a couple of times, and she was reminded of a reptile behind glass. The afternoon was completely still. Then he seized the decanter and flung it. She flinched and threw up her arm as the window shattered in her face. She stumbled away, feeling the shards prickling.

Michael came running. 'Neen, what happened?' Unable to speak, she touched her face: her fingers were red and wet. His expression told her she was covered in blood. He was panicking. 'Are you OK? Are you OK?'

'I'm fine,' she said, trying to stay calm so that he would, too, shaking the glass out of her hair and off her clothes. ‘Come on, let’s get out of here. We should never have come.’

Michael stared through the broken glass at the old man. ‘Whatja do that for, you old dickhead?’ he yelled.

She grabbed his arm. ‘Come *on,* Mike. Leave it, please, just leave it.’

He shook her off. ‘Why?’

‘Come on, Mike. Come *now.*’ She dragged him around the corner, back to the car. She sat in the driving seat, dabbing at her face with a handkerchief. ‘It missed my eyes. I’ll be OK.’

Then there was someone beside the car, bending down to the window. ‘What happened? Are you all right?’

She looked up. A fair guy in a white t-shirt. An expression somewhere between puzzlement and suspicion.

‘I saw you from upstairs,’ he said. ‘What do you want?’

‘I was photographing the house. I didn’t know there was anyone in. I’m a photographer.’

He looked at her face, then at the camera beside her on the seat.

‘John gets alarmed easily,’ he said. ‘He probably thought you were trying to break in. Why don’t you come in, get cleaned up?’

‘Come on, Nina!’ Mike was off on his bike, yelling from halfway down the street.

She shook her head and started the engine. ‘No thanks. I’ll be OK.’ In her rear-view mirror she could see the guy watching as she drove off.

Her injuries healed in a few days. But not Michael’s pride. He moped about, blaming himself.

‘It was my fault. I took you there.’

‘I wanted to go.’

'Next time I'll go by myself,' he said miserably.

'Mike, no.'

'But we didn't find anything out, did we?'

'Let's just leave it, OK? We've got the pictures.'

'Something weird's going on there. Why did he chuck the bottle at you?'

'It doesn't matter. Don't.' She touched his arm. 'Promise.'

'OK,' he said, shrugging her arm off.

'Really?'

'Really.'

A few seconds later he was back on his bike, riding away without even a wave. She heard nothing from him after that. She rang him a couple of times, but received no answer. By the time he called her in the middle of the night, she hadn't seen or heard from him for two weeks.

She broke into a run, her feet slapping on the wet pavement. Rounding the corner into the main street she crashed into a group of revellers, *heylookwhereyagoingcan'tya?* She had Michael's words looping in her head: *Are you there, Nina?... Please pick up the phone!... Are you there?* The sirens had stopped but as she closed on the station she saw lights, cars, uniforms, tape, the ambulance. She overheard *a kid on a bike ... train ... didn't see ...* and she knew the whole story. She stopped, gasping, at the boom gate. The ambulance was parked beside the tracks, its light strobing. The paramedics had gathered twenty yards away. They were looking down at something. In the midst of her panic, there was still a desperate hope: perhaps it wasn't too late, maybe they could do something — an operation, a transfusion. She took a few steps onto the tracks before an orange arm snapped across in front of her.

‘No closer, ma’am.’

‘What happened? Please, I’m a –’

‘Back onto the road,’ the policewoman ordered her. Ignoring Nina, she spoke into her radio: ‘We have a blocked line and a fatality.’

Nina moved back into the shadows, watching helplessly. A stretcher was carried out and something was lifted onto it. The policewoman picked up a tangled mass of metal that used to be a bike and carried it from the tracks. Shadowy figures gathered on the other side. Cars were banking up at the gates, their headlights dazzling her. Then another light fractured the darkness. *Flash. Flash.* It was a photographer. He was out on the tracks, circling the paramedics like a crow round carrion.

The stretcher was lifted into the ambulance, but there was no urgency from the crew, no lights, no siren, and she knew what that meant. *Flash.* She couldn’t move. *Nina, are you there?... Please pick up the phone!* Rain in her hair, snot on her face. *Flash.* Someone was speaking to her. She didn’t hear at first, didn’t want to hear. *Oh shit, he’s behind me* ... A face had come too close. Someone was forcing himself into her space. ‘Did you know Michael?’ The voice sounded as if it was coming from very far away. ‘What a tragedy.’ She was forced to look, saw him. ‘How did you know him?’ Hearing that question, every drop of hope evaporated. ‘Haven’t we met before?’ He wouldn’t be shaken off. ‘I’m Philip Trudeau from *The Messenger.* What’s your –?’ She thrust him away. *Nina, are you there?* She was blind with tears and rain. ‘Did you know him?’ She shouted something, dodged round a car, and then she ran, ran, ran.

19

Nina walked to the window and stood gazing out, as if she believed that Michael might appear, pedalling furiously round the corner. Philip reflected that at last he was getting to know Michael. The kid had lived a secret life that his friends, his teachers, even his mother had known nothing about. Philip's brief investigations had revealed shamefully little of it. No wonder Nina hadn't wanted to talk to him at the funeral. He looked at her silhouetted in the window, and again he seemed to hear the mournful phrase from Coltrane.

'So it was you who left the photos on my kitchen table?' he said.

'What photos?' Her puzzlement seemed genuine.

Philip decided to leave the question open. 'Never mind. Did you know he'd been back to Price's place?'

'I told him not to. But ...'

'You knew he would?' She nodded. 'Stefan must've followed him from there.'

'Why?'

'I don't know.'

'I didn't see Stefan at the station,' she said, but her voice was no longer as certain as before.

'He'd gone before you got there.'

'How can you be sure it was him?'

'My witness described him, and the car.'

'Can I talk to her?'

'I don't know where she is.'

'If Stefan was there, other people must have seen him,' she said.

Philip nodded without optimism. He could try to track down the other witnesses and ask them if they had seen anyone answering Stefan's description. But it was unlikely, and how reliable would their memories be? Philip attempted to picture the scene that Nina's description had brought back to him: the rain, the cops, the ambulance, the crumpled bike, the shocked groups of onlookers. It had been hard to make out faces in the darkness. There had only been the lights of the ambulance, the less-than-perfect street lighting, and – yes – a flash that repeatedly punctuated the darkness.

'Just a minute,' he said. 'Ted!'

'Who?'

'The photographer. Works for *The Messenger*.' As Philip had leaned on the boom gate, talked to the witnesses, tried to coax some details out of the cops, Ted's flash had been going off repeatedly. Philip remembered Ted coming up to him in the office, a sheaf of pictures in his hand. *Took 'em the other night, at the station. Whaddya reckon?*

'Do you think he saw Stefan?'

'Maybe.' How quick had Ted been this time? Quick enough to capture Stefan's presence by the tracks?

Philip reached for his phone. 'It's worth checking the photos. I'll call him now.'

'Will he show us?'

'I think I can persuade him.'

'Welcome to Ted Gross Fine Art Studios,' Ted said, opening the door, swallowing a mouthful of pizza and extending an oily hand for the beers. 'Lunatic soup? My favourite.' He glanced at Nina. 'Didn't realise you had company.'

'This is Nina.'

Ted gave her an appraising look. 'G'day. Have we met before?'

Flash. Rain, darkness, a body on the tracks. 'I don't think so.'

'Heard you got the flick, Phil,' Ted said.

'Ron wants to be leaner and meaner.'

Ted snorted. 'So he sacks the only decent journalist he's got.'

He led the way into a dark, putrid room. The floor was deep in styrofoam and cardboard. The windows, like the curtains, hadn't been opened for weeks. The only light came from the glow of half-a-dozen computer monitors.

'What is this, Ted, the place where old pizza comes to die?' Philip said.

'It's the maid's day off. And I've got more important things to do.'

'Such as?'

'Setting up my website. Check this out.' He sat down at a computer and clicked the mouse to bring up a succession of images. 'They dragged this chick out of the river. Strangled, they reckon. Choice, isn't it?' They all looked.

'What do you think, Nina?' Ted said. Testing her.

She breathed in. 'Too bright. You didn't expose for the shadows.'

'Bullshit.' Ted stuck his nose up to the screen. 'It's hardly noticeable.'

'You're putting *that* on a website?' Philip said.

'Realvictim.com. Pay for access, hosted in the Netherlands. Totally untraceable and outside Australian jurisdiction.' Looking at Nina, Ted went on: 'I'm striking a blow for artistic freedom. Hey, if you think this is bad, check out Goya. Ever seen *The Disasters of*

War? It's all there: murder, torture, rape, you name it. Take a look at this.' Determined to get a reaction, he slid another CD into the computer and brought up a new image set. 'This old woman died in her house, right? It was weeks before they found her. When the cops arrived, they couldn't get in till they'd shot the Dobermans, which had gone crazy 'cause they hadn't been fed. And look what the dogs had done to the corpse.' A series of clicks: the body in close-up.

Philip stared. 'How did you ...'

'A few contacts. Ten minutes, that's all I need.'

'Ron's never gonna use these.'

'Fuck Ron. My clients'll pay a packet for 'em. And when the site takes off, it'll be bye bye *Messenger*.' He closed the pictures, spun his chair round. 'But you didn't drop in for a chat. How can I help?'

'Remember that train accident in Yarraville?'

'The kid who played chicken with the express. Yeah, I remember. Why?'

'We think someone was chasing him. There's a chance the bloke might still have been there when you arrived. What time did you get there?'

'A long time before you, ya lazy cunt. Picked it up on the radio. It's only round the corner.' Philip gave silent thanks that Ted's personality ruled out any more sociable evening activities than eavesdropping on the cops. 'Even beat the ambos. Course, when they arrived, they told me to fuck off. Already had the shots by then though.'

'Can we see them?'

'Lemme find the job bag,' Ted said. He delved into a filing cabinet and fished out a CD. 'Hope you've got a strong stomach.' He slotted the disk in and a series of thumbnails appeared. He scrolled rapidly. 'The early ones are abysmal – the light was a tad shit.'

'We need to see all of them,' Philip said. 'Especially the ones you took first.'

'Check these out, then.' Ted scrolled back to the top. 'Took 'em when I got there. It was mayhem.' He sat back, ripping the cap off a stubby.

Philip and Nina leaned forward, staring at the screen. Blurred figures, splashes of light, shadows, headlights, rain. No sign of Stefan. 'You must have been too late,' Philip said.

Nina pointed at the screen. 'That car.'

'Where?'

'At the boom gate. It's a four-wheel drive.'

Ted nodded. 'Toyota.'

'That's what Stefan drives,' Philip said. 'Pity we can't see the rego.' But it was an encouraging sign. Philip scrolled quickly through the next few pictures. *Where are you, Stefan? Come on you bastard.* Faces were hard to distinguish. He heard Nina breathe in sharply as she saw the images of Michael. Subscribers to realvictim.com would not be disappointed.

Nina put her hand on Philip's. 'Stop – there.'

'Where?'

'In the corner, behind the signal.'

Philip frowned. In the foreground a group gathered around the body. Behind them, on the edge of the frame and partly obscured, a figure was bending to retrieve something. 'Is that him?'

'Could be,' she said. 'It's hard to tell.'

'Want me to enlarge it?' Clicking the mouse Ted zoomed in on the stooping figure – 150, 200, 400 per cent – till it filled the screen. 'Can't go any higher, it'll res out.'

'It's good,' Philip said. The face was turned away from the camera, but light from overhead spilled onto fair hair, a shiny leather jacket. 'What do you reckon?'

Nina nodded. 'Yeah.'

'What's he doing?' Ted said.

'Zoom in on his hand,' Nina said.

The hand, a pixellated blur, was lifting something from beside the tracks

'What's he picking up?' Philip said.

'Wouldn't have a shmig, mate. It's just a red splodge,' Ted said.

'Mike's mobile was red,' Nina said.

'Yes! The witness said he was on his mobile.'

'But why would that guy want it?' Ted asked.

For Philip, it was as if the nine letters had magically sorted themselves and revealed the anagram. 'To find out who he'd been talking to. The kid was on his mobile while Stefan was chasing him. Stefan saw him. He found the phone – the call was in the memory. That's why he got so friendly with you, Nina: he wanted to know what Mike had told you. Ted, I need a print of this pic – as large as you can.'

While the enlargement of the photograph uncurled from the printer, Philip and Nina checked out the other pictures, but Stefan didn't appear again.

'He must have left as soon as he found it,' Philip said.

Ted handed them the A4 print. 'It's a bit clearer now. I Photoshopped him. But you can't see his face.'

He had cropped out the other figures. What remained was the enlarged figure of Stefan, bending over the tracks.

'Ted, you're a sick genius,' Philip said.

'Any time. Bugger off, now – I've got two murders to upload before the footy starts.'

Philip drove Nina from Ted's back to her place. Unused to passengers, he had to sweep rubbish from the passenger seat to the floor to make room for her, so bottles and cans rattled around their feet. Philip glanced at her. She sat hunched up on her seat, a cigarette between her lips, staring out the window. He could tell that her mind was back at the station on the miserable night he had first seen her, her old coat wrapped round her night clothes, her face a mess.

'How could Stefan do something like that?' She threw her cigarette stub out of the window. 'I can't believe I fell for it.' She was chewing her ragged nails, her face full of anger and pain.

'Don't be too hard on yourself.'

'I really thought he liked my work. What an idiot.'

'He's been fooling people for years,' Philip said, remembering his conversation with Vandenberg. 'And your photos are great. Best thing in his gallery.'

She gave him a small smile. 'I guess I owe you an apology.'

'Forget it.' It was a good sign. He had earned a tiny amount of trust, but he would have to invest it carefully. She was still wary of him. He couldn't blame her – only a few hours ago he'd wedged his foot in her door. In a few minutes they would be on the bridge, heading back across the city towards her flat. He had promised to leave her alone after she told him what he wanted to know. Now that moment was approaching. It gave him an empty feeling.

A kid came round the corner on a bike and rode swiftly past them. Philip heard Nina breathe in sharply. Her face had become tense. 'I keep thinking, what if I'd answered the phone?'

'It wouldn't have made any difference.'

'Maybe. I don't know anything anymore.'

'Nina, there's nothing we can do to bring him back. But at least we can nail Stefan.'

'You reckon?'

'Yeah. He's only good at intimidating people,' Philip said, thinking of Zayley's panicky voice: *He said no one would notice another dead junkie.*

'Is he dangerous?'

'I don't have much to lose.'

'How come you lost your job?'

'It's a long story. I have a bad habit of breaking rules.'

She looked at him. 'Why are you doing this?'

It was a fair question. Even if he could complete the story, no one would publish it. What was driving him on? A memory flashed into his mind of the first time he had ever got a good story into print. Writing for a uni newspaper, he'd stumbled on the clumsy attempts of student politicians to rig an election. That had been kids' stuff, but not so long afterwards there'd been his first front page at *The Biz & Fin*, about the Mirage Property scandal. It had led to a flurry of resignations, enquiries and ultimately prosecutions. He remembered the elation of getting the truth out there, of knowing that he had been the one to lift up the rock, sending the bugs scurrying for cover. That had been the high that made everything worthwhile.

'I just want to know what happened. The real story, the stuff that no one else can be bothered about. I guess that's why I became a journalist. And besides ...'

'What?'

'I'd like to see you again.'

He waited, his heart pounding ridiculously. She looked out of her window, then back at him. 'So what are you going to do now?'

'Show Stefan the photo, and see how he reacts.'

'I'll come with you.'

'No, it's better he doesn't know we've been talking.' The last thing Philip wanted was Nina on the wrong side of Stefan. 'I'm going to the gallery tomorrow. There's an exhibition opening that I've been looking forward to. Oh, and one other thing. I'll talk to Ted about those photos of Mike. Tell him not to put them on his website.'

‘Thanks. But you may not have to.’

‘Why not?’

She put her hand in her pocket and showed him the disk shining in her palm. ‘I don’t always follow the rules either.’

20

The gallery was buzzing. Making his way inside, Philip was confronted by dark Italian suits and tanned, expensive bodies. Waiters circulated, their trays rattling with flutes of champagne. High-volume networking was underway. Among the throng were faces he recognised from business, politics, TV. What had brought Stefan's A-list connections out tonight? Less the attraction of the arts, Philip supposed, than the lure of money and power. He had to scan the room for several minutes to find Stefan himself, and eventually spotted him in a corner, chatting to Roger Sterling and his wife. Philip helped himself to champagne. Dr O'Day's warning flitted across his mind, but he pushed it away.

'Phil Trudeau, as I live and breathe!' Philip turned to see Richard.

'I've come to talk to Stefan.'

'I'm after a few words myself, for the Thursday page. I've always respected James West, but I must say, I wasn't expecting anything like this. These pictures are incredible. Are these the ones he got from that old man you told me about? Frankly, they put West's later work to shame. I'd never have expected it. Everyone wants a piece of Stefan now. He's even dragged Peter McKendrick back from New York to launch the show.'

'How much are they worth?' Philip asked.

'Who knows? With the publicity this is going to get, Stefan can name his own price. Love your work, Phil.'

Richard glided away with a wave of the hand. Philip picked up a shiny catalogue from a table. He skimmed the introduction: *... amazing discovery ... exceptional collection ... remarkable feat of restoration ... unique ... one of Australia's finest painters ... startling new light* ... There was no mention of John Price, nor an explanation of how the paintings had come to Stefan. The only person who might have provided an alternative version of events was Price himself, and he could no longer dispute anything.

Something was happening at one end of the room. A man in a bow tie, face glowing with champagne and self-importance, was fiddling with a microphone. Philip assumed this was Peter McKendrick. The roar of talk subsided to a buzz. McKendrick tapped the microphone a couple of times and began to speak.

'I'm delighted to be here to open Stefan's marvellous new exhibition. Years ago, when I was a struggling young critic' — McKendrick beamed at the audience to convey the distance between his former and his present status — 'James West's *oeuvre* was not held in the high esteem it is today. I think my biography caused a little revaluation, and today he holds a pre-eminent place in Australian art, indeed international art. As State Gallery Director I purchased several of his works, and I was proud to regard him as a personal friend. But even I never suspected that a vast cache of early masterpieces was awaiting discovery in a shabby attic. It is the kind of discovery of which every art historian dreams.'

Philip surveyed the audience. His eyes came to rest on a bespectacled grey-haired man who was standing in the front row, watching benevolently. David Stevenson. What was he doing here? As Philip was wondering this, Stevenson's head turned towards him. The man showed no sign of recognition but his eyes, behind large-framed glasses, locked onto Philip's for several seconds before he looked away and murmured something to the person next to him.

'Why are these paintings so important?' McKendrick went on. 'Because they mark a key point in Jim's development. We have – or rather, we had – too few paintings from his early period. When I wrote my little book, there were only a handful of known works painted before 1951, the year Jim exploded on to the scene with his tour de force in Paris. Looking at these newly discovered, astonishing, terrifying paintings, one detects a vigour, an *esprit*, a radical imagination that exceeds the strength even of his later *chefs-d'oeuvres*. They are brilliant, yea, breathtaking. In these paintings we can already see the themes that obsessed him for the rest of his career. I certainly hope that my successor at the gallery – hello there, Henry – will ensure that some of these works end up in the state collection. Living in New York, as I now do, one gains a more international, indeed global, perspective ...'

As McKendrick's torrent of self-congratulation flowed on, Philip turned back to the catalogue. It listed over fifty paintings. Could Price have owned so many? Thinking of the boxes piled up in his house, Philip decided it was perfectly possible. Had Price known their value? It seemed unlikely that any collector, however eccentric and reclusive, could be unaware of owning works with values running into the millions. Philip scanned the list of titles. *Lovers. Evening over the river. Sailors. Slaughterhouse. Portrait of a woman. Self-portrait. Night flight.* Could Valerie be among them?

Philip had not yet glimpsed the paintings; the crowd was too thick. Now he elbowed his way to the perimeter of the room and began to circumnavigate it. At once he saw what Richard and McKendrick were talking about. The paintings were far stronger than anything – save the portrait – he had seen at Price's place.

Some were outpourings of violence and pain, inscribed in thick layers of paint, while others, just as powerful, almost glowed with warmth. Philip pushed his way around the room, not caring how many bespoke shoulders he barged aside, or how many flutes he overturned. Then he stopped.

He had last seen the picture nine months before, in Price's library. It had been a cracked piece of canvas, thick with dust; now it was clean and in a timber frame. She stared out at him. He felt his heart pounding, his cheeks flushing. He remembered the ice clinking in John Price's glass, the face in the window on a sunny afternoon. This was the woman James West had returned to again and again, even at the end of his life, a wreck of a man in a wheelchair. Like West, Philip was unable to move. Her gaze bored into him. A young woman, red-haired, her eyes black, her bones showing through the taut pale skin. He felt paralysed, as if electricity was flooding through him.

'Mr Trudeau.' Philip turned. Stefan was standing behind him. 'I must have forgotten to post your invitation. I see you made it anyway.'

Philip indicated the portrait. 'I thought you said he didn't paint this.'

'Excuse me?'

'At John Price's place – remember? Not by West, you said. Now here it is in your West exhibition.'

Stefan said nothing. Determined to provoke a response, and noticing some guests heading towards them, Philip raised his voice. 'You told me it was a piece of crap. Was that the expert advice you gave John? Funny, I don't see any mention of him in this catalogue.'

Stefan glanced around. 'Come in here for a moment.'

He fished in his pocket for a key and opened a door leading into a tiny office. It contained a table heaped with papers, a computer, filing cabinets. 'Now, Philip, what were you saying?' His tone was patient, humouring, a little weary. Philip wanted to grab the guy and shake him out of his complacency.

He reached inside his jacket and took out Ted's photograph, which he tossed onto the desk. 'Recognise anyone?'

'What's this?'

'Yarraville station, the night Michael Maher was killed.' Philip pointed to Stefan's blurred figure. 'Find what you were looking for?'

Stefan glanced at the picture with a faint smile. 'This picture's been tinkered with, mate. I've never been near Yarraville station.'

'There's a witness, *mate*. She got a good look.'

Stefan walked to the door and stood looking through the glass panel. 'Have you seen who's out there, Philip?' he said conversationally. 'The Minister for the Arts. The Director of the State Gallery. Roger and Lady Sterling.' He tossed the photograph down. 'I don't think any of them will be interested in this.'

Philip put out his hand to retrieve the picture. As he did so, he noticed on the desk a yellow Post-it note with a name and email address written on it. He quickly glanced away, trying to work out the implications of what he had just seen.

'How did you get the paintings?' he said.

'I bought them.'

'Price would never sell them. You ripped him off.'

Stefan looked at him like a psychiatrist confronted by a patient who believes he is Jesus Christ. 'Oh, I ripped him off! And what about you, Philip? He told me he paid you $500. Exactly what did he get in return?' His eyes locked onto Philip's, who blinked first. Stefan went on: 'All right, I'll say this once, in very simple terms. John loved my father. And he appreciated my help. He wanted to show his love and appreciation. So he sold several paintings to me, providing a nest egg for his old age. The rest he was generous enough to leave me in his will.' He turned the palms of his hands towards Philip — nothing to hide. 'What's your problem?'

'He'd never leave them to you,' Philip said. 'He wanted the gallery to have them. He may have been eccentric, but he wasn't stupid.' Outside the door the party was in full swing, the roar of chatter and the clinking of glasses drowned out a string quartet that was gamely attempting to perform.

'It's been a long time since you left *The Biz & Fin*, hasn't it?' Stefan looked at Philip sympathetically. 'It must have been difficult to adjust to life on a suburban newspaper. No big stories. No prestige. Just local stuff. And now, you don't even have that. No family, either. No one to come home to. An empty flat. No one to notice when you're depressed.' He glanced through the door again. 'Oh, there's Callum, I must say hello in a moment. Look Philip, I'm concerned about you. I once had an associate in your situation. I had to cut him loose, and he took it badly — started imagining people were out to get him. He had a problem with the booze, like you. One day it all got too much for him. He got pissed, took a jump from eight storeys. There were spiked railings at the bottom. Coroner said it was one of the most tragic suicides he'd ever come across.'

'Is that a threat?' Philip said.

'He was depressed, broke, a heavy drinker. They found a note. I'm just worried about you.'

'And what about Michael Maher?' Philip said. 'Had to cut him loose too, did you?'

Stefan reached for his phone, murmured something into it. Turning back to Philip, he said: 'You're talking shit. People who do that eat their words.' The door opened and the bearded guy from that night at Philip's flat appeared. He folded his arms and stood watching Philip. 'I'm sorry, Philip, but I must get back to the party,' Stefan said. 'Let's catch up when you're feeling better. Don will see you out, all right?'

Back in his car, Philip removed his tape recorder from his jacket. It wasn't the most sophisticated recording device, but it did the job. He pressed play and heard Stefan's voice: *All right, I'll say this once in very simple terms* ... Stefan hadn't let slip anything incriminating, but he must be concerned or he wouldn't be making clumsy threats. Philip regarded them as a positive sign that he was getting close to the truth. He was certain now that Stefan had stolen Price's paintings. But what was his next move? He needed Maureen. He missed her ideas, her quick thinking.

He reached for his mobile, dialled. *The number you have called is not connected*, a robotic female informed him. He cursed and shoved the mobile back in his pocket.

Then he thought of the yellow sticker he had seen on Stefan's desk. What was it doing there? Time to fast-track an answer to that question.

The lights were still on at the offices of *The Messenger*. Philip's key and swipe card – which Ron had forgotten to demand back from him – got him through the door and up in the lift. In the newsroom a couple of people were still at their desks: Steve the sports reporter, deep in a phone call; and the keen young cadet, pounding away at her keyboard. Ron would have loaded Philip's allocation of stories onto her. She was ambitious, and probably welcomed his dismissal. She glanced up curiously but didn't speak. The sports reporter paid no attention whatsoever. Perhaps they thought that Ron had un-sacked him; such a thing was not unknown. Philip walked to Ron's office and sat down at the computer. The Post-it note had read:

Ron Mitchell
editor@westernmessenger.com.au

Why would Stefan have Ron's email address? Philip could think of a few possible answers to this, none of them good. The machine came to life, blurting and bleeping, before a password was requested. This wasn't a problem: Ron was known to alternate between a small selection of his favourite obscenities. On the third go, Philip got it. He glanced down the office: the sports reporter was still running up the phone bill, the cadet frowning at her screen. Philip turned back to the computer.

A list of Ron's recent emails appeared. Philip scrolled down. He didn't have to look far to find a message from Stefan.

I just heard Philip Trudeau has been making more accusations against me. If anything appears in your newspaper, I'll be taking legal action. I thought Callum had already told you Trudeau is out of control. If you can't rein him in, find another job. SW

Ron had replied to the message the same day:

Dear Stefan,
I'm sorry Trudeau is still hassling you. I was completely unaware of it. I kicked his arse when Callum first told me. You won't be bothered again. Phil was taken on as a casual and he won't be staying at the paper. Ron Mitchell

Spineless bastard. Philip continued scrolling down the list of names, hunting for more messages from Stefan or Callum, but another name jumped out: Graeme Kelly. Graeme was editor of *The Biz & Fin*, Philip's old boss, the mate who'd worked with Ron before the Flood. The message was over a year old. The subject line was 'Trudeau'. Philip opened it.

G'day you old bastard. How's life in the 'burbs? Interested to hear you are thinking of hiring Phil Trudeau — I thought he'd dropped off the face of the earth. Mate, it's a hell of a risk — he was a good journo once, but he's a stubborn bastard and gets some crazy ideas. His fuck-up with Stevenson knocked the stuffing out of him, and I heard he had a breakdown, but maybe he's straightened himself out by now. Anyway, it's your call. I know you have a taste for lost causes. Cheers, Graeme.

Rereading the words 'a good journo once, but a stubborn bastard,' Philip saw himself in the tenth-floor office at *The Biz & Fin*, watching Graeme pace to and fro in front of his huge window.

'Phil, are you out of your mind? You can't possibly –'

'It's the only way, Graeme. The proof is in that office.'

'It's a fucking crime, mate. Do you realise the risk?

'You want them to get away with it?'

'No, but if you just wait until the cops –'

'By tomorrow, everything will have been shredded.'

'No way. You're on your own. I don't know anything about this.'

A cough: someone was standing behind him. Philip turned. It was the cadet, looking uncomfortable.

'Hey Phil, 'sgoin'?' she said, faking a smile. She glanced at the screen, where Ron's emails were in full view. 'Back with us?'

This was terrific. No doubt she'd be telling all to Ron first thing in the morning. Well, what difference would it make now? 'Nah, Sal. Just wanted to check something. I'll push off now.'

She watched as he closed down the computer, stood up and walked out of the office.

'Phil!'

She caught up with him at the lifts. She had a note in her hand. 'Somebody rang yesterday. Wanted to talk to you urgently.'

'Maureen Eastley?'

'No, a young dude. Found you on Google. Left his number.' She handed him the note.

He stared at the name. *Nathan Shearwood*. 'Thanks.'

'Are you gonna be coming back?' she asked.

'Nah, I'm finished with *The Messenger*.'

'Oh, I'm sorry. I'll miss you.' She stepped forward and unexpectedly hugged him. 'See you, Phil.'

Caught by surprise, returning the hug, Philip looked over her shoulder and around the newsroom. Here he'd stacked up his twenty stories per week: the minor robberies, golden wedding profiles and fluff pieces. When he'd started, *The Messenger* had represented a humiliating come-down. He'd accepted the job because it was better than nothing. He hadn't expected to form friendships. How weird, then, to feel a sense of loss on leaving – as unexpected as the hug. Maybe the experience at *The Messenger* had not been as empty as he'd thought. Perhaps *The Messenger* had kept him sane.

Once out of the building Philip called the number Sal had given him. As he waited for an answer, he stared at her handwriting. *Shearwood*. The name came into focus. Bill Shearwood had been one of the Maribyrnong Group, the one who had a fight with West, the other young man in the photograph. He'd turned to cartooning. Philip had phoned every Shearwood in the book without success. Who the hell was Nathan?

A young man answered. Philip identified himself.

'You rang a few days ago, asking about grandad. We were talking and then Mum came on.' The young man spoke quickly, and so quietly that Philip could hardly hear.

Philip remembered the conversation. The woman, Bill Shearwood's daughter-in-law, had given him an earful and hung up. 'Yeah.'

‘Hang on a minute,’ said the young man. There was a pause. ‘I just had to close the door. Listen — there is some stuff that grandad left us. Some photos. Cuttings. Even a diary. I could show you if you like.’ Eagerness in his voice.

‘A diary?’

‘Yes, it’s all about the artists you’re interested in,’ the boy said excitedly. Philip heard the rustle of pages turning. ‘Listen, Mr Trudeau, I’m ... I’m really keen to be a journalist. I write articles for the school paper, and, um, if I could meet you and ...’

‘Thanks ... Nathan, but I’m not interested in Bill Shearwood anymore. And I’m sure you can find a better role model.’ Philip prepared to end the call. His experience with John Price had made him dubious about the reminiscences of old men. Besides, events had rushed on. Now that he knew what had become of Price’s collection, what he needed was evidence against Stefan. More anecdotes about the Maribyrnong Group weren’t going to help.

‘The diary’s not by him,’ the boy said. ‘It’s by someone else.’

‘Who, then?’ There was a pause.

Philip could hear the flicking of pages.

‘Someone called Valerie Elliott.’

21

The diary was a small book with plain white pages: an artist's sketchbook. It contained a few rough drawings, but most of the pages had been covered with handwriting in narrow, cramped lines. The entries began at the top of the first page and continued for a dozen or so more, the handwriting becoming progressively more unreadable. In places words had been heavily crossed out and there were complicated doodles in the margins. The inside cover of the book was inscribed: *Valerie Elliott, Williamstown, 1951.*

Philip held the diary in his hands and stared at it. She was here, in these pages — the woman who had obsessed him for months. Nathan had told him that the diary had been lying at the bottom of a box of his uncle's personal belongings. When Nathan's mother had told him the full extent of Philip's call, he had gone rummaging through the box, and found in the diary the artists' names Philip had mentioned.

Philip had no idea how Valerie fitted in, but she had been on his mind ever since the first time he had seen her portrait. Her face had affected him just as powerfully that second time, in Stefan's gallery. Something about her compelled him. And there was the girl he had seen in the window at John Price's place – who was she? And what about James West's obsessive painting of Valerie, at the end of his life? Even if nothing in these pages could help him find out the truth about Price and Stefan, Philip had to know what they contained. He began to read.

20 February

Went to see Doc Clay this morning. Told him I wanted the truth. He said the results were back and the radiotherapy's helped a bit, but not as much as he'd hoped. And there seems to be a secondary growth. So I'm a goner. He says I have three months at worst, maybe six or twelve at best. Doc told me there is a chance of remission but I must take things easy. No exertion at all. But I *have* to paint.

Afterwards I went down to the Strand and walked up and down, watching the ships. How bloody unfair it is. There's so much more I want to do. It's like writing a letter, and finding you've reached the last page when there are still a million things to say. If I could at least do a few good pictures, that would be something. To know one hasn't lived a meaningless life, like one of the herd lined up to be knocked on the head. I feel as if my whole life has been spent looking — I don't even know what for. I've always loved Plato's myth of the cavemen, huddled in their little circle, watching the shadows on the wall and believing the shadows are reality, when just behind them, if they cared to look, is the world of brilliant light.

I won't tell Jim. Don't want him rushing home when things are going so well. Who knows, the quack could be wrong. Anyway, he's there for both of us. I can revel in his success, as if I was there myself.

Lumps have broken out on my neck, and my glands are swollen up. Had the curse worse than ever. Feel so weak, as if I had bad flu. Breathless all the time. Have been reading up on the subject. Doc Clay was telling the truth when he put on his hanging cap. The book lists famous people who have died of it — as if that's supposed to make you feel better. One is Marie Curie, who caught it from her experiments. Strange that a ray can cause it, and a ray treats it. A wonderful quote from Curie: 'Nothing in life is to be feared. It is only to be understood.'

But I am afraid.

28 February

Bill came to visit this morning. Kind old Bill, with his endless pauses, his eyes that were meant to gaze across paddocks, not tally invoices. He brought me new paints and brushes, and showed me his latest drawings, sweet sketches of gum trees. He wants to get up another Group exhibition. Told him I wouldn't be part of it.

No one in this town has the right idea about painting. All they talked about at school was 'craft' and 'technique', by which they meant all the tricks they already knew. None of that matters. When I walk past the slaughterhouse I hear the bellows of the cattle, the anguish, I imagine the stamping, the bulging eyes, the blood. If I could capture that in a painting, it would be something worth doing.

No letters from Jim. Why?

5 March

Started a picture of Jim and me today — exactly as I remember him — his sweet, blue eyes, soft lips, the blonde hair in his beard that catches the evening sun. I captured us rather well, I think. This thing has forced my hand, and instead of endless time wasting, now I must work. It exhausts me, but I mustn't stop. I showed Sarah the picture. She was horribly shocked, started in on my loose morals and God knows what. Isn't it typical of this town? That same attitude had Jim's nudes thrown out of the school exhibition, so he sold them to a shopkeeper in High Street, before the police were called to seize them. No wonder the good painters are leaving in droves.

Lying in bed last night, exhausted from work, just before sleep, had a weird sensation — as if warm electricity was flowing through my body. Was unable to move — totally paralysed. My body a network of humming wires. Terrified at first — thinking 'so this is how death feels' — I gradually relaxed, let it happen. After a while the feeling subsided, I was myself again. Could move again, feel my body. Felt strangely happy.

26 March

At last, a letter from Jim. It's like a miracle — he's met a bloke who works for the Aussie embassy over there, a cultural attaché with the job of promoting Aussie artists to *les frogs*. This fellow wants to show our work in a gallery attached to the embassy. The show's to be called *New Australian Painting*. Jim met him at a party, took him to his studio and showed him our stuff. The bloke was so impressed he promised the show then and there, made all the arrangements in a few days! It's not till July though, so I have time to paint more and send them over — that's if I last long enough. I must.

29 March

A horrible dream last night. Dreamed the doc told me all my tests were clear, they'd mixed up my results with somebody else's. Woke up feeling so happy, till the truth slowly materialised, ugly as the lumps on my neck.

I lose myself in work. Rise at six, paint like a maniac till ten, when I have to rest. Again in the afternoon till six or eight, if it's going well. Doc Clay looks suspicious when I swear I only do an hour a day. But I can't stop now. The thought of Paris is all that keeps me going — it'll be bloody marvellous. Waiting to hear more news from Jim. With this show behind us, together we'll take on the world. Somehow my work will be there, even if I have to force my stupid body, flogging it like a mule.

5 April

Keep expecting another letter from Jim. Too busy working I suppose. Had a dream about him last night. He was standing in a lighted shop window. I was outside on the street, staring in. Inside the window, money was blowing all around him and he was grabbing it, snatching for it. I knocked on the window, trying to attract his attention, but he didn't hear me — or wouldn't. Eventually he was submerged under a great mountain of money.

8 April

Bill here again, bringing more canvas and paints. He's kind, but too solid and loyal, like a dog that comes back when it's been kicked. He stayed for almost an hour till I told him to go. The souls I love are the solitary, bright beings — the hungry and mistrustful. I had thought Jim was one of them, but now I am beginning to wonder. Was he ever, really, what I wanted him to be?

20 April

Tried to take a walk today, back to the places I used to go with Jim. Too tiring: had to stop every few minutes. How useless my body is. Drugs don't help, just make me sluggish and dizzy. Rested on a bench near the park. A still, peaceful arvo. Saw a boy riding past — a kid with sharp eyes and a sharp face, pedalling furiously, no doubt playing truant from school.

Envied his speed, his eagerness, his energy — then he was gone. Home to work, too exhausted to do more than a few minutes.

14 May

No letters for over four weeks. Feel like I'm in a vacuum. Why doesn't he write? Doc Clay prescribes rest, but I can't stop. I'm desperate, and I paint out of desperation. When I work, it takes me over completely.

I know, I feel, nothing else. But it shatters me. And the time gets shorter and shorter.

18 May

Don't know how to write this. Last night I had the most amazing — no, not dream, 'cause I was fully conscious the whole time — not a hallucination, either — is there a word for what happened? Maybe a vision, like poor mad mystical virgins used to have. Anyway I can't tell anyone about it, they'd think me bonkers and lock me up.

It started as I lay in bed. Couldn't sleep — my mind was buzzing too much. But too weak to keep working. Then the warm, strong, electrical feeling began, just like before. This time, felt no paralysis — but when I moved my hand, I couldn't see it move — instead my arm stayed by my side, though I *knew* my hand was in front of my face. Be calm, I thought. Remember Marie. Nothing is to be feared, it is only to be understood. As I was saying this to myself, over and over like a prayer, I came out of my body like an orange coming out of its peel. When I say 'I', what do I mean? I was somewhere else, looking down on my body — like Eliot says, a still point above the turning world. How sick and pale I looked, like a dead seagull. And then — I *flew*. How to describe it? A rush, a brilliant light. Like swimming through diamonds. I was miles above the city, all spread out below me like a map, the details incredibly clear. Saw the ships unloading at the docks, men heaving crates from the hold. Flew over the flophouses, and saw the sailor boys heaving and groaning on top of the tarts. Saw the cattle herded into the slaughterhouse. A boy setting a charge at the quarry. The lads of the basher gang on the corner. Bill, on his office stool, staring out the window. Felt filled with an amazing sense of love. How long did this go on? I don't know. But at the end of it, I was reeled in, as if I was a fish and my body was the net. I swooped back towards my house, my bed, and landed gently. And there I lay, myself again, in the world of time and space, flesh and my disease.

Maybe it was just the drugs, or the ray. Or maybe I really did leave old Plato's cave, and step for a few moments into the light.

30 May

Now finished a dozen or so paintings. Sent Bill to the post office — told him send them by air, to hell with the expense. What is there to save my money for? He didn't want to go — told me the French customs are absolute buggers about letting paintings in — something about protecting French culture from outsiders — as if Matisse and co would tremble in their boots at the arrival of a few Aussie pictures. *Sacrebleu!* Bill reckons they hold on to them for months, then put the official stamp slap bang in the middle of the canvas. Made him send them off anyway. They should get there just in time.

Only Bill comes to see me. The others hate me for taking Jim away from them. I couldn't care less — those months with Jim were the times I was most alive, though sometimes we fought like cats in a sack. But we connected with each other — and how rare is that? The others hate me 'cause I refused to worship him like they did, but before he met me his pictures were gutless. Those pretty landscapes belonged on a drawing-room wall. It was me who made him look at the docks and factories, streets where the air stinks of slaughtered animals, and sailors brawl in the corner pubs. We've brought all that back to the studio, and transformed it into pictures. We're like Picasso and Braque. Jim's done his best paintings with me — the ones that won him the scholarship. I made him an artist. So why the silence now?

8 June

Today I saw that quick, sharp boy again. I was sitting outside Salvation Hall when the door burst open and he came dashing out, grabbed his bike and rode off full pelt. A daring look on his face. Would love to know who he is — he's like a symbol of everything that is hopeful, wild and curious.

15 June

No word for six weeks now. I write to Jim every day to every address I can think of. Has something happened? If I wasn't already sick, the worry would kill me. I know one thing: he'd never let me down on purpose. He wanted recognition more for me than for himself. If he doesn't write, there has to be a reason.

19 July

Today Bill showed me a report in *The Argus*. The show's opened in Paris — great stir — a hundred people at the opening — Jim the star, no mention of me at all. He is pictured (new suit) on the arm of 'English heiress Pamela Flett' — in front of the slaughterhouse painting — my painting! — beside a rave review — 'West's unique, powerful vision'. Then Bill told me it's been like this all along — Jim's been using me, taking my ideas, copying my style. Those paintings that won him the scholarship — they were copied from mine. Bill says he saw it all — that's why they fought at the Hall. Bill knew I wouldn't believe it till I saw the proof myself. Then he tried to kiss me, begged for another chance. I pushed him away, told him for God's sake go.

Nothing to live for now. It's all over. Pamela doesn't matter. Could cope with any betrayal except this.

Such loneliness.

20 July

Only a few more weeks now. Perhaps days. Only time for one more picture — a self-portrait. Myself as I truly am. Pale as a corpse, flesh bruised, eyes sunken, neck swollen. It's OK working if I'm propped up by pillows, just for ten-minute stints. Want to leave this skin behind, like a snake. Nothing is to be feared. Just finish.

Doc Clay comes, gives me drugs. Losing all sense of time. Memories crowd around my bed. Mum and dad. Jim. Myself as a girl. That boy on his bike. Time past and time present.

26 July

Dreamed I woke in the dark. Moon shining onto the picture. Her skin glowing. Her eyes watching me. Heard her breathing, her whispering voice: *I will survive you.*

28 July

Painting finished. No more strength. Told Bill to package it up, send it to Paris. My last gift to Jim. May he look at it, and remember.

Philip closed the diary slowly. So James West had abandoned Valerie. Maybe that betrayal had haunted him all his life, leading him to imagine her presence during his last days at the nursing home. Kathleen O'Regan had said such delusions were common enough: *They get the past and present all mixed up.* West's obsessive drawings and night frights were probably the results of dementia and isolation.

Yet Philip had seen someone too, in the upper window of Price's place, the day of the auction. He remembered Maureen's contemptuous response: *What was she, a ghost?... a wispy maiden ... dressed in white?* She was right to be sceptical. They were journalists, dealing in facts. Ghosts belonged in the world of superstitious peasants huddled around a fireplace — or in its modern equivalent: late-night TV. Whatever had preyed on the minds of James West and John Price, it didn't affect him.

Philip forced himself to consider more material questions. Who had painted the pictures from Price's collection, now in Stefan's gallery? The picture of Valerie was a self-portrait – *Myself as I truly am*. What about the others? Had Valerie painted the slaughterhouse series?

Philip remembered James West's letters from Paris. He'd been ambitious and full of hope – until his ambition was gradually poisoned by doubts. *What if I'm not good enough?* Doubts that grew more insistent every day. Then, at last, the breakthrough. The guy from the embassy. The chance of an exhibition. Reviews, sales. His career launched. It was a perfect story of determination triumphing over adversity, except for the lie at the heart of it. How much of West's work was actually Valerie's? Had he passed off her pictures as his own, or copied them? Justifying it by telling himself: *We were a team, our ideas were shared, her work or mine, it comes to the same thing ...*

It was understandable, Philip thought. Christ, you could almost sympathise with the guy. Lacerating self-doubt: you didn't have to be an artist to feel it. Philip remembered an episode towards the end of his time at *The Biz & Fin*. He'd filed a thousand words on Stevenson and gone to the pub on a high, convinced that the story would run the next day, maybe even on the front page, smashing apart Stevenson's façade of legitimacy. In the morning he'd grabbed the paper, rifled through it in disbelief: nothing. He'd stormed past Graeme's secretary, into his office. 'Where's my story?'

'It's not gonna happen, Phil. It's all speculation. We'd be in court in five seconds if we printed it.'

'You've run it past the lawyers?'

'Didn't need to. There's no substance to it, Phil. You're accusing the guy of big-time corruption on the word of a few disgruntled ex-employees.' Seeing the expression on Philip's face, Graeme tried to placate him. 'Look mate, you've got six weeks of leave owing. Get away from the office, spend some time with the wife and kid.'

'Fuck off, Graeme, I'm not going anywhere. You want evidence? I'll get you the evidence.'

'Forget it, Phil. The story's dead. I'm not giving you advice now, I'm telling you. Take a break, you need one.' He tossed Philip's story back at him over the desk. 'Five years ago you'd never have given me this shit.'

Yes, Philip knew what West had been going through. You ignored the voices as long as you could, but they got to you in the end. *You're finished mate. You're a talentless hack.* And at that point, given a chance to save yourself, any chance at all, you'd grab it. Whatever the damage to other people, or to yourself. So West had passed off a few of Valerie's paintings as his own – what was the harm in that? No one would ever know – not with Valerie dead. But someone *had* known. Bill Shearwood had seen it from the start. As early as the Group exhibition, he'd suspected that West was stealing Valerie's ideas and taking the credit – that his growing reputation was unearned. No doubt jealousy had fuelled his anger, but he'd been right. And what about John Price? Hadn't he seen it, too? But he was an admirer of West, practically a shrine-builder; once the paintings were in his keeping, it was unlikely that Valerie would ever be heard of again.

Philip needed help to untangle all this. He reached for his phone.

22

Richard closed the diary, laid it down beside his plate, looked at Philip and gave a long whistle. 'This is amazing. Where did you get it?'

They were eating in a cheap restaurant in the city, at Philip's suggestion. His first choice would have been one of his usual haunts, but he knew that Richard would no more cross the bridge to eat in the western suburbs than he would visit a drug house in Marrakesh. Instead Philip had opted for a place in the CBD run by septuagenarian Italians, where he could just about afford to shout lunch. Richard had read the diary in the time it took to eat a bowl of pasta and drink a bottle of chianti.

'From a kid called Nathan Shearwood. His uncle was the Bill in the diary.'

'Bill Shearwood the cartoonist?' Richard prided himself on his knowledge of minor figures in art history. 'I must say, you haven't lost your knack, Phil.' He took a drink, so absorbed in the diary that he neglected to pass comment on the dubious quality of the wine. 'If this is the real thing ...' He raised his eyebrows. 'Do the facts back it up?'

'Yeah.' Philip flipped through his notes. 'The Maribyrnong Group held an exhibition in 1950. According to the catalogue there were paintings by James West, Bill Shearwood, Vic Smith and a V. Elliott.'

'I've never heard of Valerie Elliott.'

'Not surprising, if her paintings disappeared.'

'Until now,' Richard said. 'And Stefan's saying they're by his father. Where did he get them from?'

'John Price – the old guy who died.'

'Did Price know who the painter was?'

'He thought they were Wests. He hero-worshipped West. He never said he had any paintings by Valerie Elliott.'

'It would slash their value if it came out.'

'But they're great pictures – even I could see that.'

Richard shook his head. 'The art market's all about names. It's like paying twenty grand for a designer watch. The last thing you use it for is to tell the time. In art terms, James West is a Rolex. People like Peter McKendrick write books about him. David Stevenson invests in him. Everyone has heard of him – even you, Phil.'

'Thanks.'

'But this Valerie Elliott – who the hell is she? If this' – he gestured at the diary – 'becomes public knowledge, those pictures aren't worth a quarter of a million apiece. It'll be a few hundred, if he's lucky.' He glanced at the newspaper by his elbow, which contained a full-page splash on the exhibition, complete with a photo of Stefan. 'That'd wipe the smile off his face.'

'It'd be a pretty good story, wouldn't it?'

'The best story in Australian art since the stoush between Bradley Black's wife and boyfriend about his estate.'

'Front page stuff?'

'Graeme's allergic to art, but in this case it's possible.'

'You can have it, Richard,' Philip said, pushing the diary towards him. 'Who better than the arts editor of *The Biz & Fin* to break the story?'

Richard hesitated. Philip remembered his warning: *Don't get on the wrong side of Stefan West.* He also remembered Stefan's story about his associate who landed on spiked railings.

Eventually, journalistic instinct, or just plain desire, won out. Richard slid the diary into his jacket pocket. 'Thanks. I'll try and get it in next weekend.'

'And while you're at it, how about a story asking how Stefan got the paintings?'

Richard shook his head. 'No way, Phil. The identity of the painter is one thing. Stefan's business dealings are a different matter.'

'But it stinks. Price wanted to leave his pictures to the State Gallery. But his will – drawn up by a mate of Stefan's – has him leaving *the residue of my estate* to Stefan.'

'Has anyone challenged the will?'

'No.'

'Then there's no story. I can't touch it unless you get something tangible.'

'Oh, come on, Richard. He was ripping the old guy off. Millions of dollars worth of art – and no mention of where it came from?' Irritated by Richard's smile and shake of the head, Philip went on: 'This isn't just one of my crazy ideas. Maureen's talked to Stefan, she reckons he's a crook.'

Richard shot a look of surprise at Philip. 'Maureen?'

'Yeah, but I haven't heard from her for days. Mobile's turned off or something. Hey, has she been in touch with you?'

'What are you talking about?'

'Maureen Eastley – she used to work with us at *The Biz & Fin*, remember?'

'Yes, of course I do.'

'Well, I've seen a bit of her lately. But I don't have her number.'

Richard lifted the bottle and slowly emptied the final dregs into his glass. 'I don't understand,' he said eventually.

'I'm just asking if you've seen her.'

'No, I haven't seen her for years.'

'I ran into her a few weeks ago. She was interested in the story, offered to help out. Now she's disappeared. It's weird.'

'But Phil, you can't have seen Maureen.'

'Well, I have.'

'It's not possible.'

'Why not?'

'She's dead.'

In the silence that followed, a waiter cleared their plates. When he withdrew, Richard continued in a low voice.

'She died three years ago. While you were ... away. You must have heard about it. She took her own life, Phil. Somewhere overseas. There was a memorial service. The whole office was there. Graeme said he'd told you. Phil, are you all right?'

But Philip could no longer hear him. Richard's voice, and the whole restaurant, seemed to dissolve. Instead he was back in the prison hospital, confined to bed. His marriage was over, Sarah and Amy gone, his career in ruins. A cocktail of antidepressants and painkillers swilled around his bloodstream. In the midst of that, a letter had arrived from Graeme at *The Biz & Fin*. *This is to tell you some very sad news about your former colleague, Maureen* ... That had been the moment when it all tilted: he had tumbled into the darkness that swallowed him for eighteen months. Eventually he had dragged himself out, but only by slamming the door on the knowledge. He had focused on small tasks; getting through each day, each hour, was a kind of victory. He wasn't strong enough to handle anything bigger. Could he handle it now? Richard's flushed face rematerialised in front of him. But as he groped for words, his mobile went off. Automatically he took it from his pocket.

'That you, Trudeau? It's Gary Fennelly here.'

‘Gary? What?’

‘It’s Zayley,’ Fennelly said with a choking sound. ‘She’s in intensive care.’

‘What happened?’

‘Hit by a car, last night. Bust her neck. She’s critical.’

Philip tried to formulate a question, but nothing would come out. How many times had he spoken to people in distress, and never been lost for words? But all he could think was: *Not Zayley, anything but that*. ‘What ... how ...?’

‘The kids said a car came out of nowhere, no rego, mounted the kerb and hit her.’

‘Where is she?’

‘The Western, in a coma,’ Fennelly said. ‘Listen, Phil, you asked about her two weeks ago. You knew something was going to happen, didn’t you?’

Philip fumbled for words. ‘Gary —’

‘Listen, Trudeau, if you know anything, fucken tell me. Who did it? What’s going on?’ Fennelly was yelling now.

Philip ended the call. *I did it, Gary*. He hadn’t been driving the car, but he might as well have been. His questions had pushed her under its wheels. His need for the story. He remembered Zayley’s defiant face in the streetlights, and her voice on the phone: *They said no one would notice another dead junkie*. In trying to find the truth about one dead kid, had he killed another?

He stood up. ‘I’ve gotta go.’

‘What’s happened?’

‘Someone’s hurt.’ Philip made for the door.

Richard called out: ‘What about the diary?’

‘Do what you like with it.’

The restaurant door closed behind him.

By seven that evening Philip was back in his flat. He had gone straight to the hospital, but had not been allowed to see Zayley. She was not expected to last the night. He had spoken to several kids, who had told the same story: a car with no licence plates, driven by a guy with a beard and shades, had mounted the kerb and hit Zayley so hard she had flown into the air and bounced off the roof. The car then drove off at high speed. Philip hung around for a while, feeling useless, until Fennelly's aggressive questioning became too much for him.

It seemed impossible that only a few days earlier he had felt happy. The edifice of deception he had painfully built for himself had been shattered, as if by a wrecking ball. No – *he* was the wrecking ball, bringing disaster on those around him. First Maureen, now Zayley – their lives had been destroyed by his actions. Then there were those who had been closest of all: Sarah and Amy, driven away by his obsessiveness. And all for what? Stevenson was more prosperous than ever. Stefan West, whatever temporary embarrassment the diary might cause him, was likely to escape justice. Philip's life had been a failure of monumental proportions.

After leaving the hospital, Philip had stopped at a pharmacy and picked up a repeat prescription of sleeping tablets. Then he'd crossed the road to the bottle shop and bought his favourite Scotch. Back home, he'd slotted a CD into the player – Coltrane, of course – and poured himself a drink as the first notes echoed around the room. He took out his wallet and looked at the creased picture of Amy riding on his shoulders. That little girl was long gone: she had no need of him now. She had other shoulders to ride on, other necks to fling her arms around. Likewise Sarah. How would she hear about it? Philip wondered. Who would ask her, *Do you feel numbed by his death?* He doubted she would feel anything much. Like John Price, he would die alone and unmourned. He raised the glass to his lips, then took the bottle of sleeping pills and read the label. How many would do the trick? A dozen? Two dozen? The whole bottle?

But he couldn't bring himself to rip the cap off. *Get on with it, you coward.* No, it wasn't cowardice: it was the memory of Nina that came into his head, summoned up by the phrase Coltrane was playing. A few days ago he had been so hopeful that they could get to know each other. Maybe it was a remote hope, but was he prepared to slam the door on it completely? He put the bottle down, refilled his glass and sat motionless, listening to the joyous, spiralling sounds made by the sweetest of all players. Nina was in every riff, in every note: standing by the railway tracks; pushing him away outside the cemetery; turning to him in the car, saying: *Why are you doing this?* When the track ended, he still hadn't moved.

Creak.

The noise had come from the hallway. That was odd. Had he left the door open? He didn't think so, but the latch had been playing up. The music began again, drowning out other sounds, but at the same moment a slight draught blew under the door. An open window? Philip got unsteadily to his feet and walked out into the darkened hallway.

Two men were waiting for him there. One had a baseball bat which he swung at Philip's head. The hallway was so narrow he couldn't land a clear blow. Philip half blocked the first one, but the second cracked the top of his head as he ducked. Then everything became a confused welter of blows and kicks. It was a bad place for a fight: narrow, cramped and dark. In slow motion, he felt himself fall to the floor. He passed out briefly and came to lying in a foetal position while the two guys aimed kicks at his stomach and groin. The bat smashed down again on his head — then darkness.

23

Philip didn't know how much time had passed. He was slumped in the passenger seat of a car, speeding along a deserted road. His head felt as if nails had been driven into it. Blood was oozing over his left eye. One of his attackers – it was the bearded guy, Stefan's offsider – sweated beside him in the driver's seat. Don – that was his name. The car reeked of whisky – Philip's mouth was full of it, his clothes stank of it. He groaned.

Don stopped the car, grabbed the back of Philip's head, tilted it and forced a bottle into Philip's mouth. Philip swallowed several times. Scotch spilled onto his face and clothes. Then the car took off again and sped through the darkness. The road was unlit. Philip noticed the time on the dashboard clock: 10.24. An intersection approached, and the car swung onto an unsealed road. Philip realised they were somewhere in the outer western suburbs, on one of the long, straight roads that seem to lead nowhere and pass nothing, save for the occasional factory or warehouse and signage advertising land sales and housing developments.

'Where are we going?' Philip slurred his words.

Don glanced over. 'Shut the fuck up, dog.'

Philip realised where he had heard the voice before: that evening at the Irish pub, from the next cubicle: *You're a dead man, Trudeau.*

The car slowed down and halted with a scrunch of gravel. A short distance ahead were signs indicating a level crossing. A second car pulled up behind them. There were footsteps on the gravel and another man appeared at Don's window.

'What time's it due?' he said.

'Ten minutes. Put it on the tracks.'

''Sgoing on?' Philip said.

'The V-Line,' Don said. 'It's going to pick up an extra passenger.'

The second guy walked back to the other car and drove it slowly onto the level crossing, where he parked on the tracks. Philip recognised his own Kingswood. The driver killed the lights and got out, leaving the door open.

'You're not serious,' Philip said.

The guy looked at him with the kind of eyes Philip had seen often enough in prison, eyes like nails, from which all human feeling had long gone. Philip realised there was no point in saying any more. People like this would take a life as casually as if they were deleting an email. Then the guy's mobile rang and he reached for it. 'Everything's sweet. Yeah, shitting himself. Five minutes. OK.' He held the phone to Philip's ear. 'He wants to talk to you,' he said.

'Hello, Philip.' It was without surprise that Philip recognised the voice.

'Why are you doing this?' Philip said.

'You've become a nuisance, Philip. I don't have much patience with that.'

'So you're killing me?'

'Of course not. I just want you to seek help,' Stefan said. 'Middle-aged male, depressed, drinking too much, divorced, unemployed. You fit the profile perfectly.'

Only too true, Philip thought: not long before, he had almost done the job himself. But this was different. The knowledge that

Stefan wanted him dead filled him with the desire to live.

'I'm sure neither of us wants another rail tragedy,' Stefan went on. 'Train accidents are so messy.'

Philip remembered the policewoman at Yarraville station three months before: *There are bits of him everywhere.*

'I've filed a story, you know,' Philip said.

Stefan laughed. 'I don't think so. Ron knows what's good for him. But it doesn't have to be this way, Philip.'

In the distance a horn sounded, long and deep. The bearded guy glanced at his watch, then at Philip.

'What do you mean?' Philip said.

'Just cooperate with us, mate,' Stefan said.

'How?'

'Tell us who you've been talking to.'

Philip tried to think, his head fuzzy with pain and Scotch. If Stefan believed only Philip knew what had been going on, it was all the more reason to get rid of him. Better for Stefan to believe that others knew, too. Then again, if these goons really meant to kill him, they would do it anyway.

'A few people ...' Philip said vaguely. His tongue felt like a slab of meat.

'We know about that little slut – Zayley, wasn't it? Very silly of her to get involved. Your obliging editor gave me her name. Anyone else?'

The bearded guy was getting impatient. Any second he'd snatch the phone and end the call. 'Yeah, maybe,' Philip said.

'Who?'

Philip was silent. He was thinking of Nina walking home with her shopping, moving around in the lit window, alone in her flat. *Alone in her flat.* Don stretched out a large hand for the phone.

'Something strange happened a few days ago,' Stefan said.

‘Portelli’s came to the gallery, saying we’d booked a delivery to Nina Fletcher. Someone had rung them, asked for her address. That was you, wasn’t it?’

‘No.’

‘Tell me what you told her.’

‘I haven’t seen Nina for weeks.’

‘Don’t make it hard for yourself, Philip. We don’t have a lot of time.’ Philip said nothing. ‘I’ve noticed a change in Nina,’ Stefan went on. ‘Last time we spoke, she was quite hostile. Maybe we’d better visit her, just to put the record straight.’

‘No. No.’

‘Tell me what you told her, Philip,’ Stefan said soothingly. ‘Just tell me, and Don’ll drive you home.’

‘Nothing. Nothing …’ Philip began, chilled by the realisation that Stefan and his thugs would now go after Nina. Surely there had to be a limit to the number of people he could bring trouble upon? There was another long blast from the approaching train. In the distance, two points of light appeared.

‘Look, Stefan, I’ll explain it all to you,’ Philip said. ‘But we have to meet. I …’

‘I don’t think so, mate. You have a train to catch. Goodbye, Philip.’ The line went dead.

The two men dragged him out of the car. The cold night air, like a splash of water, brought a moment’s clarity. As Don pinioned Philip’s arms, the second guy headbutted him. Philip sank to his knees on wet gravel. They half dragged, half carried him to his car. They shoved him into the driver’s seat, slammed the door and retreated into the darkness. Lights began to flash at the level crossing to warn of the approaching train. Nine-tenths unconscious, Philip slumped over the steering wheel. His car had been parked directly facing the oncoming train, whose lights poured through the windscreen, dazzling him. The train, very close now, gave a long, angry blast of its horn as the driver realised there was an obstruction on the track.

The train was travelling – so its driver told police – at eighty miles per hour when it struck the car head on, crumpling it like an empty can and shoving it backwards over a hundred yards before tipping it down a bank where it came to rest on its roof.

24

Dazzle. Noise. Pain chiselling his skull. Where was he? There was something he had to do — and fast. There was danger. But he was tired. He needed to rest, to sleep a little longer. His head rolled against something hard. *You're a dead man, Trudeau. It's all become too much for you*. Dazzle. Noise. The train, that was it. Someone had been hit. Who was the victim? He had to find out. Wake up. He must wake up.

Philip raised his head from the steering wheel. It felt like a sandbag. Lights needled his eyes, as if for an interrogation. Flinching away, shielding his face, he saw the shadowy figure in the passenger seat beside him.

'Hello, Phil. You look like shit.'

She looked tireder, older. She wore no make-up and her hair was unkempt. She was wearing jeans and a t-shirt, and still had the scarf around her neck. But something was wrong. She shouldn't be here. Something Richard had said. He touched his head. What had happened?

'I think someone's trying to kill me.'

The corner of her mouth curved slightly. 'You probably deserve it.' A match flared. She lit up at the third attempt, her hands shaking, and tossed the match out of the window.

He frowned, struggled. A memory rose sluggishly to the surface, like a bubble in a pool of mud. 'But aren't you ...'

'Yeah.' She inhaled deeply, then let the smoke out. 'It's like being an actor. You just step offstage, that's all.'

'Why are you here?'

'Why?' She looked at him in mock amazement. 'Don't you remember, Phil?'

'I can't remember anything.'

'Can't or won't?'

A blast from the horn cut through Philip's daze. 'The train ...' he mumbled.

'It won't hit yet. We've got a little while.' She was silent.

Philip waited. He felt neither conscious nor unconscious, but suspended in some intermediate state where there was no car, no train, only him and Maureen and the pain that pounded in his head.

Then she spoke again. Her voice sounded very far away. 'You're asking me why? Let me tell you all about it. All I ever wanted to be was a journalist. Had my first piece in the paper when I was thirteen. I still have it, that is, I *had* it.' She smiled briefly. 'Straight out of uni, I joined the local paper. Fetes and rates, you know the drill. I loved it, but I wanted more.

'When I got a job at *The Biz & Fin* I was rapt. I thought, this is where I belong. And who was I working with? Philip Trudeau. The journo I admired the most. I was assigned to the Stevenson story – the kind of thing I'd always dreamed of. My name was there, next to yours. OK, it was just a supporting role – *additional reporting by Maureen Eastley* – but hey, at least I was in the mix. And y'know what? I was good at it. People didn't always want to talk to Philip Trudeau. They didn't trust him. But Stevenson's ex-CFO gave me a two-hour interview. Remember that?'

Painfully, Philip nodded.

‘All the same, you never really believed in me. You put it down to beginner’s luck, or my face, or my legs, didn’t you Phil? Not the hours I worked, or talent. But I didn’t care. I was doing what I loved.’ She glanced at him. ‘Any of this coming back?’

He nodded again.

‘Then something else happened. Philip Trudeau liked me, and I liked him. He had a wife and kid, but he never mentioned them, and I never asked. It was exciting. Intoxicating. And I thought it meant as much to him as it did to me.’

It did, he wanted to say. *It meant the world.* But, as in a dream, he was unable to speak.

‘Then everything went pear-shaped. Stevenson’s lawyers were hitting the phones. Graeme got toey, started pulling our stories. And we were so close! Remember Stevenson’s assistant? It was my idea to talk to her. She told me about his lunches with the minister – the one who’d denied ever meeting him. She told me about his secret diary. She knew about the kickbacks, the promises, the lies. And she’d had a gutful.

‘When I look back, she was the only decent person in the whole thing. All we wanted was the story – we didn’t care how we got it. She could see what they were doing, and she risked her career to blow the whistle.

‘*Get us the diary,* we said. *Photocopy it.* It took a week to persuade her. *The public’s right to know* – your favourite phrase, Phil. But before she could do it, they sacked her. Cleared out her desk and escorted her off the premises. They must have suspected something. But they didn’t know she still had a key. And you said: *Let’s go in ourselves.*’

Now Philip groaned, his head in his hands. Maureen’s voice went remorselessly on.

‘You’re crazy, I said. We can’t do that. *Course we can,* you said.

Piece of piss, it'll take two minutes – like it was something you did every day, not a crime at all. We chose an evening when Stevenson was out of town, the staff at Friday drinks. Remember how close we got? Up in the lift – she'd told us the security code – past reception, into his office. But the diary wasn't where she said. So we tried the desk, the filing cabinets ... and that was what we were doing when the security guards found us.

'Stevenson had been waiting for a chance to go for *The Biz & Fin*, and he set the dogs loose. The government leaned on the prosecutors, and they chucked every charge in the book at us. Course, they wanted to know our sources – when we wouldn't tell them, they threw in contempt. The judge couldn't stand journalists – remember what he said? *An exemplary sentence is necessary to deter these appalling practices by journalists who hold themselves above the law.* There were questions in Parliament. Writs, apologies, retractions. Gutless Graeme backed down and settled out of court. Then he told me I'd never work again. Course it was you they really wanted – I only got four months. But that was bad enough. I thought we might get a fine, but I never expected to go to *prison*.'

She stopped, biting her lip, and looked away. The dazzling lights were still pouring through the windscreen, but the train seemed to have come no closer.

'After I came out, I was a mess. I went to a counsellor; she gave me antidepressants. Then I tried to visit you, but they told me you weren't seeing anyone. So I decided to travel round for a while. Bali, India, Sri Lanka. I sent cards but you never replied. I ended up in Tibet. A little village. That's where I got this scarf.' She plucked at the bright material, rubbing it between her fingers. 'I spent a couple of weeks just hiking, visiting monasteries, stuff like that. It was so peaceful. In the end my money ran out. I thought: do I go back, start temping, work in a bar? Pretend I never had a career? Even then,

Phil, if I'd heard anything ...' She almost glanced at him, seemed to think better of it. 'I couldn't see any way forward. It was like being at the bottom of a well.

'On the last night I smoked the rest of my dope. I didn't have any pills left. I thought, I wish it was all over. No more hassle. I realised what I had to do.' She slowly loosened the scarf. 'I tied one end around a roof beam, the other round my neck. I stood on a chair. Then I kicked it away.' She took off the scarf and turned towards Philip. At first he thought the colours in the silk had run into her pale skin. Then he realised that the dark circle around her neck was bruising. 'It took a long time. The drop wasn't far enough. I thought, I've even stuffed this up. It was horrible. But it worked in the end.' She was silent.

In the shadowy car, her face had the same look of despair he had seen in the painting of Valerie. He turned away. 'I had no idea about any of that. I had ...'

'Problems of your own. Yeah, you said.'

'What do you want from me, Maureen?'

The train had still moved no nearer. They seemed poised in space, like a swingboat at the top of its arc, before the rushing descent.

'They told me you tried to visit,' he said finally. 'And I did get the postcards. But I couldn't face you.'

'Why not?'

'You'd trusted me, and I let you down. I should have looked after you.'

She sighed. 'I didn't need to be *looked after*. We were a team, Phil. We may have stuffed up, but we were still a team.'

'I stuffed up, not you,' Philip said. 'I always knew you were a good journalist – it wasn't luck that got those interviews. You were young, smart, ambitious – like me, fifteen years ago. I was over the hill, I hadn't broken anything big for years. Then the Stevenson story came along.

'I only realised how big it was when we started digging. The politics. The corruption. It was the sort of story that makes careers, that brings down governments. But it was too big for me — I couldn't handle it anymore, but I couldn't let it go either. I was drinking too much, working eighteen-hour days, blowing up at everyone. I remember standing in the lobby of the Grand one night, using their phone. I didn't even know who I wanted to call. I was yelling at the phone, abusing everyone in sight 'cause I couldn't get through. All I had in my hand was a bunch of receipts: I was trying to call the numbers on them. There were bits of paper all round me on the floor. I was totally out of it.

'I got scared. I didn't know what was happening to me. When we went into Stevenson's office that night, I knew we'd get caught. I *wanted* us to get caught. 'Cause then at least it would be all over. I was finished, Maureen. But I shouldn't have taken you down with me.'

'Why didn't you tell me all this?'

'Tell you what? That I couldn't hack it anymore? I couldn't fail in front of you, Maureen. You looked up to me, and I failed big time.'

'But Phil, none of that mattered. I didn't expect you to be perfect. I just — liked you.'

He lowered his head to the steering wheel. 'I'm sorry, Maureen.'

In the darkness he sensed her face close to him, her voice urgent.

'All I wanted to tell you was that I never blamed you. Not for a second. We were dumb, we threw it all away. But it was my choice to be there in Stevenson's office, not just yours. If you'd read my letters, if you'd let me visit you ... Stop beating yourself up, Phil. It wasn't all your fault. We were in it together.'

Philip lifted his face and looked at Maureen. He didn't

understand what was happening. The events of the night were too unreal. But he seemed to feel the first lightening of the weight he'd been carrying for the last three years.

'So what now, Phil?'

'I dunno. I guess it's all over.'

'No, Phil. The story's not finished.'

'There's nothing more I can do.'

'Don't be pathetic. Stefan faked the will and stole the pictures.' Her voice had taken on its familiar decisive tone. 'He's tried to kill you and Zayley. And what about Price?'

'What?'

'The old bloke just happened to take a dive, after making a will in Stefan's favour? Bit convenient, isn't it?'

'You think Stefan —?'

'Hurried things along a bit? Sure. He's an impatient man. Probably had a buyer all lined up.'

Philip thought of Stefan showing him around his gallery, boasting about the slaughterhouse painting: *It's just been bought by one of the country's most successful businessmen ... He wants to donate it.* Then he remembered Richard's warning about Stefan's powerful friends, and Richard's comment: *Stevenson's keen to be the next chairman of AMOMA.*

'Stevenson?' Philip said.

'Bit slow, Phil, but you got there in the end.'

Stevenson had been at the exhibition, too, Philip remembered, rubbing shoulders with the arts minister and the gallery director.

'That's why Stefan needed the paintings,' Philip said. 'To sell them to Stevenson, so he can donate them to the gallery and get himself made chairman.'

'Sounds good to me — and Price was in his way.'

'But what can I do?'

'Proving Stefan stole the paintings would be a start.'

'How? Where's the proof?'

'Well duh, Phil. Do I have to tell you everything?'

He tried to think. 'Wait – the will. There was something dodgy about it. None of the paintings were listed. What was that solicitor's name ... Parker?'

She nodded. 'Maybe he's got the real will somewhere.' She refastened the scarf neatly around her neck.

'I can't do it alone, Maureen.'

'You've got to, Phil. Giving up is not an option. There are other people involved.'

Philip's head began to clear. He thought of Zayley in her hospital bed; of Nina in her flat, unaware that Stefan's thugs were on their way to pay her a visit. There was another blast from the train.

'I gotta go,' Maureen said.

'Wait, Maureen. I need to know –'

'Not now – the train.'

He looked up: it was almost upon them. They were back in real time again: the rails were humming, and a draught of air hit the car, pushed by the approaching train, whose lights now filled the windscreen.

'Will I see you again?'

'No, Phil. It's up to you now.' She leaned towards him, and for an instant her cold lips brushed his cheek. 'Quick – go.'

With a half-fall half-dive, he rolled out of the door and off the tracks. As his shoulder met the gravel, the train hit the car, smashing it like an egg.

Philip rolled down a grassy bank. He saw a kaleidoscope of wheels, earth, lighted windows, shocked faces. The train came to a slow, deafening halt. At the bottom of the bank was a dry ditch. He tumbled into it and oblivion.

Philip's eyes opened. Stars. Voices. A blue light strobed the darkness. At the top of the bank, figures moved around. He saw torches, orange jackets, heard the buzz of radios and fragments of official conversation.

'Found anything?'

'Only the car. No body.'

'Driver swears there was someone in it.'

'He must've jumped.'

The voices faded. The figures had gathered around the wreckage of the car, fifty metres away. They looked like participants in some nocturnal ritual. It was a scene Philip had witnessed many times: normally he'd walk up to the nearest cop and ask for details. Not on this occasion. There would be questions, interviews, statements. He had no time for that. Philip got clumsily to his feet. He scrambled along the ditch in the opposite direction. A safe distance away he crossed the tracks and headed back towards the road. The level crossing was still clear – the train had stopped well past it – and occasional vehicles were coming through.

A car was approaching now. Philip staggered into the middle of the road, his hands up in the air. The car halted a couple of inches from him and Philip toppled onto the bonnet. An incredulous face stared at him through the windscreen.

'Phil?'

'Ted! God, I'm glad to see you.'

Fairy godmothers rarely came in so unprepossessing a shape, but at that moment Ted seemed the answer to a prayer.

'Can you take me back to the city?'

'Sure, hop in.'

Ted moved camera equipment from the passenger seat, allowing Philip to get in. As the car took off, Philip put his head back, closed his eyes and groaned.

Ted glanced at him. 'Rough night?'

'Someone just tried to kill me.'

'Mate, you need a hospital.'

'There's no time for that. What are you doing out here?'

Ted made a noise indicating disgust. 'Train driver reported a suicide – said he'd hit a Kingswood on the tracks. It came through on the radio. I thought, you beauty. Cops, ambos, firies – we all headed out here.' Ted spoke as if he too was providing an essential service. 'When we get here, there's no body. Bastard must've lost his nerve.'

'Inconsiderate of him. Put your foot down, Ted – I'm in a hurry.'

'OK, I know a shortcut to the freeway.' Ted accelerated, at the same time adjusting his radio. There was a static-laden exchange about a stabbing in a nearby suburb. Ted looked wistfully at his camera. 'We couldn't just take a quick detour?'

'Keep going, or there will be a body. Yours.'

'OK, steady on.' Ted glanced at Philip. 'You drive a Kingswood, don't you?'

'Used to.'

Ted lifted a stubby from its resting place between his thighs and took a swig. 'The cops'll be looking for you. It's a crime to obstruct train tracks. Recklessly endangering other lives besides your own.'

'It wasn't my idea.'

'What's been going on, Phil?'

'I'll explain later.' Philip's head was about to explode; red hot needles seared through his guts. 'Just tell me when we get there.'

'When we get where?'

Philip told him Nina's address.

25

Philip knew little of the drive back. He could have been in a storm at sea, tossed on waves of nausea, illuminated by flashes of pain. He closed his eyes and surrendered to it. Once Ted stopped the car so his passenger could vomit painfully onto the verge. For the rest of the trip Philip curled up, semi-conscious, his brain shuffling words and images like the computer generating cards for solitaire. The train, Mike's photograph, Maureen's face. *I realised what I had to do.* John Price in his armchair, ice clinking in the glass, the portrait of Valerie. *The curtains ... please ...* Zayley at Yarraville station. *He said no one would notice another dead junkie.* Among these fragments, one refrain hammered insistently: *Price's death was no accident. No accident. No accident ...*

'Hey Phil, you alive?'

Philip cautiously opened his eyes. 'Just.'

They were in Andrews Street. He tried to focus, recognising the ugly apartments, the run-down houses and the ripped billboards. He looked up to the unlit window of Nina's apartment, then back to street level. He saw Nina's car. *Oh shit.* Another car Philip recognised was parked directly outside the apartments. Philip could make out the shapes of the two men inside.

'Pull over!' Ted trod on the brake and swung into a space a few cars back.

'Thank God – she's not home. What time is it?'

'Eleven-thirty. What's going on?' Ted said.

'Those guys tried to kill me. Now they're after Nina.'

'What do you wanna do?'

'Get to her before they do.'

'They'll see us.'

'They don't know your car. And they think I'm dead.' Philip groaned and doubled over again.

'What's up with you?'

'My pancreas. They filled me full of Scotch.'

'Why?'

'To make it look like suicide.'

Between staving off bouts of pain and nausea, he told Ted what had happened. Ted was so astonished he turned off his radio. The night's accidents, potential fodder for realvictim.com, went on unphotographed.

'How much of this can you prove?'

'I'm working on that.'

Ted pointed down the street. 'There she is.'

Nina was crossing the main road at the end of Andrews Street, making her way towards her flat. Her path would take her directly past the other car. Its occupants had seen her, too: there was movement as cigarettes were extinguished.

'Go!' Philip said. Ted stamped on the accelerator. Nina stepped back in alarm as the car slammed to a halt beside her.

'Nina!' Philip shouted. 'It's me – get in.'

'What?'

'No time to explain. Come on.'

She hesitated and looked round. The lights of the other car came on like searchlights. Dazzled, Nina opened the back door and got in behind Philip. Ted's foot hit the floor and with a screech of rubber they were into the main street.

Philip looked at Nina. 'That was close.'

She took in the blood on his face. 'My God – what happened?'

'Those guys are mates of Stefan's. They just tried to kill me. Now they're after you.'

'They're following us,' Ted said, his eyes on the rear-view mirror.

'Look out!' Philip said. Ted slammed on the brakes to avoid a crowd of partygoers.

'Is it because of Mike?' Nina said.

'Yeah – and John Price.'

'They're gaining,' Ted said, accelerating.

'Take this left,' Nina said.

'Nah, it's a dead end.'

'There's a way through. *Take it.*'

Ted flung the car into the street Nina had pointed out. They immediately hit a series of speed humps, each one jolting them violently. At the far end a narrow exit led down an alley between two houses. They sped through and out.

'Neat,' Ted said. 'How'd you know that one?'

'I take photos round here.'

'Are they still there?' Philip said.

Ted checked the mirror. 'Yeah – but further back.'

'What about John Price?' Nina said.

'Stefan killed him.'

Ignoring a 'no entry' sign, Ted swerved again. There were no speed humps this time and he gunned up to eighty. Short-skirted women looked up as the car approached. 'Sorry girls, not this time,' Ted muttered. He took another sharp turn, down a ramp to an underground car park.

'What are you doing?' Philip said.

'Relax, they'll never see us down here.' Near the entrance were several large rubbish skips. Ted manoeuvred behind them and killed the lights. They waited. The other car sped past on the main road. Ted reversed up the ramp and turned in the opposite direction.

'How did you know those skips were there?' Philip said.

'A job a few months ago. You don't want to know what was found in them.' Ted smiled at the memory. 'Where to now, chief?'

Philip told him.

They pulled up outside Gordon Parker's office. It was closed, like the shops around it. The street was deserted but well-lit.

'This the place?' Ted said, squinting.

'Yeah. But I can't go in the front,' Philip said. 'It's too risky.'

'Try the back,' Ted said. 'Don't be long. Take my torch.'

Feeling as conspicuous as if he was on stage, Philip made his way around the back of the shopping strip, into an alley full of garbage bins. A couple of stray cats fled but no other living thing was about. He saw a rear window to the solicitor's office. Looking around the alley he found a brick, which he used to break the window. Then he crashed through it himself, landing in a heap on the floor.

Picking himself up, Philip groped his way through the darkness. Parker oversaw a small operation and apparently didn't worry about burglars: no alarm sounded. Despite this, Philip's heart began to race. He felt an overwhelming urge to run, but couldn't take a step. A tsunami of fear was about to crash over him. He reached for cigarettes, lit one and inhaled. Now he was in Stevenson's office. There were footsteps outside. Maureen's hand on his arm: *Phil, someone's coming!* He forced his breathing to slow down. *Relax – there's no one here.* He tried to remember the day's word puzzle, telling himself he would not move until he had twenty words. He concentrated fiercely on vowels and consonants. Gradually the panic receded. He was OK. Clinging on by his fingernails, but OK.

He shone the torch around, remembering his previous visit. There was the waiting area where he had sat unsuccessfully prompting the receptionist for information; and there was the receptionist's desk and filing cabinet. This was locked, of course, but Price's original will would surely be inside. Philip grabbed a paper knife, forced it into the crack and attempted to lever the drawer open. The knife snapped, the blade flew across the room and he was left clutching the handle. Furiously he attacked the filing cabinet. The metal buckled, but the drawer remained obstinately shut. He paused for breath, and delivered a kick to the recalcitrant object. *Use your brain, you idiot.*

He shone his torch over the receptionist's desk. She was a tidiness Nazi. Everything had been put neatly away. What about the computer? Maybe the files would be stored electronically. He switched it on and it blinked into life. Immediately a dialogue box came up. *Username: JMoffett Password:*

What had her name been? Jan, that was it. He tried various possible spellings of her name and surname, but nothing worked, and after a few attempts the computer locked him out. He glanced around her desk for clues, but her mind was not as easy to read as Ron's. Jan defeated him.

Next to the computer stood the jar of multicoloured jelly beans. He opened the jar, slid his hand in and took a few. As he did so, he remembered the receptionist doing the same thing, reaching for lollies with one hand, then dropping something into her desk drawer with the other.

Her keys!

The desk drawer was unlocked. The bunch of keys lay there.

Philip removed them. Moving to the filing cabinet, he tried one at a time. As he did so, another jolt of agony hit him like a punch, bending him double, gasping, until it receded. Then one of the keys turned and the damaged drawer scraped open.

Rapidly he fumbled through the files. There were dozens of manila folders, each marked with a name, stored in alphabetical order. Miller, Newton, Palmer, Quinn ... nothing under the name Price. He searched again with increasing desperation. The original had to be here somewhere. He slammed the drawer shut.

He went to the window and saw Ted and Nina looking anxiously towards him. He made gestures to indicate that he was nearly done. Turning away from the window he faced the door to Parker's inner office. Maybe Price's will wasn't out here, with the rest of the files. Maybe it was too sensitive to be stored among his regular clients' files. Maybe Parker kept this one to himself.

The door to the inner sanctum was locked, but again the receptionist's keys did the trick. Philip stumbled in. The mess of papers and files put him in mind of John Price's house. He tried Parker's own filing cabinet. He was right, here was another drawer full of manila folders, among them one marked Price. He extracted it, and removed a sheaf of papers. Yes, it was the will – but exactly the same as the one he had already seen: this would get him nowhere. He stuffed the folder back and shuffled through the papers on Parker's desk. Finally he unlocked and opened the desk drawers.

The bottom drawer of Parker's desk contained a surprise: two small oil paintings. Philip could see little of them in the dark. Were they James Wests? Maybe. He leaned them against the desk and rummaged in the drawer. Under the paintings were some magazines. Philip lifted them out and laughed: Parker's private papers were half-a-dozen copies of *Schoolgirl Lust*. On removing these, and digging right to the bottom of the drawer, his hand settled on a dozen disks. He took them out, and shone the torch on them. One of the disks was marked with a single word, scribbled in biro: *Price.*

This would have to do. There was nowhere else to search. Besides, the wave of panic was beginning to rise again. Replacing the porn and the paintings, he closed the drawer, slipped the disk into his pocket and left the office as he had entered it.

'Hope it was worth it,' Ted grumbled, placing a mug of tea and a print-out in front of Philip half an hour later. 'I missed a smash on the bridge thanks to you.'

They were back in Ted's flat. Philip was prone on a lumpy sofa, poring over the print-out, riding the waves of pain that kept washing through him. At first sight it didn't look good. This will, printed from the disk he had stolen, looked identical to the one from the Probate Office – same date, same pedantic listing of possessions. Had his break-in been in vain?

'Total waste of an evening,' Ted said. 'More bodies than a vampire movie out there, and I missed the lot.'

Philip riffled through the pages, trying to separate the words swarming together. And then, like a sign appearing in headlights, a name appeared. Philip's finger leapt to the place, as if the type might jump off the page. 'Here.'

'What?' Nina looked over his shoulder.

'It says James West.'

They all stared at the page. 'It's there, too,' Nina said.

'And there,' Ted said. 'It's all over the bloody page.'

And now they could all see it – James West's name was everywhere. The Lovers *by James West, oil painting.* Slaughterhouse *by James West, oil painting.* Night flight *by James West* ... Some thirty paintings were listed, including many of those currently showing in Stefan's exhibition. Philip laughed, until the laughter became a bolt of pain.

'What's the big deal?' Ted said.

'There were no paintings by West in the will that I saw.'

'So this is a different will?'

'Yeah, well, it's the complete one.'

'Who'd he leave the paintings to?' Nina said.

Philip read aloud: *'I leave my collection of artworks to the State Gallery, for the establishment of a permanent collection, to be known as the John Price Collection, to be kept together and exhibited in perpetuity.'*

'Why was the other will different?' Ted said.

'This is what Price signed, but the one I saw before was all that was kept.' Philip flipped rapidly through the document. 'All the West paintings are on these two pages. Only Stefan and Parker know about them. All they had to do was take these pages out.'

'I don't get it,' Ted said. 'If there are no paintings by West in the will, how did Stefan get them?'

'Because of this.' Turning to the end of the will Philip read aloud: *'The rest and residue of my estate I leave to Stefan West.* Everything else, in other words.'

'So Stefan gets everything that's not listed?' Nina asked.

'Yeah. They're part of the residue of his estate.'

'This doesn't prove Stefan killed him,' Ted said.

'It proves the paintings don't belong to Stefan. The State Gallery should have got them. And there's something else Stefan doesn't know.'

He was about to tell them about Valerie's diary – that she, not James West, had painted the pictures – when Nina said: 'Oh God.'

'What?'

'Do you think that's what Mike found out? That the will had been altered?'

'Maybe.' Philip said. 'But how could he?' Then another pain hit him with the force of a chainsaw.

'You really need a doctor,' Ted said. 'I'm driving you to the Western.'

'No. All I need is painkillers and sleeping tablets. I'll stay here tonight, Ted. And I'll need your help tomorrow.'

'What are you gonna do?'

'Visit Stefan.' He glanced at the clock. It was two in the morning. 'But right now I have to rest.'

26

At first Philip thought the gallery was deserted when he arrived there the next morning. The desk was unattended and, though lights were on, he saw no movement. He pressed the buzzer and waited, looking through the large glass door at the pictures. Almost all had red dots beside them indicating a sale.

Then Stefan appeared from the inner gallery, stopping abruptly when he saw Philip through the glass. After a long pause he opened the door.

'What a pleasure, Philip,' Stefan said, with an expression that suggested it was anything but.

'Surprised? Did those clowns tell you they'd done the job?' Determined to make the most of his temporary advantage, he advanced into the gallery. 'I want to show you something.'

'What's this?'

'John's will. The complete one, that is. This one has no pages missing. Look at page six.'

'Where did you get this?'

'Price left his collection to the State Gallery, including the pictures you have here. Care to comment?'

He waited. Stefan flipped through the pages and handed them back with a weary smile. 'It's not signed. It's worthless.'

‘This is just a print-out,’ Philip said. ‘I’ve got the disk in a safe place.’

‘Anyone can alter a document on a disk. It means nothing.’

‘I’m sure the Gallery’s lawyers would like to see it.’

Stefan attempted a laugh. ‘Are you blackmailing me? You’re not improving, Philip.’

‘I want to hear your side of the story before we publish.’ It was a line that had served Philip well many times in the past, creating the dilemma of either leaving a damaging allegation unanswered, or giving too much away. As he spoke Philip slipped his hand into his pocket and pressed record on the Sony. ‘Let’s start with last night. My car was hit by a train.’

‘I heard about your suicide attempt, Philip. I can’t say I’m surprised. Thank God you’re all right.’

‘I was assaulted in my flat.’

‘How terrible. Who saw it happen?’

‘OK – what about the car that hit Zayley? We’ve got witnesses for that.’

‘A bunch of junkies? I’m sure their testimony is reliable.’

Philip paused to gather his wits. His mind and body had taken too much abuse recently. He wasn’t sure he had the stamina for another duel with Stefan. Perhaps it had been a mistake to come. The pain in his guts had returned – he had left the painkillers at Ted’s. These surroundings didn’t help. The paintings unnerved him. He tried to close them out, but everywhere he looked nightmarish images intruded. After his initial surprise, Stefan seemed to have recovered his composure. Sensing Philip’s discomfort he kept on the move, pacing the gallery, his slim figure reflected in the shiny wooden floorboards.

‘Let’s talk about Michael,’ Philip said. ‘You were at the station that night – we’ve got photos. Michael had been at John Price’s place — my guess is you were, too. You were there the night he died.' He held up the will. 'Now we know why.'

Stefan turned his back to Philip, examining one of the pictures. Holding the frame in both hands he adjusted its position on the wall. The animals' hooves seemed to batter at the frame to escape, their mouths open in a scream, their nostrils flaring. Stefan glanced at his watch, and turned to face Philip.

'OK, mate. You've found out more than I expected, I'll give you that. But you've put it together all wrong.'

'Then tell me what happened.'

'You're right, I was at John's house that night.' Stefan took a packet of cigarettes from his pocket, lit one and offered another to Philip, who accepted after a moment's hesitation. 'I was working late. The project was almost complete, a few more paintings needed restoration. I let myself in, went upstairs, packed them and brought them down.'

'Where was John?'

'In his library. He was used to me coming and going,' Stefan said. He paused. 'The relationship between a collector and a dealer is very delicate. People are passionate. Tempers fray. Anyone in the business would tell you that. John and I loved each other, but we had our differences. You know what he was like.'

Philip nodded.

'That night, John had been drinking.' Philip remembered that Price had been found with a glass in his hand. 'He became confused and belligerent. I tried to reason with him, but the poor guy was out of control. He stumbled against a pile of boxes, and they fell on top of him. Of course, I tried to drag them off, but they weighed too much. It was horrible.' Stefan passed his hand across his forehead.

Philip watched carefully. He didn't believe the story, but Stefan told it well. In the absence of counter evidence, and with a good lawyer, he might get away with it. 'Go on,' he said. 'What about Michael?'

'I heard a noise and looked out the window. The brat was there, watching. I'd seen him before, snooping around. John threw something at him once, smashed a window. I realised he'd seen us arguing. I thought I'd better explain, so I called out to him. But he jumped on his bike and disappeared. I got in my car and followed him.'

'You left John there?'

'It was too late for John – I had to find the kid. But he knew all the back streets. I lost him. I drove into Yarraville. Then I saw him again. He was heading towards the station. He looked back and saw me. I didn't want to scare him, but he panicked. He rode straight onto the tracks. I couldn't do a thing.'

'You went onto the tracks, too. Why?'

'Trying to help,' Stefan said. 'But it was so dark, I couldn't see. Then the ambulance arrived. There was nothing I could do.'

'What happened then?'

'I went back to John's house. But it was as I thought. John was dead.'

'You could have reported it.'

'I know, I should have called 000. But it wouldn't have helped John, and there would have been inconvenient questions. You saw that house – it was a disaster waiting to happen. There was bound to be an accident one day.'

'You stole the pictures.'

Stefan shook his head. 'I was entitled to them. That will you've got is meaningless – when the State Gallery ignored him John changed his plans and left the Wests to me. There's no evidence to prove anything else – and you know it.'

He looked calmly at Philip. Philip felt Stefan's force of will. It was a wall against which he could batter himself all day without result. Nevertheless, he had to go on.

'Nice try, Stefan. But it's bullshit. John didn't die immediately – it took several hours. If you'd called an ambulance you could've saved his life. But you didn't. Why?'

'You tell me.'

'Because he didn't just fall under those boxes, Stefan – you pushed him.' Ignoring Stefan's burst of laughter, Philip ploughed on: 'Maybe you didn't plan it, it could've been on the spur of the moment. But that's what Michael saw. You couldn't risk him telling anyone, so you chased him. Perhaps you didn't know the train was coming. You were planning a hit and run, like Zayley. But the train saved you the trouble.'

'Oh, Philip – ever the tabloid journalist. That would make a good story, wouldn't it? Not one, but two murders! But I had no reason to kill John. All I had to do was wait. Have you spoken to his doctor?'

'Why should I?'

'John was a very sick man. That was why he was so obsessed with sorting his will and writing his memoirs. He knew it was only a matter of weeks. You can easily check.'

Philip remembered the old man reaching for his medicine bottles, his comments about how weak he was, how close to the end. *We don't have much time, Mr Trudeau.* Stefan could be telling the truth. If so, what possible motive was there to kill Price? The paintings would be Stefan's anyway.

'Then he'd twigged what you were doing. Realised you were trying to steal them.'

'John trusted me completely. I was like a son to him. Do you think that, if he didn't trust me, he would have had me in his house at all? So you see, I had no reason to push a pile of boxes onto him.'

Philip was silent. Stefan had every move covered. Like an expert fencer he parried Philip's clumsy swipes. And yet Philip was right – he knew he must be right. How hard would it have been for Stefan to throw the old man to the ground and shove half a tonne of boxes onto him? But he couldn't think clearly. The pain was returning. And he couldn't keep his eyes off the corner where the portrait of Valerie was hanging. Those few square inches of paint dominated the room. The more he tried to close it out, the more insistently it drew his eyes.

Stefan took a step towards him. 'You don't look well, Philip. Maybe that's why you keep imagining things.'

'It's not imagination,' Philip said doggedly. 'I knew John, too. I was his ghostwriter. He'd never have given you his paintings.'

'I was his ghostwriter,' Stefan mimicked. 'You poor bastard. Haven't you worked out why he hired you?'

Philip looked at him, wrong-footed. 'Why?'

'Because I recommended you,' Stefan said, clearly amused by how easily he had turned Philip's momentary advantage back against him. 'When John started talking about a ghostwriter, I discouraged him. I didn't want a hack crawling over the house. But he insisted. So I agreed to help. I saw your name in *The Messenger* one day. I made some enquiries. He's finished, they told me. Lost it. He's an alcoholic, a loser. I thought, perfect. I'll tell John to hire Trudeau, that'll keep him quiet and there's no danger of that drunk finding anything out. It worked out beautifully. How many times did you visit? Twice? Write anything? Thought not.' He raised his voice, revelling in Philip's discomfort. 'You should have heard the way he talked about you. *Philip Trudeau – what a professional! Such a dedicated man! Splendid writer!* The vain old fool. He loved having a well-known writer working on his memoirs. Just like he loved having a collection of James Wests. He didn't realise you were a phoney, too.'

Philip slumped against the wall. Remembering Price's words – *you've been recommended to me* – he realised that the commission, which had seemed a possible lifeline at the time, had been a gamble placed by Stefan on his incompetence, a bet which subsequent events had proved to be a safe one. But through the haze of that recognition, Stefan's words hung in his memory, and he sensed that some meaning lay hidden in them, as an anagram lurked in the letters of the puzzle. He frowned, grasped for it.

'What do you mean, "too"?' Philip said.

'What?'

'You said "He didn't realise you were a phoney, too".'

'That's right, you're a drunk, a loser – and a phoney, too.'

'No,' Philip said. He pushed himself off the wall and advanced a few steps. 'You were talking about the pictures, weren't you?'

'What?'

'John's collection looks authentic, but they're not genuine. He thought I was a writer, but I'm a phoney, too. That's what you meant, isn't it?'

Stefan laughed. 'I don't know what you've been smoking, but these pictures are genuine.'

Philip walked up close to the portrait of Valerie and looked hard at it. 'James West didn't paint them, did he?'

'Of course he did.'

'Really? Then where's his signature?'

'He often didn't sign his pictures.'

'So you can't prove they're his.'

'No one else painted like this.'

'Valerie Elliott did.'

'Who the hell is Valerie Elliott?'

'I think you know, Stefan. The question is: how do you know? Have you seen the diary?'

'What diary?' This time the surprise in Stefan's voice was genuine.

Philip stared at the whiteness of Valerie's face against the black background, her dark eyes, her expression. He shivered again as he had at John Price's house, but he did not drop his gaze. He remembered the words from the journal: *I will survive you.* Remembered the first time he had seen the picture, remembered the old man's reaction. Now the letters in the puzzle had fallen into place, revealing the word he had struggled to find. Here was Stefan's reason for killing Price: the single fact provoking the events that had led Michael onto the tracks, Zayley under the wheels of a hit-and-run driver, and Philip to this confrontation. He turned to face Stefan.

'It was John, wasn't it?' Philip said. 'He told you the paintings weren't by West. But that wasn't what you wanted to hear. That would slash their value, and blow the whole deal. So you had to shut him up, didn't you?' His words ended in a gasp as another bolt of pain hit him in the belly. He bent over, supporting himself against the wall, waiting for it to pass. As he did so, the door buzzer sounded. Stefan quickly opened it. Turning, Philip saw the bearded guy from the previous night.

'Where the hell have you been?' Stefan said. 'You should have been here half an hour ago.' He pointed at Philip and Philip realised why Stefan had kept him talking.

In other circumstances, Philip would have enjoyed the expression on the guy's face when he saw his victim alive in Stefan's gallery.

'What the fuck is he doing here?' he said.

'Missed my train,' Philip said.

'You —'

'Shut up,' Stefan said. He turned to Philip, grabbed his throat and shoved him against the wall. His strength was surprising: Philip, in his weakened state, couldn't fight back. 'Where is it?'

'What?'

'You said there's a diary. Where?'

Now Philip knew he had been mad to take him on. It had been as crazy as trying to punch a hole through a wall with his bare fist. The man was implacable. There was nothing he would not do.

'Where – is – the – diary?' Stefan's thumbs dug into Philip's windpipe. 'In your flat?'

Philip shook his head. He was close to blacking out. He couldn't tell Stefan about Richard — couldn't bring trouble on someone else. He caught sight of the painting of Valerie, her face turned towards them, the same face he had seen in the photograph printed by Michael and Nina. He forced a syllable out in an almost soundless cluck.

'What?' Stefan's fingers relaxed slightly. 'What did you say?'

'Car.'

'Your car?'

'Yeah. Jacket. Left it there.'

Stefan released his grip for a second, then shoved Philip towards the door.

'Right. We're going to get it.'

As they went out onto the street, Philip saw Ted get out of his car, where he and Nina had been waiting, and approach across the road. 'Everything all right, Phil?'

The bearded guy glanced at Stefan, and at a nod from him, grabbed Ted and flung him onto the street. As they scuffled, Stefan hustled Philip into his car, got into the driver's seat and took off.

Stefan's foot was on the floor, his knuckles white on the steering wheel. They were heading west along the freeway, the city already far behind. Philip felt as helpless as a passenger on a fairground ride.

He had given no thought to what would happen when they reached their destination. He had told Stefan the first thing that came into his head to get the man's hands off his throat. When Stefan realised the diary was not in the car, he might do anything, and Philip was in no state to put up a fight.

'What if the diary's gone?' Philip said. 'The cops have crawled all over the car.'

'You'd better pray it's not.' Stefan was staring through the windscreen as if he was watching the paintings and his deal with Stevenson vanishing fast into the distance. He swerved from lane to lane, heedless of the horns and the squealing brakes of trucks. The speedo nudged 150. Stefan began talking.

'Stupid old fool. If he'd kept his mouth shut, I'd have made us both a fortune.' He executed a rapid manoeuvre across three lanes, then took his hands off the wheel to light a smoke. 'He didn't deserve those pictures. Didn't even know he had them. I was up in the attic one day – What's in these crates, John? *Oh, nothing of importance.* When I opened them up – my God! – I'd never seen anything like it. A house full of garbage, and these jewels hidden away. I said: I'll restore them for you, I'll sell them, I'll make you rich. But he didn't want that.'

'Why not?'

'A bequest to the nation,' Stefan said with contempt. 'That's what he wanted. A room in the State Gallery named after him. A grand opening, the Governor and his lady wife sipping Veuve in honour of the great philanthropist. That little nonentity! The John Price Collection!' Stefan laughed. 'Fine, I said, fine, that's what we'll do. I know just the man who can fix you up. And I sent him to Gordon.'

An exit approached. Stefan swung the car off the freeway and onto a road between paddocks of listless horses. Philip guessed it was the route he had been driven the previous night. Soon they would reach the scene of the crash. Philip had hoped there might still be some cops around, but in the distance he could see only the level crossing and the crushed wreck of his car, now parcelled with orange tape, resting beside the tracks. The empty road swept down towards the level crossing, trees on either side. Stefan accelerated.

'I was completely justified in what I did,' Stefan went on. 'Morally, those paintings were mine. Price didn't even know what they were.'

Philip said: 'When did he tell you about Valerie?'

'After we found the pictures he got crazier and crazier. He started talking to himself – I'd hear him muttering in the next room. Then he'd grab me, like this' – Stefan unexpectedly grabbed Philip's arm – 'and say: *No, no, Stefan, please don't go, please don't leave me* ... Shit like that.'

'What was he scared of?'

'*We've got to change the will,* he said. Why? *Because your father didn't paint them.* What do you mean, I said, these are by my father, anyone could recognise them. *No,* he said, *no, it was Valerie, she painted them.* He was out of control, crazy. – Listen to me, John, I said, if you want to leave your collection to the nation, they have to be by James West. *No,* he said, *I don't care about that, I've changed my mind. I have to tell the truth.*'

'And that was when you killed him, wasn't it?' Philip said.

Stefan didn't answer for a long time. When he finally spoke, it was in a low tone. 'None of it was meant to happen.' He glanced at Philip. 'Can you believe that, Phil? Everything just got out of hand.' He stared through the windscreen, hardly seeming to see the road. 'But what I did was right. John had no right to ruin my plans. And neither do you.'

The car's speed was insane as it reached the bend. Gravel

spewed from the wheels and the tyres screeched as Stefan took the corner, somehow keeping the car on the road. Sunlight streamed across the bitumen. 'That diary had better be there,' Stefan said, 'because if not –'

Philip was about to speak but the words died in his mouth.

A woman was walking towards them down the road. She walked calmly, confidently. She had on a white blouse and brown corduroy trousers. Her arms were tanned and her reddish hair gleamed in the sun. She had a companion: a boy on a bike, standing up on the pedals, laughing. Sunlight dappled their faces. They made no attempt to evade the car, walking straight into its path. It was impossible to miss them. Stefan wrenched at the wheel. Instinctively Philip flung up his hands and braced himself for the thump of bodies bouncing off the hood. It didn't come. He had a glimpse of their faces – the kid's all sharp nose and freckles, hers pale, dark-eyed, fragile and wearing the faintest of smiles. The car plunged off the road, down a slope, snapping saplings and flattening bushes, jolting uncontrollably before it skidded into the creek, toppled onto its side and slammed against a rock with a sickening smash. An airbag exploded against Philip's chest and the last thing that crossed his mind was a half-admiring thought: *You've done it Valerie, you've had your revenge*, before, with more relief than pain, he blacked out.

27

'You've made a good recovery,' Dr O'Day said, when he came through the ward on his morning rounds. He studied Philip's charts and added a few notes. 'We're sending you home. You'll need a few weeks of rehab, and we have to keep an eye on the pancreatitis. No more grog till it's completely cleared up. All that Scotch could have killed you, even without your other little mishap.'

Philip had been in hospital for four weeks. His assortment of broken bones and internal injuries had required several operations and constant attention. But O'Day had just laughed when Philip complained about the discomfort. 'You're lucky to be alive at all,' he'd said, which, Philip knew, was the truth.

O'Day sat on the edge of the bed. 'There's one thing I wanted to mention. Your CT scan came up mainly clear, but –'

'Mainly?'

'Don't be alarmed – there's no brain damage, which is obviously the risk after head trauma. But there were a couple of odd things. They looked as if they'd been there for a while. Have you suffered any head injuries in the past?'

'Yeah.'

'Another accident?'

'Something like that,' Philip said, though there had been

nothing accidental about the batterings he took in Castlemaine.

'Your scan showed up a few anomalies. I was wondering if you've experienced any symptoms.'

'Like what?'

O'Day sighed. 'It's hard to say. The brain is the last medical mystery. We've unlocked the genome, but we don't know what goes on in our own heads. Some patients with your kind of ... anomalies have reported enhanced perceptions. An ability to see or hear things that other people can't. As if they were tuned into some kind of higher frequency. Any of this make sense?'

Where to start? Philip thought. With the woman he had seen in the city, or the figure in the window? With Maureen? With the conversation in the car, moments before the train hit? Or with what he had seen before the final accident? He had kept these things to himself. No one but he had seen the expression on Stefan's face while wrenching the wheel in an attempt to avoid the two figures on the sun-drenched road. James West's face must have looked like that, Philip thought, when the old man sat in his wheelchair on the lawn at dusk while a figure in a white blouse walked slowly towards him, a light smile on her lips.

He shook his head. 'I haven't noticed anything unusual.'

O'Day looked disappointed. He stood up and shook Philip's hand. 'Take care on the outside. Oh, by the way, I've got an update about the girl you asked after — Zayley Marshall. She's out of the coma and responding well. We expect her to make a full recovery.'

After O'Day departed Philip picked up from his bedside table yesterday's *Biz and Fin*. Richard's feature story had made the front page. Philip had read it so many times he had almost memorised it.

In connection with his celebrated exhibition 'New Directions West', the late art dealer Stefan West claimed to have made an astonishing discovery in an attic: a cache of unknown paintings by his father, Sir James West. What followed has proved to be even more remarkable. A diary — published for the first time in these pages — shows that the paintings were not by James West, but by his sometime lover Valerie Elliott, who died in 1951 aged twenty-seven. Elliott's work is now certain to receive overdue attention. Leading art critic Peter McKendrick has hailed her as: 'One of the neglected geniuses of Australian painting'. Unfortunately her works are unlikely to be seen publicly until their ownership is settled. They are the subject of a legal battle between the West family, the State Gallery and Rosemary Price, daughter of the eccentric collector John Price who had kept the paintings for some fifty years.

One person inconvenienced by this outcome is David Stevenson, who had paid an estimated six million dollars for the paintings, only to find that they are not by James West and did not legally belong to Stefan West when he sold them. Since the death of Stefan West in a car accident three weeks ago, allegations have surfaced about his business methods. The homicide and fraud squad are investigating, and Stefan West's business partner Gordon Parker has been charged with several offences (see the special feature 'The Art of Murder' in The Weekend Business and Financial Review*). Stevenson's close association with Stefan West is likely to damage his bid to chair the Australian Museum of Modern Art, widely seen as an attempt to enhance his public credibility …*

The facts in the special feature had been drawn largely from what Philip had told Richard about Stefan's activities. The police had been interested, too, and had interviewed Philip several times in hospital.

Philip had also spoken to Sally Maher, Michael's mother. She had sat beside his bed, watching him intently and plucking at her hair while he told her all he knew about Michael — his friendship with Nina, his curiosity about the photograph, his discovery of Price's house, his presence outside when Price was murdered and his fatal flight from Stefan. Philip had hesitated when he came to the last part, but Sally had said, 'Go on', so he continued the story to the end.

'Thank you,' Sally said when he finished. 'At least I know now. Funny, isn't it? My own kid, and I need a stranger to tell me what he was up to. Working so much, it separates you from them. I needed the overtime, but maybe if I'd been there more ...'

'It wasn't your fault, Sally. You did all you could.'

She nodded, but he knew that the rest of her life would be haunted by regrets and what-ifs that no amount of consolation would cure.

'Have you got kids?' she asked.

'One. A girl.'

'Do you see a lot of her?'

'She's with my ex-wife.'

'That's a shame. They grow up so fast,' she said. 'There's so much you don't know.' She fiddled with her hair. 'After you came to the house, and said he'd been doing photography, I remembered something. There was a camera in his bag. I didn't know where he'd got it from.'

'You found his camera? Why didn't you tell me?'

'I didn't want to bother you.'

'It wouldn't have ...' Philip began, but then he remembered how exasperated he had been the first time she had called, how he had nearly cut her off. He didn't finish the sentence.

'I wanted you to have his pictures. Thought it might help. So I looked for you.'

Philip thought of the night he had returned from meeting Zayley at the station to find his door open and the bundle of photos on the table. 'So it was you who left the pictures? Why didn't you wait for me?'

'I don't know,' she said, flushing. 'It's just ... you were so kind, when you came to see me.' She dropped her eyes.

Philip was silent, shamed by the realisation that his pretence of concern, put on to help him get the story, had affected her so deeply. She had barely crossed his mind after the interview, yet he had obviously been in her thoughts. She was on her own – no family or friends. Was it surprising that she had feelings for one of the few people who had shown her any sympathy? She wasn't to know that the sympathy was fake, part of Philip's professional equipment, as bogus as the outrage he adopted when interviewing council officers. Now that he wanted nothing from her, he felt a burst of warmth for this meek woman, prematurely aged, in her t-shirt and tracksuit pants. At least Philip still had a child, even if it was one he never saw.

She stood up to leave. Philip put his hand out. She squeezed it between her thin fingers. Philip wanted to give her something more.

'He was a special kid,' he said. 'He was brave, smart, resourceful. He helped uncover a murder. You should be proud.'

She wiped her eyes, and forced a smile. 'I know.' She patted his hand. 'Try to spend more time with your daughter.'

'I will.'

She went to the door, then turned back. An unanswered question clouded her face.

'But why wasn't he more careful?' she said. 'Why did he go onto the tracks like that?'

The question bothered Philip, too. His only answer was the one he gave Sally now. 'He was scared, and desperate to get to his friend's place, so he took a risk. Ninety-nine times out of a hundred, he'd have got away with it.'

Later Philip left the hospital, walking out into bright spring sunshine. Ted had come to pick him up.

'How are things?' Philip said as they drove off.

'Fantastic. I've given *The Messenger* the flick. The website's going crazy, takes up all my time. Got another hundred subscribers last week.' He glanced at Philip. 'My shots of Stefan are very popular – everyone's downloading them.'

Philip gaped at him. 'You don't mean ...'

'Well, why not? It was an opportunity. Hey, don't look at me like that. The guy was dead – what difference did it make?'

'Lucky I wasn't or I'd have ended up on realvictim.com, too.'

'I did get a couple of you, as it happens,' Ted said with a grin. 'Won't be using them though. You don't bleed enough.'

'You're a sick bastard, mate. Drop me off here, will you. I've got something to do.'

Ted left him on the main street of Yarraville. The suburb's much-vaunted 'village atmosphere', beloved of real estate agents and property writers, was in evidence. The street bustled with shoppers strolling from deli to café to cinema to bookshop. Ahead of him Philip saw a father bouncing a little girl on his shoulders. The bells at the level crossing began to ring; half-a-dozen people waited patiently, but a young man pushed his way through the gate and crossed briskly with cocky disregard for the oncoming train.

Philip's mobile rang. 'This is Sarah.'

When they had been married, she had never used her name on the phone – in the early days it had always been 'It's me, darling', later on just 'It's me'. They hadn't spoken for more than a year and now her voice had the warmth of an automated call centre.

'How are you?' Philip said.

She didn't waste time on small talk. 'We're moving back to Melbourne.'

'All of you?'

'Just me and Amy.'

'What about Gavin?'

'I'm not calling to talk about that,' she said sharply. 'It's about Amy.'

'What about her?'

'She's developed an interest in music.'

'Really? On his rare visits to Queensland Philip had encountered an increasingly silent teenager who had been unwilling to tell him anything. But Philip had been wrapped up in his own problems. It was possible she had mentioned it and he just hadn't heard. 'What instruments?'

'Piano and clarinet. They say she's a natural. She remembers you playing your sax when she was little. She's got some crazy idea about you two playing together. Of course, you're probably too busy, but I promised I'd mention it.'

Philip said cautiously: 'I'd love to. I'm not working at the moment, so I've got plenty of time.'

'Sacked again?'

'No, I resigned. I'll be doing some freelance work, but that doesn't start for a week or two. Anyway, I'll always have time for Amy.'

Sarah responded sceptically to the mention of freelance work, but it was the truth. On the day Richard's feature had appeared, Philip had taken a call from Graeme at *The Biz & Fin*. He had congratulated Philip and asked if he was available to write an article on the financial side of the art market. Philip had considered a heroic gesture of refusal, but only for a tenth of a second. It wasn't the big time. It wasn't even a regular job. But it was a step in the right direction.

After Sarah's call Philip was in no hurry to get back home. Instead he stopped at a café. Once seated at a table he took out his phone and dialled.

'Hi, it's Phil. I've just been discharged from hospital.'

'That's great.' She sounded happy to hear from him. He remembered the time when he had sat in his car outside her flat watching her talking on the phone and envying whoever was at the other end. She was out of that flat now, with its Stefan overtones, and back in her old place in Yarraville.

'It's thanks to you I'm alive at all,' Philip said. It had been Nina who had called the ambulance, after taking the wheel of Ted's car and following Stefan and Philip on their breakneck drive.

'Where are you?'

He told her. 'Are you busy?'

'I could use a break. See you in ten?'

Philip put his phone away and gazed out the window. The idea of seeing Amy scared him a little. Did she really remember him playing the sax to her? In hospital he'd decided to take it up again; he'd lain there improvising solos in his head. He would need to get back into practice, get the instrument cleaned and fixed. He flexed his fingers, and as he did so, as if divining his thoughts, the waiter slipped a CD into the player and the café filled with the sound of Coltrane. Had Amy ever heard of Coltrane? Philip doubted it – her mother's tastes hardly stretched beyond Van Morrison. He would fix that. It was the track that had been on his mind for months – the one with the phrase he had never quite been able to master. After a dizzying series of chord progressions in minor keys, played at an incredibly fast tempo, it made a sudden switch into a major key. That was the part that always threw him. But he reckoned he'd got it now. He was sure of it.

Philip closed his eyes and let the sweet and gorgeous sound fill his head. The music summoned up three women. First Maureen, as she was the last time he had seen her, on the day her life and career crumbled around her. Then Valerie, whose face had seemed so familiar when he first saw the self-portrait. It was her despair that had resonated with him: the anger and pain of her betrayal. And finally he thought of Nina beside the tracks on the night of Michael's death. He saw himself walking towards her, compelled to intrude into her grief – he relived the strange sense of familiarity he had felt on witnessing her distraught face. Then the change came, with a series of soaring, joyous notes. Yes, he had it now: he knew how it went.

The bells jangled at the door. When he opened his eyes Nina was coming into the café to meet him.

Epilogue

Lungs bursting, heart pounding, Mike's feet pistoned the pedals. Wheels hissing on the wet tarmac, he swerved off the road and biked furiously along the track beside the creek. It brought him out onto a quiet residential street. He was safe here, but to get home he'd have to risk the main road. Reaching it, he took a look back over his shoulder. At first he thought he was OK, but then he saw them again, the lights that had been chasing him from the old man's house. Immediately the driver put his foot down and the car ate up the distance between them: it would catch him in a few seconds. But Mike knew Yarraville better than the driver, better than people who'd lived here fifty years. As the car closed on him he swung the bike across in front of oncoming traffic and headed down a side street, forcing the pursuing car to slam on its brakes. Halfway along the side street a tiny alleyway ran between two terraces. As the car came up behind him again he could hear the driver yelling. It was only a few inches from his back wheel. Like a fish darting out of a shark's mouth he swerved down the alley, where no car could follow, and was away. By the time his pursuer had worked out how to get around, he'd be in the clear.

But now he had gone out of his way; the chasing car was between him and home. He paused at the end of the alley to get his breath back and weigh up his next move. Then the idea hit him: *Go to Nina's*. Her place was closer, only half a k away, the other side of the railway line. In the distance he heard the faint blast of an approaching train.

It was late; he'd been out for hours. He'd pretended to be asleep when his Mum came to check on him, but as soon as she went to bed he'd snuck out of the house. He'd been shivering outside the old man's place for what seemed like ages. He didn't understand what was going on, but he couldn't tear himself away. The younger, blond-haired man had been going up and down the stairs, carrying stuff out of the house and loading it into his car. The old man had seemed upset. Mike had lurked behind the bushes, watching them. It was the first time he'd been there in the evening. Normally he did his detective work by day, but that afternoon he'd heard the blond man call 'I'll be back tonight to finish off' and he'd realised this might be his last chance. It was cold and dismal, and he was falling asleep on his feet. He'd just decided he might as well go home when he heard raised voices. Mike crept as close to the window as he could.

Mr Loony was upset, pink in the face and speaking loudly in his piping voice. The old man reminded Mike of a yappy little dog he knew that loved to take on other dogs twice its size. Mike strained to hear.

The younger man said: 'They've got to be by my father, do you understand?'

But the old man wouldn't shut up, he kept jabbering: 'No, we have to tell them the truth, Stefan, we have to tell them ...' What was all that about?

The other guy had his hand on the old man's shoulder. 'But why didn't you tell me this before, John?'

The old man had tears running down his cheeks. 'I loved your father, Stefan. I always had my doubts about those paintings. Bill told me, but I didn't say anything ... I just wanted to protect his reputation.'

'Good, then protect it, and shut up,' said the younger man.

'But I can't, Stefan. I can't, not now. It's her, she's come back, Stefan please ...'

'What the hell are you talking about? Who's come back?'

Now the old man's face was full of agitation. 'I see her, Stefan. Valerie. I see her every night.'

There was a moment's silence while the younger man stared at him. Then he said something that sounded like, 'We're not telling them anything', and gave the old man a shove that sent him sprawling onto the floor, where he lay feebly wriggling like a beetle on its back. The younger man stepped towards him and at first Mike thought he would help Mr Loony to his feet, but instead he leaned on the pile of boxes and gave them a shove. The pile swayed like a tower in a breeze, then toppled onto the old man.

Mike heard a cry, but then realised he had made the noise himself. The younger guy turned to the window and saw him, his face clearly visible, his nose pressed up against the glass.

From the alley Mike took off again, riding towards the station. *Call her first, check she's home,* he thought, and reached for his phone. Steering one-handed, he keyed in her number. Her phone diverted to the machine. 'Nina, are you there? Answer the phone if you are.' He heard a car behind him, looked over his shoulder and saw the familiar lights. 'Oh shit, he's behind me!'

He pedalled frantically towards the tracks. The bells began to ring and the boom gates descended. He rode harder than he'd ever ridden, mouth wide open to suck in the air. If he could just cross the tracks, the car would have to stop and he'd be in the clear. Ahead of him, the train pulled into the station. He could cut around the back! But then he heard the horn of the second train – the long, sonorous blast that meant a V-Line express coming the other way. He wouldn't make it. The car was close behind. He yelled into the phone, begging her to answer, looking back at the car, with its lights on full beam, bearing down on him. At the last second he decided to swerve off to the left, into the side road that ran parallel to the railway tracks, and conceal himself in the darkness behind the toilet block.

Then, looking up, he saw her in the shadows on the other side of the tracks. She was wearing a white blouse and her hair was blowing in the breeze. He stopped pedalling, and strained to see in the darkness. Was it really her? She raised her arm and beckoned him forward. He hesitated for another second – surely the train was getting close – but the car was almost upon him, and now she lifted her hand again and he saw her white fingers waving impatiently, heard her call out *Come on, don't be scared, I've been waiting for you.* 'Oh Neen, I can see you!' he shouted joyfully, coasting round the boom gate and onto the tracks. She stepped forwards to meet him. It was only at the last moment that he realised it wasn't her, it wasn't Nina at all, and as the train hit them he fell gently, through an eternity of time and space, into her waiting arms.

About the Author

Nick Gadd is the author of the novels *Ghostlines*, which won a Victorian Premier's Literary Award and a Ned Kelly Award, and *Death of a Typographer*. He was the winner of the Nature Conservancy Australia Nature Writing Prize in 2015 and was shortlisted in the essay category of the Melbourne Prize for Literature in 2015. He is the author of the blog Melbourne Circle and his essays on place have recently appeared in *Meanjin*, *Kill Your Darlings*, *Griffith Review*, *The Guardian* and several anthologies. He lives in the western suburbs of Melbourne.

www.ingramcontent.com/pod-product-compliance
Ingram Content Group Australia Pty Ltd
76 Discovery Rd, Dandenong South VIC 3175, AU
AUHW020859161224
404293AU00003B/59